PRAISE FOR EARTHCYCLES
BOOK ONE,
SONG OF ALL SONGS

"This rare blend of naked imagination, careful story-telling, poetic flair, and meticulous language is reminiscent of Ursula K. Le Guin at her best."
　　—*Self-Publishing Review,* ★★★★★

"When anthropologist Donna Dechen Birdwell turns her keen sense of how societies evolved in the past toward imagining a post-apocalyptic future, the result is a thoughtful, nuanced, intelligent thriller."
　　—Robert J. Sawyer, Hugo Award-winning author of *The Oppenheimer Alternative*

"*Song of All Songs* is a beautifully written and richly realized vision of the future, informed by a deep under-standing of humanity."
　　— Christopher Brown, Campbell and World Fantasy Award-nominated author of *Tropic of Kansas* and *Failed State*

"*Song of All Songs* is a lovely book. It is sad and hopeful both, and I thought about it long after I read the last page."
　　—Patrice Sarath, author of *The Sisters Mederos* and *The Unexpected Miss Bennett*

BOOK OF ALL TIME

BOOK TWO

EARTHCYCLES

DONNA DECHEN
BIRDWELL

Wide
World
Home

Book of All Time, EarthCycles Book Two

Cover design by Robin Vuchnich, mycustombookcover.com
Author photo by Lucero Valle Archuleta

Published by Wide World Home.
8944B Parker Ranch
Austin, TX 78748 USA
wideworldhome.com

First Printing—August 2021

Birdwell, Donna Dechen
Book of All Time, EarthCycles Book Two
362 pp.
1. Science Fiction – Fiction 2. American – Fiction
I. Donna Dechen Birdwell
II. Book of All Time, EarthCycles Book Two
ISBN: 978-1-7355569-2-5

Printed in The United States of America.

To those who became our ancestors,
in spite of everything.

"Within the expanse of spontaneous presence
is the ground for all that arises.
Empty in essence, continuous by nature,
it has never existed as anything whatsoever,
yet arises as anything at all."
—Longchen Rabjam

"People like us, who believe in physics,
know that the distinction between
past, present, and future is only
a stubbornly persistent illusion."
—Albert Einstein

1.

I don't know where I am or how I got here.

I fell.

Yes, I remember that. But I was already divided, dispersed, as the twinned lives in my womb clamored toward awareness. Impinged upon consciousness. Or magnified it?

I remember there were five of us at the table, talking, as we often do, about the photographs that Damon is making, the pictures that shimmer with life.

There was pleasant conversation, back and forth, but I grew weary of all the words and excused myself to go for a walk.

I promised we wouldn't go far.

We didn't go far. But something tripped me up and we fell.

Now we stand outside myself. Beyond ourselves. Three beings—Meridia and her twins.

No. One being.

The Migrant saturates our awareness, obliterates our will.

We go with the Migrant wherever they take us.

The Migrant is everywhere.

Donna Dechen Birdwell

2.

Out there, Amergin was called blind. In here he guides their way.

The Migrant has brought us here. How else could we have found Amergin, here in this musty darkness sparked with color and ambient, ancient tremolo? It's a deep time, crusted with danger.

Amergin is young, nearly a man. He's not Melfar like us. Not like Abél and Brân and Avienne. And yet he pertanges the colors. Discerns almost-images from vibrations. Verberations. He walks at the front of a small group, all children except for Naomi, the youth who clings to Amergin's belt, and three older women. They make their way cautiously, fearfully through the cavernous obscurity. "Un poco mas adelante hay un cuarto grande. Con aire. Por allí podemos descansar." The sound of the words is strange to us, but we understand the verberations perfectly. He's shown them a big room ahead, with air, where they can rest.

"That's welcome," a woman says. She feels her way along a wall, fretting over the smaller children. They've been walking for...how long they can't tell. In here there is neither day nor night. No moon to measure the count of days. There is only hunger and thirst and the effort to satisfy those needs at frequent enough intervals to keep going. And the periodic need for sleep. The crying child in the woman's arms is a reminder of all of these things.

The woman is troubled. She's clothed in filthy gray garments that enfold her head and body. The rope around her waist is adorned with a metal ornament, two bars crossed to form four equal angles. Around her neck, inside her blouse, a strand of beads supports a similar shape. We can't tell what stone the beads are made of. The material is inert.

How is it that we know what she looks like? This place is shrouded in the deepest darkness imaginable. We pertange her through the verberations and memories of the girl Naomi. She keeps scanning their surroundings as if she, too, pertanges something. She does, but not so clearly as the blind boy. Naomi's eyes are open wide, and they are fully functional, but there's nothing for them to see. It's only sensations she responds to. Vague colors emanating from the cold stone walls. The kinds of colors shown to the mind without need of the eyes. Pertanged colors, carried by an undulating hum that caresses her awareness as she moves through the cramped space, ducking to avoid contact with the stones overhead.

Out there Naomi was considered dull for her inability to read, her stubborn silence among grownups. Down here the Sisters trust her. She's begun to trust herself.

Sisters? She's referring to the three adult women who are with the group, which includes maybe seven children in addition to Amergin and Naomi. All three women are dressed in identical fashion.

They're nuns. Like monks, only women. Naomi tells us this, though she isn't at all clear who she's speaking to. Who she imagines that she's speaking to. She's done this all her life. It's part of what relegated her to the care of the Sisters of Saint Odilia at the children's refuge.

A shudder of memory sends blue-green arcs along Naomi's arms and across her chest. She feels it again, that brilliant flash, the strange wind, the cloud rising like a giant mushroom on the near horizon as the Sisters, pretending to be calm, hurried all the children down the stairs and into the big stone room, closing the doors heavily behind them. There was a murmur of prayers as they sat listening, wondering when they would be allowed to go outside and play again, not knowing that the answer might be "never."

We fall into the girl's memories, memories from the moments just after the white light, the swift wind.

Naomi sits next to Amergin as she always does. Amergin reaches for her hand. "Are you okay, Omi?" he says.

"I'm sad for my mother." She shows Amergin, as she has many times, the place where she lived before coming to Saint Odilia's, a place now in ruins.

He squeezes her hand. He's glad his own mother is here with him. He calls her Sister Berta now, like everyone else, but she's still his mother. Back at their home in a city called Cochabamba, she was la Profesora.

Sister Berta and the much younger Sister Antonia have completed their count of the children and verified that they're all here.

"What about Sister Carnelia and Sister Rosa?" Antonia says to the older nuns. "Of course we'll let them join us when they return."

"Of course," Sister Maggie Marie says.

Naomi knows that won't happen. The two Sisters in question went to the city early this morning to do the weekly shopping for supplies. In other words, they went to beg for donations. They'd taken the smallest child with them, a blind boy who was born with only half a brain. They always got more donations when they took him along. They were undoubtedly still in the city when the explosion happened. *Bomba. Bomba nuclear.* Naomi picks up those words from Sister Berta.

We pertange a blinding brightness. A brief rush of fear. A deathly shattering.

Naomi can't tell us exactly what the words mean, but she knows the effects. She experienced the dazzling light. Knew the wind that took her mother, the two Sisters of Saint Odilia, and the little blind boy with half a brain. She knows they're all dead.

"Are you crying?" Amergin lifts Naomi's hand and holds it against his forehead. "You're crying. Please don't cry, Omi. Surely they'll be back soon."

"No, they won't. You know they won't."

Amergin knows. He cradles Naomi's hand against his chest and sends her azure waves of comfort.

"Where were we?" Sister Maggie Marie stands up and clasps her hands together. "Oh, yes. We were about to go into the common room for snacks. Well, guess what, children? Today we're going to have our snacks here."

There's a vague murmur of disinterest among the children. Sister Maggie Marie and Sister Antonia walk among the stacks of boxes, examining labels. They select a smallish box and carry it to the long table that runs down the center of the room, calling the children to gather around and sit on the benches next to the table. Sister Antonia opens the box and begins taking out chunks of some kind of food. Each chunk is wrapped in a transparent material stamped with words in bright colors. Each child gets one little package.

"I'm thirsty," comes the voice of one of the tiniest children at the far end of the table.

"Of course, Alfrin. Right away." Sister Maggie Marie scowls as she stares at the sink next to the wall, wondering if the water in the pipes is still safe. It would be fine if this had only been a bad storm. But this is a nuclear explosion. Maggie hopes Sister Berta remembers the protocols. They're written down on a piece of paper somewhere. The paper says what's safe and what isn't for how long and how far from wherever that monstrous weapon fell. The paper was sent to them by the authorities after the first bombs dropped in a few other places. Other countries. They knew there would be more.

The two Sisters go to the first of a very large stack of bottles. Sister Berta pulls some of them toward her and when one of the bottles hits the floor, it bounces a little. It doesn't break.

What strange substance is this?

3.

"How is Meridia this evening?" Our partner Damon sits down in the chair next to our bed. The chair knows him well by now. His arms rest on his knees as his tall form bends toward us. He's here most of the day and sleeps curled next to us at night. His dark skin is grayed with worry and his thick Mundani eyebrows droop.

"There's no change." Maddie thinks about how many passages we attended to her every need in her own illness. She regrets her emotional distance during that time, her unkindness to her only child. Her dark hand caresses our tawny skin. She regrets not having been able to shield us from the prejudice levelled toward anyone even half Melfar in a Mundani world.

"And the nens?" Our hearts warm with Damon's fervent concern. Though he didn't place them here, he loves these twins as his own.

It feels so strange. Being here and elsewhere at the same time.

"Bekanz says they're both okay for now."

Damon is grateful that this sister of Emba, the Melfar woman who first knew of our pregnancy, is here in New Beniford taking care of us, taking care of the growing nens. In our mind, Emba and Bekanz merge—they have the same healing touch, the same pale orange hair. But Bekanz is younger and Bekanz is still alive.

Damon tries to think how long we've been asleep. Bekanz calls it a coma, but Damon prefers to think we're only sleeping and that soon we'll be awake again, happy and rested. He thinks we ought to awaken soon. He tells us that we need to eat and drink, nourishing not only our body, but our two interior lives as well.

He's probably right.

How long has it been since the accident? Our fall. It didn't seem bad at the time. We only slipped on the path. Tripped over something. There was a bump on our head that raised up quickly into an impressive but unsurprising lump. We recall feeling disoriented, dizzy. They took us to Bekanz, who advised us to lie down and rest for a bit, assuring us that the dizziness would soon pass.

We lay down. We went to sleep.

They wait impatiently, fretfully, for us to wake up.

But there's so much more for us to learn.

4.

While the children eat their snacks and drink their rations of water (to which Sister Berta has added carefully counted drops of something from a small bottle), the Sisters converse in quiet tones.

"There's enough here to support us for at least three weeks. A month if we're frugal." Sister Berta has been doing mental calculations. When they planned how to stock the shelter, the children were younger. Amergin and Naomi are almost grown now. They eat far more than they used to.

"Don't forget about the flood last spring when we couldn't get into town for supplies," Sister Maggie Marie says.

Sister Berta had just recalculated to account for the absence of Sister Carnelia and Sister Rosa and the little boy with half a brain. Now she has to revise her projections again, subtracting the two boxes of packaged meals they'd consumed when the river overran all the bridges. They hadn't been able to afford to replace those supplies. "I still think we can make it for three weeks. Close to that."

"And then what?" Sister Maggie Marie picks up the cross hanging from her belt and cradles it between her palms.

Sister Berta was a scientist before becoming a nun. She still is, really. She only went through the taking of vows here at Saint Odilia's so that she could stay near her son, Amergin. They'd been living in the city and it had become impossible to care for Amergin while continuing to work there. Her mother's heart wouldn't let her send him away. At Saint Odilia's she could continue to observe him and others like him as well. She thought it might even further her research into the effects of blindness and other impairments on the mind and other senses. How it affects the way such individuals experience the world.

We pertange most of this through Naomi and Amergin, as they observe what their caregivers are planning.

"And then what?" Sister Maggie Marie repeats her question without expecting Berta to answer it. She has her own answer. "Then we pray," she says. She has greater confidence in this thing she calls prayer than Sister Berta, who discounted it altogether back when she was Profesora Rigoberta Mendoza. Berta is the one who insisted that the emergency shelter contain equipment that could allow occupants to communicate with the outside world.

What kind of equipment?

Naomi tries to show it to us. All we pertange are some boxes filled with twisted wires and slices of an inert substance inscribed with intricate designs. *It's how we get messages from the outside. The devices pick up vibrations that come through the air.*

We're astounded that inert machines might be capable of such things. We search and find some of the odd vibrations. They're very faint. We can't make any sense of them. They're deep shades of red we've never experienced before.

Sister Berta moves to a far corner of the room where she takes a small rectangular object from her pocket and attaches it with a long piece of cord to a receptacle. She places two objects into her ears. She listens. After a few moments, her face goes ashen pale and her hand goes to her mouth. Tears slide down her cheeks.

It's during their first night in the shelter that they feel more than hear a second explosion.

Some of the children sit up suddenly and begin to cry. Amergin has both hands over his forehead as his face contorts and his shoulders press toward his ears. Naomi's wide-open eyes search for the source of the bright sparkles she feels certain just swept across their underground room.

"What is it?" Sister Berta runs to her son, holding his hand as the child next to him clambers into her lap, attaching himself like one of the creatures that encrusted the Old Mica Benison.

"There was a light," Amergin says, his sightless eyes roving across impenetrable blackness.

Amergin has always been able to sense light, to know the difference between outdoors and indoors, between night and day. But Berta has seen nothing, though she did feel something like a vibration. Not a jolt, exactly. It came and went.

Naomi joins them. "I saw something, too," she says. "Or maybe I didn't see it. I only knew it when it came." Naomi trusts Sister Berta to understand such things. The good Sister has always been receptive to hearing the children's descriptions of what they imagine they see or hear. When she first arrived at Santa Odilia, Naomi had been gratified to find that here she was not alone in her strangeness.

"What do you see now?" Sister Berta asks. It's a question also for Amergin and for little Alfrin, who clings to her, burying his head in her breast.

"The ceiling is so much stars," Alfrin says.

"It was the same light like we saw yesterday," Naomi says. "But coming from a different direction. It swept right over our heads."

Alfrin's face tilts up toward the ceiling. "Falling stars," he says.

Across the room, Berta's eyes meet those of Sister Maggie Marie where she kneels, giving comfort to other children. The lamp she carries offers scant illumination. They're all awake now. Little deaf Frida is sobbing loudly. Lourdes, Frida's constant companion, is undisturbed by her noise. She strokes the older girl's arm to console her.

Berta takes the rectangular device from her pocket again and presses a button. It lights up and everyone turns toward the brightness. Berta shuts it off quickly, but not before she's seen what she didn't wish to see. Again she catches Sister Maggie Marie's eyes. She shakes her head and the two women sigh in concert, their eyes drifting heavenward. Earthward. Toward a surface that is no longer habitable.

"Let's all settle down and get back to sleep," Sister Maggie Marie says. "God's angels and our beloved Saint Odilia will watch over us."

Sister Berta trusts more in science than in the benevolence of saints and angels. She tucks the children's blankets around them, furtively planting an extra kiss on her son's head. Amergin has his sightless gaze fixed on the northwest corner of the room.

"Do you see something?" Berta asks.

"Blue," he says. "There's blue in the corner."

A shudder runs through Sister Berta. She doesn't know how her son can describe colors, but Naomi has been helping him with that for years and Berta trusts that the words he uses are fairly accurate. "That sounds pretty," she says. "I wish I could see it."

Berta walks with the calm pace of a good Sister over to the corner where Amergin said he saw the blue light. She takes some translucent sheets that had wrapped the bottles of water and stuffs them into the vent.

She approaches the table where Sister Maggie Marie hovers over some papers. Berta recognizes them as the inventory sheets for their shelter stores. She sits down and reaches out to place a hand over the sheets. "We have a more urgent consideration, Maggie."

The elder nun removes her glasses and waits.

"I think there's radiation coming in through the ventilation ducts."

"But we have the filters. You said those would remove all the radioactive particles."

"They should. But if this latest detonation was closer, the filters could be overwhelmed."

"What should we do?" This is not the first time that Sister Maggie Marie has thanked her younger self for having been willing to take on a scientist as a Sister of Saint Odilia. What the woman lacked in faith and devotion to the saints was more than compensated by her practical and technical knowledge. Besides, there hadn't been any young women coming to them professing a pure and holy call to the service of Saint Odilia in many years. There was only Sister Antonia, who had been sent to Saint Odilia's as a young child and took the vows because she didn't want to leave.

"One problem is the power failure. The filter pump has switched over to auxiliary power. The batteries, you know? But that won't last more than a few days, even if we use our power exclusively for the filter."

"And the other problems?" Maggie's head drops toward her papers as her eyes angle up to find Sister Berta's eyes.

"Obviously we can't block the ventilation shaft. Well, we can. I just did. But that's a very temporary solution. We have to breathe. I'm thinking maybe the dust out there will settle a bit if we can keep it blocked for a while." Berta's eyes probe the dimness, calculating the volume of air held within the room against all the pairs of lungs requiring it. "I'm thinking we can keep it blocked for six or seven hours with no harm to anyone. We'll use less air with the children asleep."

"And after that?" Sister Maggie Marie's folded arms rest on the table as her shoulders slump.

"We'll think of something," Berta says.

Sister Maggie Marie presses her beads against her lips and begins mumbling something that sounds almost like song.

5.

We've never before been with the Migrant for so long. The Migrant taught us the Song of All Songs, but this is different. The Migrant also showed us brief glimpses of...something...when we were on Selbourne with Prophet Amos Quint. Father says that what we saw then was from the past. Could that be so? We feel certain that Naomi and Amergin are in the past.

Where are we now? There are voices, clear enough, though they sound far away.

One of the voices is Damon's. Our heart's partner, Damon. Even though he's Mundani, he was drawn to us when we lived in Temur. After Mother had gone away and we were all alone. Damon had been struggling to make photographs of what he called biophotonic images. We knew little about such images then, knew nothing about how they're generated by the Melfar aurynx, pertanged by the gnosic orb, contained in the crafted stones called Benisons. But Damon was already Revelant and he'd had glimpses of such things. We've learned so much since then.

"It's okay, Damon, I know you need to be here with Meridia." That's Vidvana's voice. Without using our eyes, we see her dark face, her converging fringe of eyebrows, her eyes wide behind her glasses, her hair wild as always, despite her efforts to bind it into a knot.

"She's with the Migrant. We have to trust that," Zara says. Her tone shows us her golden face, glowing as it always does when she speaks of the Migrant. Her amber eyes are bright and her yellow curls quiver. Zara is a scholar like Vidvana, but, being Melfar, her methods are different. The two women—one Melfar, one Mundani—are writing a history of our two peoples.

It will be called the *Book of All Time*.

Maybe the Migrant wants Amergin and Naomi to be part of Zara and Vidvana's book. Is that it? But what does their story have to do with Melfar and Mundani? The people trapped in the subterranean room are clearly neither.

We're drawn to them. We're curious to know more, but we're also afraid. We ought to go home.

The nens of us are not so frightened. Perhaps it's the nens' enclosedness that forges this bond with the children in the underground room. If only the Migrant would explain themselves. Other than through songs and images, the Migrant doesn't speak. We remember when they showed us what happened to Mother, how she was killed. How they restored her life. They spoke then. Or do we only remember it that way?

We should try thinking of Mother. Maybe that will take us home. We've been thinking repeatedly of Damon and that hasn't helped.

We're so tangled up in this story, captivated by this group of... we aren't sure what they are. Only one of them is as dark as Mundani. Most have lighter brown skin. The old Sister Maggie Marie and Sister Antonia and the small one they call Alfrin are that odd shade of pink we've seen before on a journey with the Migrant. We saw many people like that in our brief vision of some ancient city. That vision came when we were on Selbourne. Our father Abél was there. And the Mundani Prophet Amos Quint.

Breathe with your mind, Meridia.

Did the Migrant say that or are we only remembering what our uncle, Brân, told us that day when he introduced us to the workings of the gnosic orb and aurynx? We think Amergin and Naomi must have these organs. Weak, perhaps. Not so well developed as they are among Melfar. But how else would they be able to pertange the lights and colors and sounds the way they do? To generate such things the way we do?

Someone is creeping through the darkness of the underground room, feeling their way along the wall. It's Naomi. She stands for a moment next to Amergin's head and reaches out with a soft rosy sound to caress his forehead. He stirs and reaches a hand toward her, lifting his blanket with the other hand. She stretches out beside him and their two bodies settle together. They hum a few silent blue notes that hide their trespass from the Sisters. They lie quietly, comforting one another.

Our hearts ache for Damon.

"I'm here, Meri."

We feel his hand grasping ours and his kiss is warm on our cheek. We want to reassure him, but we're too far away.

6.

By the time Sister Berta's wrist device pulses to tell her it's morning, Naomi is back in her assigned place. Berta hurries to unblock the ventilation duct and turn on the air pump. The air has become oppressive, moist with exhalation and evaporating sweat. Whether it's safe or not, they have to get air into their enclosed room. Berta has stopped trying to get information from the outside.

Sister Maggie Marie prays. She prays to Saint Odilia, patroness of the blind and afflicted. Eventually she'll stop praying for the safe return of Sister Carnelia and Sister Rosa and the boy with half a brain. Some things are too much to ask for.

The younger children accept the compacting of their old routines into this small space. Sometimes the table at the center of the room is their school desk, sometimes their games table, sometimes their refectory. During exercise time, the benches are shoved underneath it to make space for balls and jump ropes. There's laughter and singing. And prayer. They pray for the earth above and its people. There are fewer people every day.

The cracks in the ceiling lengthen, spread a little, send out new tendrils. They're impossible to ignore. Sister Berta has identified a corner of the room where she believes they could all huddle for shelter if the worst should happen. *Or would it be better*, she thinks, *to let it fall, to let God decide who should live and who should die?* Sister Maggie Marie might think that would be best, so

Sister Berta doesn't mention her observation, doesn't even call Maggie's attention to the cracks, trusting the dim light and the elder nun's failing eyesight to protect her from worrying over anything more than what already fills her constant petitions to their patroness.

The food is holding up better than Berta had anticipated, perhaps because everyone is losing their appetite for the parade of meals, each of which looks and tastes almost exactly like the last one. There should be food for another week. After that they'll have to risk going above ground again. Berta tries to remember whether she ought to give everyone a few more drops of the medicine before they leave the shelter.

"What do you suppose it's like up there?" Naomi asks.

"Don't expect things to be the same, because they won't be." Sister Berta has an aversion to lying, especially to children. "All of our buildings are destroyed."

"I know the city where my mother lived is gone. The people who weren't killed in the blast are so sick. Is that what would have happened to us if we didn't have this shelter?"

"Yes. And some of us may get sick anyway when we leave. We'll still have to stay indoors most of the time." Berta feels certain that they'll have to return to the shelter to sleep. There is no other indoors. What will they eat?

"Why am I thinking of elephants?" Amergin says.

Naomi giggles. "Elephants? Why would you think of elephants?"

"When did you first think of elephants?" Sister Berta isn't laughing.

"Just now."

"Children!" Sister Berta's voice rises above the hub-bub of playtime. "Children, we're playing follow the leader and I'm leader. Run as fast as you can after me! Sister Maggie! Sister Antonia! Come! Run!"

As the last children reach the corner where Berta leads them, the ground begins to shudder and buckle. Chunks of stone from the broken ceiling groan and crash. Children scream. They become a pile of human terror, grasping at one another as the ground rolls and jerks beneath them. More crashing. Naomi glimpses daylight and then the ground heaves again and they all slide away into darkness. Some of the children cry out in pain from injuries. Sister Antonia whimpers quietly. Another great shudder of the earth and they're dropped into a damp and spacious silence. Their cries echo back to them from what seems a great distance. The darkness is absolute.

Sister Berta is covered in rocks and earth. She sneezes from the dust and groans against what she knows must be broken ribs. Her entire body hurts, but she's able to push away a couple of large stones and sit up. "Amergin?" she calls out. "Maggie?"

"Mama!" The boy forgets to call her Sister.

"Amergin, are you okay?"

"I think so. Where are you?"

"Stay there. I'll come to you." Berta isn't sure how she'll get there, but she'll try. "Sister Maggie Marie!" she calls out again.

There's a soft moan nearby. "I'm fine. Well, maybe my leg's broken." There's a sharp intake of breath. "We have to find the children. We need to find Sister Antonia."

Sister Maggie Marie calls into the darkness the name of each child. Naomi is there. And Sister Antonia and Alfrin. Four of the children don't respond. One of them is Frida.

"How will we find dear deaf Frida?" Berta says. She's found Amergin, who clings to Naomi. They fell together. They have scrapes and bruises. Omi's leg needs binding to stop the blood. Amergin rips a sleeve from his own shirt for the bandage.

"I'm going to call out the names again," Maggie shouts. "Listen to see who's nearest to you. Listen so you can find one another." Hearing how her own voice echoes off distant, unseen walls is disconcerting. She calls the names and this time one of the children who didn't respond before emits a faint sob. "And please, everyone search for Frida. Listen for Frida. You know she can't hear us, but she may call out."

"I think she's over here," a voice says. "I'll find her."

Maggie begins singing and her song becomes their guide. One by one they dig themselves and each other out of where they've fallen and drag their bruised and bleeding bodies to the sound of Sister Maggie Marie's voice. As each child arrives, Maggie takes mental note of the name and its invisible face.

Frida announces her arrival with a breathy, nasal cry. As usual, she's in the company of Lourdes. "I don't think she's badly hurt," Lourdes says. Sign language is of no use for Frida now. No one can see her signs. Sister Berta takes Frida's hand reassuringly and surveys her body. Frida cringes a few times and shouts when Berta probes her left elbow. Berta concludes that it's strained but not dislocated.

Antonia is with Alfrin. Berta knows the little boy, the youngest child among them, is Antonia's nephew, although such things are not supposed to matter at Saint Odilia's. Sad origins are obliterated by giving all the children the same surname—Gorrión. Sparrow. They become one big family of sparrows. Alondra, who is not much older than Alfrin, also huddles next to Antonia.

"Has anyone found Dolores? Or Lasaro?" They're the only ones Sister Maggie Marie hasn't accounted for.

Sancho has a broken arm and Balbina's ankle is twisted. There are more bruised ribs and bleeding wounds for Berta to attend to, shredding garments as she goes.

"Help! Please, help!" It's Cruz, who is almost as old as Amergin. Cruz is physically strong but emotionally fragile. His voice is frantic. "It's Dolores. She's trapped and I can't get this rock off her. Please, help!"

Berta knows her broken ribs make her useless for such a task. Antonia is firmly in the grip of her two small charges. "Amergin, can you go help?" In this darkness, Amergin's lifelong blindness is an asset. He's accustomed to navigating without seeing.

Soon Amergin and Cruz return, dragging Dolores between them. She's not crying, which Berta finds odd. Dolores cries about everything.

"Oh, my," Berta says as her hands, slick with Dolores' blood, find the place where some stone crushed her skull. Berta has never felt more helpless. Out there, she'd call for help, summoning a vehicle with spinning lights and blaring sirens. Even that might not be enough. "Can we clear a space where she can lie down?"

By the time Dolores' body is stretched out on the ground, there is no breath left in her. "Let's leave her to rest for a while," Berta says. She can't lie to the children, but she's also not obligated to tell them the whole dreadful truth. At least not right away.

But Amergin sees it. So does Naomi. That brownish mist drifting up into the swirl of colors along the fissured ceiling of the cavern. They grasp hands, mourning their friend.

"Does anyone know where Lasaro is?" He's the only one still missing from Sister Maggie Marie's mental roster of children.

"He went to the latrine," Sancho says. "I think he was still there."

We sense the quiver of crimson fear in Sancho's voice, along with a sepia shudder of apology that he hadn't said anything about his friend Lasaro until this moment.

Briefly, we pertange Lasaro's panic as he digs through the tumbled debris of what used to be his life. He digs up toward the single ray of muted sunshine that penetrates his despair.

They will never see Lasaro again.

Sister Maggie Marie's leg isn't broken after all, but the swelling on her shin marks a deep bruise. "How did you know?" she asks Sister Berta. "Why did you call us to run to the corner right before the quake?"

Sister Berta chuckles and then emits a muffled cry as she grabs her side with the broken ribs. "Elephants," she says. "Elephants communicate by infrasound and quakes are always accompanied by an advance wave of infrasound. So when Amergin said he'd suddenly thought of elephants I assumed a quake might be coming. If I'd been wrong, it would have been only a silly game."

"But you were right. Thank God and all the saints that you knew that." In the darkness, Sister Maggie Marie moves her right hand first vertically and then horizontally across her chest. "I think Lasaro is the only one we're missing," she says.

"And Dolores."

"Oh, yes. And Dolores. May she rest in the arms of God's angels." Maggie wipes away a stray tear as she reviews the composition of their little band. There are three adults and nine children. The eldest are Naomi and Amergin. The youngest is little Alfrin. Maggie is overwhelmed, trying to think about what her responsibilities are toward this battered group of unfortunates.

Sister Berta places a hand on Maggie's forearm. She finds that touch far more reassuring than the oblong device that still rests in her pocket. She knows she can't contact anyone with the device. She knows its capacity to provide light will only last a short while. "We need to assess the nature of this space where we are," Berta says. "How big it is. How stable. Whether..." She stops and shifts her position to relieve pressure on her ribs. "Whether there's any way out."

"I can tell you that." Amergin's voice emerges confidently from the darkness. "It's a bigger room than our shelter. Shaped kind of like a calabaza. Curved around. The ceiling is a lot higher on this side."

"Can you see a way out?" Sister Maggie Marie long ago gave up telling her charges to stop imagining things. So much of what they told her turned out to be true.

"Maybe. I could tell more if I were closer to where I think it is. Everything still feels so noisy."

"Go, then, but take someone with you."

"I'll go." Naomi stands up and reaches for Amergin's outstretched hand. Somehow their hands touch.

Sister Berta listens to their shuffling footfalls as they move away toward her right. Naomi is limping. Berta knows their path is littered with stones, large and small, but the two youths move with increasing confidence.

We follow Naomi and Amergin. The boy has described the cavern accurately. Now he moves toward a passage, narrow and low, that leads away from this space. But where will it take them? We pertange a maze of caves and tunnels far more extensive and intricate than Amos Quint's little cavern on Selbourne. None seems to lead anywhere in particular.

"Look over here!" Naomi calls out. "I think there are a few boxes from the storeroom."

"Can you tell what they are?" Berta speaks in a normal voice. Sound carries efficiently in this space where they've landed.

"Bottles of something in one box." Naomi takes out one of the bottles and hands it to Amergin. She opens another box. "Workbooks?" Boxes scrape across the rough floor. "Sacks of dried beans. And this feels like rice. No, I think it's quinoa."

"There was a box where I was, too," Sancho says.

"Okay, we'll look for it."

Our attention returns to the nuns.

"At least we'll have something to drink," Sister Maggie Marie says.

Berta tries to remember what bottled drinks they stockpiled. Water, of course. But there were also a few cartons of some kind of sweet drink she calls Inka Kola. "Beans are useless without cooking. Poisonous," she says. "But if there's quinoa, we could eat that raw. Even soak it in a little water and sprout it."

Amergin and Naomi finally make their way back to the Sisters. Berta fishes her device from her pocket and turns on a light. The bottle contains water. The sack contains quinoa.

"We also found these over where Sancho was." Naomi holds out a handful of small packets and Berta lights up their labels.

"Protein bars! A box of protein bars!" Sister Maggie Marie's hands come to her heart in a gesture of triumphant gratitude.

"Not a box. Some of them scattered around. Also this." She holds out a jar that Berta's light reveals to be something light brown. She calls it peanut butter.

"We'll definitely need to collect up as many of those as we can find," Berta says. She suggests that Amergin and Naomi take a rest, but they insist on resuming their reconnaissance of the cavern. They like feeling important and useful.

"There's more than I thought there'd be," Berta says. "Enough to survive a few days anyway while we find a way out."

"And what if we don't find a way out that soon? Then what will we feed them?" Sister Maggie Marie's voice is quietly anguished.

Sister Berta doesn't respond right away. "Some caverns contain pools and lakes," she says. "Some pools and lakes have fish or salamanders."

Maggie almost gags, thinking what it would be like to eat a salamander. They won't even be cooked. "What else?" she says.

"Mushrooms, perhaps. Though they'd never be enough on their own."

"Would you know which ones are safe?"

"I think so." Berta tries to remember the classes she once took in school. It was a long time ago. "I'm pretty sure I'd know which ones *not* to eat." Maybe she should save the light in her device for examining mushrooms. If they find any.

Amergin and Naomi make their way back to the Sisters. "There's a passage," Amergin says, "but it's narrow and low. I smelled something, too." He tries to think how to describe the acrid odor that stained the stale air in the passageway. "You remember the cat Omi and I tried to keep in the attic? The box of sand we set up where he could poop? It smelled like that. Not so strong. But the same kind of smell."

"Bats." A surge of amethyst optimism tinges Berta's chest. "If there are bats, there must be an opening where they come and go." And maybe, just maybe, a way out.

7.

Our father Abél's awareness hovers close to our bed, bathing us in healing blue light, trying to draw us back home. Or at least to discover where we've gone. He finds no injuries that can account for our condition. Our absence. Abél has been preoccupied with the task of finding Prophet Amos Quint's son Lambert, recruiting him to join the cause of the Song of All Songs. But he knew when we fell. He knew the Migrant had taken us.

The last time Abél was physically here with us, he saw us full of amethyst hope, sparkling with golden optimism. He saw how the nens of us in our womb commingled with the Migrant more fully every day. It enabled us to help him locate Lambert. But Father could also see how the budding consciousness of the nens was confounding our sense of ourself. He noticed how Meridia often said "we" instead of "I" or spoke as if we were elsewhere, observing ourself. Ourselves.

We can't help it, Father. We drift and seem to have little control over where we go, what we see, when we are.

We yearn to share what we're seeing with Damon. Sometimes we think he knows where we are. He's Mundani, but twice Revelant, more aware than most.

Mother is Revelant, too, and sometimes we follow her thoughts, though they don't call us back into her presence as strongly as Abél's or Damon's thoughts do. Mother's mind wanders.

We pertange how troubled Mother is as she sits silently by our bedside. Her face has grown thinner, its wrinkles deeper. Strands of white escape the twist of hair atop her head. Her dark eyes have always been unusually large, giving her a surprised look. Through her eyes we see our own face, its features slack, lids closed over eyes that flit back and forth. Our brown curls are a tangled mass and there's an uncommon greenish cast to our tawny skin.

Mother is dwelling again on what she did at the Blanton Clauster. She's obsessed with it. She knows that the tincture she put into the six Palinjian leaders' wine didn't kill them, only kept them from being revived once they'd succumbed to their own foolish suicide ritual. But she wishes it hadn't been necessary to do it. Was it necessary? Mother is anxious for her beloved friend Gerd, too. Mother is safe enough here in New Beniford, but Gerd has gone out again. Out there among the Palinjians.

To rejoin the fight, she said.

There's a large group of Palinjians still there at the Blanton Clauster, tenacious devotees of the false prophet Zibal Palinj and his young successor, the late Warreth Pherson. Followers of the worst implications of the Mundani code of the Sidaya.

The Palinjians at Blanton seethe with rage. They hunger for revenge.

We recoil from them, remembering how they murdered Damon and our friend Emba. Emba is still dead. Their anger repels us, but our curiosity draws us cautiously nearer. Or is this only another thing the Migrant wants us to know?

A group of men sit in the courtyard. The space is marked by six piles of stone, crude shelter for the moldering bodies of their six leaders. Hope for their miraculous renewal has evaporated. The dead men remain stubbornly dead. Every day guards shoo away carrion crows and add to the bundles of herbs and flowers. They burn incense to shield the gathered faithful from the creeping stench of decomposition, the reek of decaying aspirations.

They've been discussing the fact that the current passage is nearing its end, talking about the five-day period known as the Binder that intervenes between the end of one passage and the beginning of the next. The first day of a new Mundani passage is required to fall on the longest day. The Binder is not part of any stint and is traditionally a period of riotous celebration when rules are broken and reckless actions go unpunished. It's always a dangerous time for Melfar.

These men are afraid they won't have much to celebrate this time around.

"They must still be in Fayredell," one man says. "They're only women. They can't have gone far." He's a big man, even for Mundani. But not in a muscular way.

"Hiding out with one of their sully weftreds, no doubt," another man grumbles. "I keep telling you, Halvor. We need to crack down on the weftreds. Find their meeting places. Root them out and put a stop to their nonsense once and for all."

"Weftreds have existed since forever, Herk. They're nothing more than sully gossip clubs. You give those women too much credit. The one who poisoned the wine was a crazy old crone, not capable of leading anything meaningful out there. She was doing someone else's bidding. I'm sure of it."

Herk appears unconvinced. There are dark circles of weariness around his eyes. "What about the one who killed the guards? Wasn't she the same one who killed some of our men out at Shadham? What was her name?"

"Gerd Finch. Yes, she may be the greater danger. We've ordered our kinrens in Fayredell to keep an eye out for her. And to kill her completely dead when they find her." Halvor slaps a fly away from his face. He has nagging doubts about the loyalty of some kinrens, but he decides not to mention it. He stands up and adjusts the stone-studded sash over his ample paunch. "I've heard rumors that there may be another Sidayen from the Prophet's lineage out there," he says.

"Which prophet? Not Quint, surely." Herk snorts in disgust. "The Quints are finished now that both Amos and Lambert are gone. No chance of them trying to start up anything against us. Pherson? Sadly, no. There's no issue from Warreth Pherson, may he rest in peace." Herk taps his chest with a fist and his eyes rest briefly on one of the piles of stone. "As for Warreth's brother, that one is far too young. Blind as well. And we know old Zibal Palinj died childless. May he also rest in peace." Herk absently taps his chest once again, eyes lifted skyward.

"That's what may not be true," Halvor says. His narrowed eyes watch to see what reaction he'll get to what he's about to say. "I've been told that there's a son of Palinj himself who's been living in hiding these many passages. Minding some shop of his mother's, they say. I think it's something we ought to check into. Track down the man and bring him in. Bring him to his senses. Show him what it means to be a Palinj. A Palinjian."

Could this be true? Our hearts flutter fearfully.

There's a mutter of low voices as the men gathered at the Blanton Clauster absorb this news. An heir to Zibal Palinj might bring them together once more, infuse them with the sense of purpose that's been slipping away ever since their six primary leaders were all lost in a single blow.

We shudder at the thought. Does Gerd know about this possible Palinj? Does she know that these Palinjians are plotting against her?

The last time we saw Gerd, she was leaving New Beniford, right after the Great Turning, to undertake her own mission. Tall and strong from her vocation of carrying burdens, Gerd has always worn her long dark hair in a single plait down her back in the masculine fashion. Most Mundani women wear their hair twisted into a knot on top of their heads.

Gerd had left in the early morning, accompanied only by her son Fergus and his Melfar friend Jalu. Gerd was sorry to leave, but grateful that our mother Maddie would be safe here with us. Gerd figured Maddie was a marked woman out there where they might know what she'd done at the Blanton Clauster, how she'd implemented the deaths of the six Palinjian leaders. But now it seems that they're not actively plotting against Mother. Only against Gerd.

Do Father and Brân know about this rumored son of Zibal Palinj?

Then we remember where Father has gone. Gone looking for a different prophet's son. Abél is searching for the son of Amos Quint, the self-exiled Mundani prophet whom many still believe to be dead. Exactly as Amos intended.

Our mind loops back again. Drifting. Unmoored. We find no one time or place any more compelling or real than any other. No sense of *now* or *then*, *here* or *there*.

We hear again what Brân said before he left, when he'd tried to convince the old Prophet Amos Quint to go with them to find his son Lambert. "If anyone can persuade him to take up the cause of the Song of All Songs," Brân said, "it will be you."

Amos was adamant. "If I'm there, he'll want to defer to me. Some of the people may even wish me to stay among them. No. Lambert needs to find his own way. I've had my day. It's imperative that I remain absent." Amos desires only to continue his solitary devotions on the island of Selbourne where we'd found him in Father's search for the Old Mica.

"But what if he doubts what we tell him?" Father said. "Even now he still believes that you died in that fire in Fayredell. How do we convince him that you live and that you support our cause?"

Amos raised his empty hands. "I have no token for you to offer him. I have no material possessions other than what I've left behind on Selbourne. But you can tell him that I saw his mirror, and that I know it was his mother's."

The old Prophet's voice echoes in our mind, dusty with regret. Amos had seen his wife's mirror in the vision we evoked of Lambert's secluded cabin somewhere in the Northern Lowlands, beyond Fayredell.

8.

~

We see the little group as it left the sheltered obscurity of New Beniford in search of Lambert Quint. Two old Melfar men in the company of a middle-aged Mundani man and a young Mundani woman who is barely more than a girl. The brother twins Abél and Brân—our father and uncle—take the lead. Willem Učen, life partner of the Mundani scholar Vidvana, follows, trailed closely by Ann Landry, Lambert's granddaughter by his daughter Keira. His daughter who was murdered by Palinjians.

Abél is gratified to see how the recent rains are bringing forth lush green grasses and even wildflowers, things not seen across this landscape in such profusion in several meeds. He marvels at the ability of seeds to remain viable after such long drought. Inwardly, he begins humming the Song of Calling the Rains, the new song of the Ancient Mica Benison. He'd promised his father that he would find that lost Benison and at long last he had found it, on the island called Selbourne, the island where the old Prophet Amos Quint had communed with the Migrant in his chamber of mirrors.

Despite the protection canopy Abél and Brân weave with their songs, the little group remains vigilant, mindful of potential danger. The Palinjians may be less powerful now, less organized, but they are also more unpredictable and volatile after the loss of their leaders. Abél had been both awed and deeply saddened by what Maddie did. Abél loved Maddie once. He still does, though in a different way. They live apart, but she's still the only partner he's ever had. He remembers how casually he left her and their little daughter Meridia, thinking to be gone only for a few days. What had happened next still troubles him. His recent experience on Selbourne caused him to think again of those two long, lonely meeds.

We want to reach into Father's memories and learn more about that period, but we find them closed off. We never understood Father's absence, always wondering why we had to grow up without him, surrounded by Mundani.

The first day of their search for Lambert Quint passed without incident, its only interruption the midmorning shower that occurs every day at about the same time. Brân wondered if the Melfar ever had knowledge of songs that offered protection from rain. If so, he knew nothing of them. It was nearing midday before their clothes dried out again.

On the second day they find shelter and avoid the soaking. Other travelers were not so prudent. Brân spots the two Mundani men before Abél notices them. They appear to be near the same age. Friends, maybe. No, brothers. The older one walks with a stick. They both carry bulky sacks on their backs. They're traveling a different road from the one Father and Brân are on, one dug into the earth. A Mundani road, now rutted and muddy from the rains. From a distance, Brân listens, breathing with his mind.

"We have to accept that the Quint line has ended. Their time is over. It's what happens with the birth of successive generations of daughters," the man with the walking-stick says. "If Keira had been able to birth a son, it might have continued after a fashion. He would have been Rolang Landry's son, too. Doubly blessed."

"So you say. I'm not sure I'd see any blessings arising from Rolang's line." Both men have shed their sandals and walk barefoot through the mud. So many passages without rain made Mundani neglect the making of boots. "What do you suppose became of Lambert?"

"Who knows? I heard that after the death of old Prophet Amos, may he rest in peace, Lambert just wasn't himself. Well, how could he be? His House was gone—father and homestead and descendants." The man's stick sinks into the mud and he stops to pull it free. "They say he was prostrate. Sold his own house and stayed with his widowed son-in-law for a while until the granddaughter disappeared. And then Lambert disappeared as well. I was told that no one noticed at first. He'd been that withdrawn."

The younger man emits a tired sigh. "The Quints were an odd lot. Old Prophet Amos, may he rest in peace, always preaching forbearance and peace and such. In times like ours, there's little appetite for that kind of message." He readjusts the pack on his back. "Though he may have been right."

"Quint didn't come from a distinguished line or House. Not like Warreth, who was a direct descendant of Prophet Razak Pherson. May the whole lot of 'em rest in peace."

"If they can."

Brân wonders what's become of Warreth's younger brother. Could he be called upon to lead the Palinjians?

"As for Warreth's brother," the younger man continues, as if he heard the question, "Saami is only a child, less than twelve passages. Not even in possession of his destiny."

The older man shifts his walking stick to the other hand as he seeks the most solid portion of the road. "Razak Pherson, may he rest in peace, was only a boy when he began to gather a following. But in his case there were signs. Poor Saami lost his eyesight when he was a nen, hardly more than a newborn. Not exactly what you'd expect as a sign of being destined for leadership."

"That was when the nacreous fever was going around. I remember. So many died over in Benbridge. At least little Saami lived."

The travelers lapse into silence and Brân pertanges their discontent. They're heading back to the farm they worked with their father many returns ago, hopeful that the rains will make the land fruitful again. Their discontent comes from not knowing in what direction their people are headed. The older man worries about the Palinjians still at the Blanton Clauster. The younger man is more concerned about the other Palinjians, the ones who have spread out across the land, vowing to hunt down the women suspected (rightly as it happens) of being responsible for the deaths of the six Palinjian leaders. Frustration has led these men to strike out indiscriminately at anyone they think might be a "Shoon sympathizer." Chanters are targeted in particular.

We cringe at the word "Shoon." It's what Mundani have always called Melfar people, and the word itself seethes with contempt. Orban warned us of the vengeful brutality of such Palinjians, men like the ones who killed

38

his Melfar life partner Emba. They did it slowly and they made him watch.

Brân sees the danger more vividly now and he almost wishes they'd denied Ann Landry's request to accompany their expedition. But Lambert Quint, the man they seek, is her grandfather. The girl has lost both mother and father. How could they deny her reunion with her grandfather Lambert?

We have to guard the girl, brother.

Abél knows. *These travelers are harmless enough, but there may be others.*

Our mind strays again, bouncing in muddled confusion from one worry to another. *Are the nens of us well? Yes, we know you're there, Mother.* We know she's concerned about Gerd. *What was it we needed to tell Gerd?*

9.

"We want no more killing, but if they attack us, we will defend ourselves." Gerd's voice has an engaging depth and resonance. She speaks with conviction and the women and other kinrens in attendance murmur assent.

We'd been concerned when Gerd told us she was leaving New Beniford to go back and fight. We're encouraged by this apparent aversion to more killing.

A lanky Mundani man rises from near the back of the group and clears his throat loudly. "I can help with that," he says. "I was trained in combat skills and I know many ways to subdue another person, even someone bigger and stronger."

Whispers of interest eddy through the room.

"Good. Stay and speak with me and we'll see about organizing some training. Does anyone else have matters to raise?" The group has been meeting for a long while and they're ready for Gerd to call adjournment.

Attendees break up into small groups, most of them remnants of old weftreds or nodes of new ones. Gerd thinks the work of these traditional secret networks has never been more important. Operating outside the official channels of the Sidayens who order the Mundani world, weftreds have always been efficient conveyers of news and rumor among kinrens. Now they're coalescing into something that makes Gerd cautiously hopeful.

The man who spoke out approaches Gerd and waits.

Gerd extends her hand and their fingers brush in greeting. The fellow is almost as tall as Gerd herself and as strongly built, though a bit thinner. More wiry. "What is your background?" Gerd asks.

"I worked for many passages as a guard at the Quint house, until we were all let go shortly before the fire that took the place. They trained us with all the best masters of combat. My name is Roqu Fulcomb."

"Well, Roqu, would you like to show us something of your expertise?"

"We should set up some mats, because the techniques I know can send bodies onto the floor rather unexpectedly."

"That sounds promising," Gerd says. "Meet us back here just past sunset and we'll see what you can do."

Gerd watches as Roqu makes his way out the door. She notices Jalu lingering near the doorway. "What is it, Jalu?"

"I'm not certain," he says. "But we may need to be more careful. You, in particular."

Gerd knows that Jalu, being Melfar, sometimes learns things through his Melfar friends. Pertanges things at a distance through Brân and Abél and Avienne. And through us. "We always work cautiously." Gerd offers a reassuring smile to Jalu.

"There appear to be instructions from the Palinjians to look for you. They know what you did at Blanton. And in Shadham?" Jalu isn't sure about that part.

A shudder of memory raises the hairs on Gerd's neck. Three dead by her own hand at Shadham. Two more in Blanton. Plus the six Palinjian leaders. They may blame her for that as well. She'd readily take the blame to protect Maddie. The approach of the Mundani Binder could well intensify their determination to take revenge. She'll need to watch her step. "Very well," Gerd says. "Thanks for telling me, Jalu. We need reminders, I guess, to keep us alert."

We send Jalu a wave of golden gratitude as he makes his way out. We hope Gerd will heed his warning. Should we alert them to the Palinjians' belief that there may be a son of Zibal Palinj somewhere? The Palinjians intend to search for him.

The only people left there with Gerd are Daedal and Shifra, two of the women who escaped from the Blanton Clauster with Gerd after Mother's cunning dispatch of the Palinjian leaders.

Gerd's reputation as a fighter and the news she brought of the survival of Amos Quint and a whole community of Melfar has vaulted her into a position of influence within this clandestine network of Chanters and other dissidents in Fayredell. She's gratified to see how many male kinrens and even a few lesser Sidayens have been recruited to their cause. Her son Fergus and his Melfar friend Jalu are eager participants. But the group is disorderly, divided about how best to move forward. The burden of their hopes is palpable.

And what is our cause exactly? Gerd wonders. They have the inspiration of the Song of All Songs, but what can they do to realize the hope it offers? Gerd is disturbed by her own uncertainty. Rebelling against the eons of Sidayen oppression of kinrens (including all women) and Melfar is strong motivation, but what exactly do they hope to accomplish? What goals are they striving to attain? This is what keeps her up at night and she broaches the subject now to the two Mundani sisters who have taken to calling themselves Daedal breth Ilda and Shifra breth Ilda after the Melfar custom, refusing to name their father or their partners.

"What do we want? We want them to respect us as equals," Shifra says. "To treat us with respect."

"But doesn't that imply that we still see them as superiors? Pleading with them for the favor of being treated well?" Gerd's hands are on her hips, her chin raised, jaw set.

Shifra takes a flask of wilderfruit wine and a jar of qaji nuts from her bag and invites the others to sit down with her. Shifra sets the open jar in the center of their small circle. She takes a long draught from the flask and then passes it to Gerd.

"Even that won't come easy," Daedal says. "They're accustomed to being in charge of everything. In charge of us. They're convinced it's the will of the Creator."

Gerd's face is drawn into a deep frown. Wrinkles have dug in next to her eyes and mouth over the last few tides. "Do we try to convince them otherwise?" *Or just overpower them.* She takes a thoughtful drink from the flask, pauses, and takes another. She passes the flask to Daedal. "I've heard a tale of how one of the younger Palinjians from the Markham Clauster was kidnapped and turned to our cause. Do you suppose that's true?"

"I know it's true," Daedal says. "I heard it from our sister-cousin Teagan. It was her own son Rio was turned. Though he wasn't exactly kidnapped."

"Of course, that was only one man." Even so, Gerd is intrigued. "Well, let's think about it. Breathe with it. Shall we chant the Song of Insight before we go?"

Amid the dusty smell of old jars and vinegar in what was once Rolang Landry's pickle storeroom, the silver notes of the chant rise.

We recognize the tune of the Old Mica Song of Reflection. The words the women sing are the Mundani contribution.

"To find our way, we open wide
Beseeching truth from every side.
Come, truth! We overwhelm all lies
With fearless heart and open eyes."

10.

⌒

Each time Bekanz places the drinking straw against our lips and we draw in a swallow or two of nourishing liquid without choking, they think maybe we're about to awaken. But we don't. The nens of us want to go back to the children. The Meridia of us wants to return to Damon. The Migrant hold us and take us where they will.

We know Damon is here. And Maddie. And even our father Abél, who sometimes wonders if he ought to join us and the Migrant. But Abél is a different *here*, somewhere far beyond our bedside. When we're in the company of the Migrant, we can be in several places at once, but since we still have only the one brain and one body to process it all, it gets muddled.

No, that's not right. Now we're three bodies, three brains. We're so confused. Overwhelmed. Is there a bigger word than that? Overcome? Annihilated.

Abél is on the northern road that skirts Fayredell. The Migrant shows him the way as he proceeds with confidence toward the cabin where Lambert Quint resides. Lambert has been there more than three tides now, immobilized by fear and desolation. He spends most of each day gazing into his mirror, hoping for some sign that will indicate what he ought to do. He doesn't even know why he took this mirror from the burned house. This mirror was his mother's and it was nearly ruined in the fire that took his father.

The mind of memory offers Lambert pale glimpses of his mother's face, wracked by her own sorrow and madness. She died when Lambert was still a boy, not yet in possession of his destiny. Lambert had idolized his older brother Rahmond, but Rahmond died in the first outbreak of nacreous fever. Lambert tries to remember when that was. So long ago. So many deaths. So many fires as Sidayens sought to burn the fever out. The Great Fires were like a fever of the land itself. Many of those who survived both fever and fires fell into madness. Later on, Lambert's own son died in an unexpected outbreak of the same fever down in Benbridge. And then his daughter Keira was killed. Murdered by Palinjians. Lambert's heart is heavy with despair. He has so much grief, so many questions. He finds no relief, no answers.

That's it just ahead. Brân lays a hand on Abél's shoulder to draw his attention and then gestures toward the northeast.

And he's there is he? Abél has been with us and he has to trust his brother twin to know this.

He's never anywhere else.

We try to tell Father what we know of Lambert, of his distraught state of mind. They know they'll have to be careful not to alarm the man after so long spent with no company other than his own.

"We should send Ann in first," Brân says, using words.

The girl willingly agrees to do as they suggest.

So the two old Melfar brothers and their Mundani companion wait while Ann Landry approaches the cabin and knocks cautiously on the half-rotted door. There's no response. She knocks again, a bit more firmly.

"Grandfather?" she calls out, her tone tentative. "Grandfather, it's me. Ann. Please let me in."

There's a scraping noise and then the metallic sound of a key in a lock. The door opens. "Ann? What are you doing here? How have you found me?" Lambert's eyes cast about in sudden panic. He sees the three men standing near the meskie tree and grabs Ann by the shoulder. Pulling her inside, he slams the door and turns the key against further intrusion.

"Should we...?" Willem begins.

"Give her time," Abél says.

The three men sit down in the shade of the meskie. The two who are Melfar attend to the conversation taking place inside the cabin.

"Listen to me, Grandfather," Ann says. "These men wish you no harm. We've come to bring you word of Great-grandfather Amos." She tries to set aside her distress at her grandfather's disheveled appearance. It's clear he hasn't washed himself in quite a while.

"So you bring me messages from the dead?" Lambert laughs. It's a staccato, hysterical sort of noise. "And maybe in the company of dead men, too. It's been loudly proclaimed that all Shoons have been destroyed. Obliterated. And yet I think I saw two Shoons standing over there outside my house." Lambert's confusion manifests in a throbbing pain in his head, invited by the deteriorated state of his health. The water jug in the cupboard has stood empty since yesterday.

"None of that is true, Grandfather. Great-grandfather Amos is alive. Alive and strong and well. I was with him all of this past stint. And many Melfar are alive, too." Ann shifts her weight to the other foot. "I can't bring myself to say Shoons anymore. They call themselves Melfar."

"Alive you say? And you've been with Amos? Where was he? How did you find him?"

"It wasn't me. It was Brân and Abél, the two Melfar men you saw out there. They're good people, Grandfather. But I think you know that."

The pain in Lambert's head intensifies and he grasps his head between his hands, rubbing his temples for relief and then pressing the heels of his hands against his forehead. A sob escapes him, but he grabs hold of the next one and steadies himself. He sits down and gestures for Ann to take the only other chair in the room. She drags it closer to the table and sits.

"It was Brân and Abél and Abél's daughter Meridia that found you, too," Ann says. "I only came along with them." She speaks quietly, wanting desperately to hug her grandfather, to comfort him, but too unsure of his disposition to risk it.

Lambert peers into Ann's face but says nothing. He always remembers her a child, but here she is a nearly grown woman and beautiful, too, like her mother. The same glowing skin, dark as polished bartlenut, the same wavy cascade of dark hair.

"Great-grandfather saw you, too, in their visions. He saw you looking into a mirror that he says used to belong to your mother, a mirror you took from the burned house. Is that true, Grandfather? Is that what you were doing?"

Another sob escapes Lambert's constricted throat, followed quickly by more and Ann rushes to kneel next to the old man, wrapping her arms around his alarmingly thin body. She can feel his ribs through his shirt. Lambert has always been slender, but now his shoulders collapse inward and his almost childishly soft features have been etched sharp by deprivation and sadness.

"It's okay, Grandfather. Things are not so bad as you thought. But my friends can tell you more. May I ask them to come in?"

We continue watching as the group assembles inside the tiny cabin. Ann brings her grandfather water and insists that he eat some of their food. They sit up most of the night, telling the stories that first amaze and then gradually quiet Lambert Quint's mind. We think Father knows we're there. We see that the son of the Prophet recognizes Abél as the man who brought his daughter Keira's body back to Fayredell after she was murdered at the Markham Clauster. He expresses his gratitude for that once again and then listens with increasing interest to how they followed the lead of a couple of stones to a remote island called Selbourne, where they found his father, the Prophet Amos Quint, and an old Benison. We relive the story as it's told. Lambert has never heard the word "Benison" before, but he knows at once that the word refers to rocks such as the ones that he's always called banestones. Abél's explanation astounds him. These stones are far more than he ever imagined.

By the time Lambert falls asleep, it's near morning and there's a faint smile on his lips.

Father, too, slips into slumber as we drift away to a far different time and place.

11.

❧

Amergin's guidance keeps them from running into the stone walls and the maze of formations that emit lovely shimmers of color for those who can pertange such things. Have these colors always been there, or are they only evoked by the subtle sounds emitted by the members of this odd company?

Amergin has followed the odor of the bats and led them to a chamber not quite so large as the one they fell into after the earthquake. But this space is lighted during daytime by a single shaft of sunlight that creeps across the floor of the cavern along a path marked by a brief line of green. We pertange their relief as they inhale deeply this air in which the distant scent of above-ground almost quells the stench of bats.

There is water, too, a deep pool of it that seems to be fed from a stream deeper underground. In the faint light, shadows dart back and forth within the pool's depths. They might be edible things, but Berta is not at all clear how they might manage to catch them.

The cavern where they've arrived houses only a small colony of bats, which is probably a good thing, since the shallow accumulation of their waste that occupies the far side of the room is unpleasant enough. There are mushrooms growing near the margins of the deposit.

The opening in the roof of the cavern provides scant but welcome fresh air, respite from the thin, dank air they've been breathing in the narrow passageways. How long did they travel to get here? Two days? Three? Maybe more. Sister Maggie Marie tried to believe that this little window to heaven might also be a way out. But Berta quickly ascertained that there would be no way to reach the opening without either a ladder or wings. They have neither. The only way out of this room may well be the same way they came in.

The children are exhausted. The Sisters think it would be good to rest here for a while where there is air and water. It will give the three adults time to think what to do next. They still have some quinoa and a few jars of peanut butter. The protein bars hadn't lasted long, even broken into pieces and carefully rationed. Sister Maggie Marie offers the children daily dollops of peanut butter scraped out of a jar on the end of the cross that hangs from her belt. Amergin discovers another dauntingly narrow passage that could lead them out of this chamber, but he's not sure what it would lead them into, if anything. So, day after day, they stay.

Frida is happier now that there is enough light for her to communicate by sign language, although she'd been surprised at how she and the others—Naomi and Amergin in particular, but also Lourdes and little Alfrin and even Sister Antonia—had been able to read each other and their surroundings in the darkness of the passageways. There were shimmers and soft bursts of color from one to another and even from the stones themselves.

Sister Berta insists that the children take daily turns sitting nearly naked in the ray of sunlight. Sister Maggie Marie was initially a bit horrified at the nakedness and had to be convinced of the health benefits. The children seem to enjoy it, except for Naomi, whose self-consciousness about her increasingly womanly breasts prompts her to expose only her back and arms and legs to the faint warmth of the sun and its nourishing effects.

Sister Antonia somehow managed to drag and carry Alfrin and Alondra, the two smallest children, through the long darkness, soothing their whimpering with play-ful songs that bounced in colorful patterns off the stones. Alondra loved the songs and sang along in a fluting voice that sounded more like a little bird than a human. She usually got the words wrong, but her tones were perfect.

When it's Alondra's turn to sit for a while in the sunshine, she sings. Antonia notices how she stops her singing from time to time and when Antonia listens with Alondra, she hears birds on the distant surface. They almost sound as if they're answering the little girl. And then one day, while Alondra is singing, something drops suddenly through the slit of sky. As the object tumbles and bounces its way down, Antonia grabs up the little girl, fearing that a rock falling from such a height might do serious harm. But it isn't a rock. It's a piece of fruit. A fresh, juicy, brightly purple fruit for Alondra.

"Look at that!" Sister Antonia crows. "How lucky for you that the bird happened to drop his lunch right into the opening." She hands the fruit to Alondra and watches in salivating delight as the child devours it, savoring every sticky drop of sweetness.

But it wasn't an accident. Time after time, whenever Alondra sings her song, a piece of fruit falls from the sky and the children share the special treat.

And so they live for a while on water and sprouted quinoa and mushrooms and precious bites of fruit. The peanut butter runs out, but Sancho—who knows how to swim—begins catching small creatures from the pool. They eat those, too. At first they didn't like the squishy texture of the flesh. Some of them even claimed that the little creatures shrieked in pain when they were killed. But hunger finally overwhelmed such sensibilities and they ate. They ate all these things and they survived.

"There's a passage under the water there," Sancho says one day. And a few days later, he dives into the water for the last time.

12.

━━

We're dazzled by the brilliant sunlight streaming through an open window where Father awakens. There's a promise of rain on the breeze. With a sigh, Father repositions himself and drifts back to sleep.

Lambert Quint has awakened, too, his mind inundated with the strangeness of his situation. He's no longer alone. Two old Melfar men snore softly near his feet and over there in the corner his own granddaughter sleeps, curled into a ball like a kitten. Lambert rises quietly, flinching at the noise the door makes as he opens it. He doesn't bother to close it again.

He watches the clouds forming to the southwest as they do every morning about this time. Now he knows why. It's the Melfar, gathered around the great stone they call the Ancient Mica Benison, singing rain into existence and sending it out across the thirsty land. Lambert clutches at the green grass with his bare toes. His heart glows with gratitude, then cringes with regret for all the times he's spoken harshly about Shoons, these remarkable people who call themselves Melfar. He tries to remember the song the two old men shared with him last night. Not the one about calling rains. The other one. The one they call the Song of All Songs. He wants desperately to believe that what the song promises is possible, that Melfar and Mundani could live together in peace. What strange words those are—Melfar and Mundani. Lambert hadn't known either of those words before, but he likes them. The words carry neither malice nor arrogance. They only describe people, making it possible to talk about differences without rancor.

Lambert isn't sure what comes next. He'd sought solitude in this remote location, refuge from a world he'd never found particularly hospitable and that he'd increasingly found downright hostile. He was looking for answers, but until yesterday he'd found none. Now he discerns at least some glimmers of possibility. Even though the Palinjians are still at large, their influence wavers and their future is uncertain. Unfortunately, based on the stories from the two Melfar brothers and their friend Willem, Lambert sees how the fury and brutality of the Palinjian loyalists has only intensified. And what was it they'd told him about the search for a son of Zibal Palinj? Lambert's thoughts careen between hope and fear.

"There are those who are organizing resistance against the Palinjians," Abél says. He's joined Lambert in the dew laden dawn outside the cabin.

It's as if Abél has read Lambert's thoughts. *Of course he has.* Such powers used to terrify Lambert, but now he reacts with more curiosity than fear. He wants to know more about these two men who seem so gifted in this art. Lambert keeps thinking his thoughts. *Would such people accept the participation of one such as I? A son of the House of Quint?*

"They already embrace your father." Abél speaks quietly, verberating in careful consonance with his words.

"And who are these people who are organizing in opposition to the Palinjians?" Lambert has turned to face Abél.

"Kinrens. Women especially. A few Sidayens, I'm told."

"Chanters?" Lambert is thinking of his late wife. Fia was a Chanter, though only in secret. She thought he didn't know.

"So they're called. They've put words to many of the songs and they do chant them together."

"Let's walk a while," Lambert says. His weakened body feels energized by what he's learning, and he longs to be active again.

The two men, one tall and dark, the other short and thickly built, with amber skin and silvered straw-colored hair, walk together through the greening landscape.

Lambert has spent much of the past stint apologizing to his dead mother, his deceased wife, his murdered daughter, and his abused granddaughter for the errors of his thinking, for his wrongs and those of all the Sidayens who assumed superiority without question, superiority over women and other kinrens, superiority over Shoons. He desperately wants to change his thinking but finds unexpected emotions springing up to impede the change he desires. Would it be possible for him to work with a group led by kinrens? By women? Maybe even Shoons? Melfar. Wouldn't he be tripped up into saying offensive things that would make them dislike and distrust him?

"I don't think you have to be too concerned about that, Lambert. Your heart is right. I think they'll see that and if you show that you're willing to work under their guidance, you'll soon gain their respect."

"Do you know these women?"

"You should talk with your granddaughter. She knows one of their leaders rather well, as did your daughter. Of course, Vidvana is still in New Beniford."

"Vidvana. You said Willem is her partner?" He'd barely stopped himself from saying she was subsumed to Willem. "I met her once. Shortly after my daughter Keira died." Despite the disturbing details Vidvana had shared about the circumstances of Keira's death, Lambert had liked the woman, liked the kindness she'd shown to poor motherless Ann when all he'd thought about was his own grief over the loss of his daughter.

"In Fayredell, one of the leaders is a Mundani woman from Blanton. She's called Gerd Finch."

"Is she one of those who implemented the deaths you were telling me about last night? At the Blanton Clauster?" Lambert had not previously known about the simultaneous demise of the six Palinjian leaders.

"That's right. Gerd is a strong and wise woman. We could introduce you to her."

Was that Father's idea or ours?

Lambert takes in a deep breath and lets it out slowly, squinting into the sunlight at a small flock of waterfowl in the distance. Where did those come from? He hasn't seen waterfowl of any kind in so many passages. "Yes," he says. "I think I'd like that."

We like it, too, and experience a pleasant sense of relief. Release.

Did you know they found Lambert, Mother? I think he's going to help us.

Maddie catches her breath as we stir in our bed. "Mer?" she says. "Mer, can you hear me?"

We watch Mother watching us. We do hear, but the voice comes from far away. Too far for us to answer. Tears form in our eyes as we dissolve once again into the vibrant colors of the Migrant, into the other story they're showing us. Back into the hue-sparked darkness of the caverns where Amergin and Naomi wait.

13.

≈

"When is he coming back?" Cruz asks, staring into the obscure depths of the pool. His friend Sancho has been gone for a whole day. Cruz has finally stopped crying, but he refuses to abandon his watch at the water's edge.

Sister Antonia folds her arms around the boy and strokes his hair. He's still a child to her even though he's now almost as tall as Amergin. "He'll come back when he's found a way," she says, struggling to convince this fragile young man that there is hope, trying to believe that somehow Sancho has escaped through the water into another cave. Or out of the caverns altogether. She wants to believe that.

The quinoa is all gone now and without Sancho to catch creatures from the pond, Sisters Berta and Maggie Marie conclude that they must try again to find a way out. Staying in this chamber means certain death, slow death by malnutrition and eventual starvation. Already the children have grown thin and listless. The three Sisters see how dry their own hair and skin have become and how readily they tire from the slightest exertion. The accumulation of their own waste led to a recent bout of intestinal distress from which they've barely recovered. If they don't go soon, they'll be too sick and weak to go at all.

"If we can find the main bat roost, surely there will be an opening where we can escape," Sister Berta says.

Sister Maggie Marie doesn't argue. She prays that this might be a release from their misery. She prays for liberation from their prison.

They collect water into the saved jars and bottles. They've dried some mushrooms, as well as some of the fruits dropped by Alondra's avian companion. They collect what they can of the lichens and sprouting ferns in the band of green things. This is what they have as they say farewell to their faint patch of daylight and make their way back into the darkness, back to where they were before they came to this cavern, in which they've now spent uncounted days.

Sister Berta actually had attempted to count the days and it is this estimate that makes her push for their departure. She knows that the rainy season is coming, and she fears what might happen if the water level in their pool should begin to rise.

The narrow exit way, deemed unfeasible when they first arrived, opens out quickly into broader spaces. Once again, Amergin leads, warning them of low ceilings, obstructing stones, and sharp turns in the passage. The rest of the group, holding hands or grasping the backs of clothing where single file is required, follow his lead. Sister Antonia finds that even though both Alfrin and Alondra are lighter than before, she struggles harder to carry them when they grow weary and plead with her for respite.

"Do you see them, too, Sister?" Alondra asks her. "The pretty lights, I mean."

Sister Antonia does see, and she now feels no shame in admitting it. "Yes, little one," she says. "I especially like the purple glow that bounces along the ceiling, don't you?"

"Yes," Alfrin says. "And the bright gold ball Amergin and Omi play with. I want them to toss it to me, but they never do."

Antonia has begun to pertange the meaning of this orb, which has recently shifted from orange to a brilliant yellow. Aren't they too young to experience such attraction?

The blindest of the group is Sister Maggie Marie, who remains unaware of the violet waves she emits, offering frail wisps of hope to her companions.

With no cues to tell them when it's day or night, they rest whenever they grow too tired to carry on. Sister Berta can tell that the intervals are getting shorter. She keeps recalculating their food consumption. Every time, her allocations are a little less. They were already far less than their needs.

"There's water ahead," Naomi announces one day. "Can you smell it?"

Amergin doesn't want to say that the smell of the water has obscured the scent of the bats that he's been trying to follow. But at this point there is only one way to go. He hopes they took the correct turning the last time he had to choose.

The passage widens as they near the place with water.

Suddenly Amergin stops. "Wait," he says loudly. "Stop right where you are." In a lower voice to Naomi, he says, "Can you see it?"

She understands what he means. "I can," she says. "It's broad. And so deep."

Amergin breathes deeply and quietly for a moment or two while everyone waits. "There's a ledge around one side where the water seems shallow enough."

"I can't see where it ends." Naomi has her eyes wide open, as if she sees the dull emanations of the rock through the undulating golden water, as if she hears it in spite of the interruptions of an intrusive voice she's begun hearing lately. The voice repeatedly calls each of them by name. *Omi! Amergin! Sister Antonia!* Naomi finds the voice confusing. Amergin doesn't hear a voice so much as sense that something is calling them ahead, offering direction. Right now, they need to concentrate on the lineaments of the water-filled cavern in front of them.

After hearing what Naomi and Amergin have to say about the way forward, Sister Maggie Marie decrees that they should rest for a while before wading through the water along the edges of the pool. Then the elder Sister withdraws into herself and, holding between her hands the cross burnished bright by peanut butter, she begins to pray. She prays for wisdom and insight, and for deliverance from their dark prison, concluding, "Saint Odilia, whose name is glorified by miracles, pray for us. Saint Odilia, patroness of the eyes, pray for us. Saint Odilia, powerful intercessor with God, pray for us. Saint Odilia, our help and hope in all our needs, pray for us." She follows up with a fervent prayer directed toward their father and finishes with another hailing someone called Mary. At last she rests. But she doesn't sleep. She waits wide-eyed for her miracle.

Our hearts break for these friends. We marvel at their persistence, their unwillingness to give in to the easier path, the resignation of death, of rejoining the Migrant. Is that what they mean by God?

Abél says willful clinging to this singular life is wrong. But is Sister Maggie Marie willful or only determined to protect the ones she's taken into her care? I remember what Brân told Damon. He said that the thought of others can sometimes override willfulness. Surely these Sisters are motivated by their thought of others, by their concern for the children and the children's future. Our future? Our hearts swell with golden gratitude for such caring.

For Mother's caring.

For our father's caring.

14.

≈

Mother wonders how much longer this can go on. Her distress is our constant companion. Her perplexity, her yearning for Gerd. Her concern tethers us. We want to tell her not to worry, that we're okay. That Gerd is okay.

Is she okay?

We watch as Gerd and Shifra help Daedal spread another blanket across the floor, covering several reed mats, producing a surface that they hope will be at least a little less brutal than the stones and packed earth beneath. The two women aren't sure what to expect from Roqu's lessons on how to defend themselves from attacks, but they have a feeling there might be bruises. Gerd's son Fergus and his friend Jalu are there, too, eager to learn what they can. Being Melfar, Jalu is considerably shorter than Fergus, though the two young men are nearly the same age.

"Yes, mainly for defense when we're attacked," Gerd says to Roqu. "But also..." She lowers her voice. "Let's say we needed to subdue someone so that we could per-haps relocate them to another place. Could you teach us a way to do that?"

Roqu's eyebrows shoot up at the word "relocate." "Those are two different sets of techniques," he says. "Are you talking about abducting someone? Taking a hostage? I need to be clear what our intentions are."

There's something in Roqu's straightforward manner that makes Gerd inclined to trust him. Here is a man who has seen much, a kinren who once belonged to the highest House in Fayredell, and he's offered to help their cause. She reminds herself of the possibility that he could be a spy, someone sent to subvert their plans. Daedal has assured Gerd that Roqu has been coming to meetings for a couple of stints now and seems fully committed, willingly divorced from the ranks of Sidayens and their still loyal kinrens. Nevertheless, Gerd chooses to speak cautiously. "Let's say that might be so. Potentially."

"Then I would recommend we conduct defense training for everyone, reserving for a smaller group the techniques of subduing and...how did you put it? Subduing and relocating individuals. Those skills will call for somewhat different training."

"Yes, that sounds good. Today we're mainly looking for demonstrations. So that we understand what the possibilities are."

Roqu and Gerd walk to the center of the mat and she addresses the group. "Today we're going to see what Roqu has to offer us." She turns toward him. "How shall we proceed?"

The man stands relaxed and nonchalant and then raises his chin and says, "Attack me."

"How..." Gerd begins.

"I believe you know how." A grin creases Roqu's face just before Gerd throws herself toward him, her right arm raised to strike. Just before she finds herself flat on her back on the mat. Her grimace of pain is quickly erased by a smile of utter delight. This is what she wants to learn to do. "Please explain," Gerd says, rising to her feet.

And Roqu does. He explains that fights are often chaotic affairs in which an attacker comes at you, flailing and punching. "Knocking them to the ground can take away their power to strike you with fists," he says, "or whatever's held in their fist. I'll show you how that's done and then we'll work on how to escape when someone grabs you by the arm or by the neck."

By the time each of the participants has gone through their paces, playing alternating roles of victim and attacker, they're exhausted and sore and bubbling with optimistic confidence.

"You have to be willing to strike at your attacker's vulnerable points—their eyes, genitals, throat, knees—and to take advantage of any weaknesses they present. Your opponents will be Mundani and those long braids the men like to wear can give you a useful grip." Roqu glances toward Gerd as he shakes his head, setting his own short locks shimmering in the light. "The sashes they often wear slung across their chests also can be used to grip and to choke. But don't get wound up in them yourselves. We'll work on that next time."

"Thank you for all of this, Roqu," Gerd says, placing her hand gingerly on the man's shoulder. "We'll arrange for you to meet with more of our people. We want everyone to benefit from this type of training."

"I'm happy to share what I know. But all of you must remember: Knowing how something is done is only the beginning. You have to practice and drill until your body knows the movements instinctively. The practice also will make you stronger," he said. "In a few stints, you'll be as strong as Gerd."

Gerd starts to say something but remains silent, watching with satisfaction as the gathering disperses.

"Thank you, Roqu," Gerd says as the two of them walk off the mat side by side. "I'm hoping this can help us to be prepared for whatever the Palinjians might be planning for the Binder." Perhaps there will be nothing more than a series of traditional bonfires, but given the current state of turmoil among Palinjians, she fears it might be worse. Mundani women and kinrens are almost as fearful of the Binder as Melfar are.

"I'm grateful for the opportunity to help," Roqu says. "Decide who you want to receive the other training. And let me know when you want to meet."

Sometimes we think Gerd is almost aware of our presence. We're sure Naomi and Amergin know when we're with them, even though they don't understand who we might be. They only know that odd things sometimes happen. They ask nothing of us.

What do we ask of them?

Thinking of Naomi and Amergin pulls us back into the dismal cavern where they still wait.

15.

Sister Maggie Marie's miracle didn't come. Instead the children awaken in puddles of water and Sister Berta knows that this means the rains have begun in earnest and are now feeding into the underground lake in front of them. She fights off the panic rising in her chest and quickly rouses the other two Sisters and the eight children.

She speaks to Amergin in an urgent whisper. "We have to go now. We have to get through this before the water gets any deeper. Can we do that?" Her trust in her blind son wavers and she strives to make her voice sound more resolute. More confident. "You can get us through. I'm sure you can."

"Yes, Mother." In truth, Amergin can't yet see to the other side, but he pertanges that his mother, Sister Berta, is trying to engender calm and he does his best to do likewise.

Amergin moves to the front of their little band with Naomi behind him, clinging to his belt. Cruz comes next, then Lourdes and Frida. Sister Berta follows; her hand is on Frida's shoulder, but her awareness is with Amergin. Sister Antonia keeps Alfrin in front of her, clinging to Berta, while Alondra, humming softly to herself, clutches the back of Antonia's skirt. Balbina, who helps Antonia with the care of the little ones, is next. Sister Maggie Marie brings up the rear, muttering prayers, increasingly insistent that Saint Odilia grant them one small miracle. She tries not to seem ungrateful for the fact that they are still alive at all.

The darkness is maddening as they move forward, cleaving to a solid wall to their right and knowing that to their left there is only water. Deep water. Those who can pertange more than simple photons are even more perplexed. They sense the depth and breadth of the waters and none can yet see where it ends. If it ends at all. Hearts pound and breath comes hard and fast. The path beneath their feet is uneven and narrow. There are places where it slopes precariously toward the water. And the water, which barely wet their ankles at first, is now halfway to their knees.

"Sister Antonia," Alondra calls out in her warbling voice, "I'm frightened. Carry me! Please carry me."

"Quiet," says Balbina. "I've got you. Hang onto Sister's skirt. You'll be okay."

"But the water's over my knees."

The tremor in Alondra's voice breaks Antonia's heart. "Hold onto Sister Berta, Alfrin. I'm going to pick up Alondra." Antonia lets go of Alfrin and turns toward the little girl. "Alondra, you're going to have to climb up on my back. I'll squat down and you climb up, okay?"

The child replies with a sniffle and Antonia imagines her nodding her head in agreement. She turns her back to Alondra, squatting down in the rising water. Frail arms encircle Antonia's neck and a little foot digs into each hip. Antonia says a silent prayer for strength and searches the wall for a handhold that might help her rise. "Hold on tight," she says. As she places her left hand on her knee to leverage herself into a standing position, the rock beneath her left foot gives way. Grasping at the slippery wall, she slides toward the water as Alondra shrieks into her ear.

"Antonia!" Sister Maggie Marie has her back to the wall, clinging, fearful lest the crumbling ledge take her, too.

"Help us!" Antonia shouts and it is unclear whether she speaks to God, to Saint Odilia, or to her Sisters.

Sister Berta answers the plea. "What's happened?" she calls, retracing her steps, pushing Alfrin along in front of her. She knows by the splashing that someone is in the water. Is it Antonia? "Where are you Antonia? Can you hear me?"

"Over here!" The plaintive voice is Alondra's. The child is sobbing. There is no answer from Antonia.

Berta sits down on the ledge and makes Alfrin step over her, sending him to the care of the others. She can do nothing about his tears right now. "I'm sitting down, Alondra. I'm stretching out my leg. See if you can grab hold of it."

A hand grasps Berta's ankle and she slips forward a little bit, barely maintaining her seat in the rising water. The hand isn't Alondra's.

"Berta!" Antonia gasps and splashes. "I've got Alondra."

"Don't pull," Berta says, trying to sound calm. "Tread water if you can and steady yourself."

Antonia coughs and Alondra sobs but there's less splashing.

"There's a ledge underneath here." Antonia sputters as she's briefly submerged again. "If I balance on the ledge, I think I can push Alondra up to you. Can you go to Sister Berta, Alondra? Go sit on her lap and then I'll come to you."

The little girl crawls up Berta's extended leg and onto her lap, never ceasing to wail and sob. We can almost see bars of light bracing the child against the walls with every cry. Sister Berta holds Alondra for a moment, seeking to quiet her as Sister Antonia treads water, clinging to Berta's outstretched foot.

Cruz has made his way toward them and he reaches out now for Alondra. The two of them retreat, clutching one another, both of them sobbing softly.

"Are you ready to try and get out, Antonia?" Berta says. "We need to think exactly how to do it. I need to move back a bit. I've slipped a little too close to the edge." Antonia relaxes her grip as Berta scoots backward, lodging her hips as firmly as she can against the wall. "I think," she says, "that if you can kind of float horizontal next to the wall and then roll up toward us, I can grab your arm and Sister Maggie Marie can grab a leg and pull you out. Do you think that will work?"

Antonia fumbles about in the water, the fingers of one hand still digging into Berta's ankle. Finally she says, "Yes. We can try that. There aren't enough footholds for me to climb out."

Berta also knows that Antonia likely is not strong enough to hoist her body out of the water without assistance. "I'm going to lie on my stomach, Antonia. Sister Maggie Marie will do the same. We'll haul you up between us. Here's my hand."

Antonia finds Berta's outstretched right hand and releases her hold on the Sister's leg. There's more splashing and then Maggie Marie announces, "I've got her. I've got hold of her ankle." The older Sister begins murmuring pleas to God and Saint Odilia.

"On the count of three, then," Sister Berta says. "One. Two. Three!" and Sister Antonia rolls and is dragged up onto the ledge. Sisters Berta and Maggie Marie sputter and cough as their faces are pressed into the water by their effort.

There's a ragged cheer of relief from the rest of the company as the three Sisters sit on the ledge, water up near their waists, and puff and sob with relief and gratitude.

"There's no time to rest." Sister Berta struggles to rise to her feet. "We're all tired to exhaustion but we have to move on because, as you can see, there's nowhere to rest here. Amergin, do you hear me?" she calls.

"I hear. Is everyone ready?"

One by one they stand and, taking hold of a hand or belt or tattered skirt, they begin to move ahead.

"I think the water's getting a bit shallower," Amergin says, just before he steps down into water that comes up past his knee. "Never mind," he grumbles. He almost says something about the ledge getting a bit wider, but then he thinks better of it.

But the ledge is wider. And after struggling about fifty paces through knee-deep water (which is nearly up to Alfrin's and Alondra's waists) the water finally becomes decidedly shallower.

There's a sharp climb upward that demands all their remaining strength, and then they are out of the water altogether. The passage is narrow, but the only water comes from slow drips overhead. They stop for a while to rest their weary limbs and eat a few crumbs of food, clustering together for warmth.

Naomi nestles next to Amergin in the blackness. She longs to see his face again, but then reminds herself that he's never seen hers. An orb of yellow light pulses between the two youths.

"Do you hear that?" Naomi says suddenly.

"The voice you mean?" Amergin has begun hearing it, too. "It sounds closer now. How do they know our names, do you suppose?"

"Do you know who it is? I think I ought to recognize the voice."

"I can't tell. It sounds so muffled and strange coming through the rocks." He thinks about their two missing companions, Lasaro and Sancho. Could one of them be out there somewhere? Or maybe Dolores, calling from beyond. The sound is that strange.

After they've rested a while in the cramped passage-way, Sister Berta gets them on their feet again, insisting that they need to keep moving.

Those who can pertange such things are pulled along by sparks of color from the cavern walls and the sub-audible hum of the slowly evolving rocks, some reaching downward, others growing upward. The way is rough and occasionally so narrow the Sisters can barely squeeze through. Sister Berta is sure their toes are on the verge of rotting off from the relentless damp and the recent slog through deep water. Legs and lungs beg for rest.

"A little farther ahead there's a big room," Amergin announces. "With fresh air. We can rest there."

"That's welcome." Sister Berta refuses to succumb to the madness of malnutrition and exhaustion. She's begun to see things in the absolute darkness of the caverns. She's hungry for sunlight.

"Ellas son monjas. Como monjes, pero mujeres." Naomi murmurs the words under her breath and glances around to see if anyone heard her. Such reflex actions still happen, even when she knows she'll see no one. She thought she heard a voice. Not the one calling their names, but a different one. Something about this voice, this presence, puts her in mind of how, as a small child, she used to sit in the little patch of garden behind her house, talking to the plants and butterflies. Listening. That habit is part of how she came to be at Saint Odilia's. She remembers that Saint Odilia's is now destroyed. There was a blast. Two of them. And after that an earthquake.

We know now the story of how they got here. How we got here is another matter.

The room they enter is not so big after all, but it's big enough so that they can all find some relatively flat space where they can sit down, where they can stretch out their weary bodies. And there is air. Moving air. The movement is barely perceptible, but the air is warmer and carries a vague scent of green. There's an unmistakable stench of bats.

If only there were light.

Naomi and Amergin sit huddled close, conjuring together an image of the contours and extent of this chamber. It connects with three passages: First, of course, the one by which they arrived, the passage filling with ever deeper water. That way is closed. A second passage is high overhead. Too high. Inaccessible. The third passage is low and narrow for a considerable distance. But after that it breaks out into a series of small, connected rooms. And somewhere, farther on, there's the chamber where the bats cluster to sleep.

"Do you think we can all fit through the low passage?" Naomi isn't sure she wants to try.

"If we crawl on our bellies, I think so. We're all thinner than we used to be." Amergin knows Naomi's arms are thinner, though they also weigh heavier against his bony, sagging shoulders.

Naomi tries to imagine what she looks like now, and to visualize Sister Maggie Marie, who was always reassuringly plump. There's no plumpness left on any of them. She fights against the thought that this is where they will all die. Here, buried deep underground, shrouded in this unremitting blackness.

We're suddenly fearful. We want to tell Naomi not to think like that.

"Don't think like that," Amergin says.

We yearn to offer comfort, something pertangible across this vast breach of time. Our hearts wrench at the plight of this pathetic group of travelers. A shower of warmest lavender spills over Naomi and Amergin and they breathe it in, wondering why they suddenly feel less desolate.

16.

"Did you see that, Damon? She smiled." Mother smiles, too. "I think she may be coming around."

Damon takes our hand and clasps it to his breast. "Meri? Can you hear me?" His words invade our hearts with rosy warmth, gentlest lavender.

Our lips move, though no sound accompanies the movement. Damon leans closer. "I think she's trying to say my name. Yes, Meri, it's me. Damon. Please come back."

As Damon watches, our lips struggle to form an "O" as our voice engages with breath at last. "Omi," we say. Our eyes blink open. "Omi?"

"I'm going to fetch Bekanz," Mother says. "Maybe she can help Mer to pull out of this."

"Yes, Maddie, of course," Damon says. His eyes try to hold ours as we glance anxiously around the room. "It's okay, Meri." He murmurs the words, reaching out to stroke our forehead, our hair.

"No. Not okay." We jerk our hand free from Damon's grip and struggle to sit up. "We need to help. We can't leave them." Our voice sounds harsh, hoarse from disuse.

Does our wildness frighten Damon? Good. There are frightening things to tell.

"We're all okay, Meri. The nens are okay. Don't fret. We only want you to get well." His words struggle to reach across the chasm, to the place that still holds us.

He wants to calm us, but he has no idea where we've been or what we've seen.

"No, no, no!" We're shouting now. We fling the sheet away and, careless of our near nakedness, swing our legs over the side of the bed and stand. Our legs are so weak. We grip the sides of our head and emit a helpless wail that starts shrill and descends into a low sob as we drop back onto the bed. Our eyes find Damon's face, all watery through our tears. "Damon? Why?"

"I...I don't know." How could he know?

Our eyes go suddenly wide and both hands go to our belly. "Oh," we say, our voice barely more than a whisper. "Are our nens okay?"

"Yes, Meri. Bekanz has been looking after you and she says they're fine." He doesn't say how worried the healer has been the past two days, concerned that so many days without adequate nourishment were beginning to take their toll.

The door opens and Damon turns, expecting to see Bekanz there with Maddie, but instead it's Avienne.

"Oh, Eldmother," we say. "You can tell us, can't you? Tell us what happened." Despite our weakness and confusion, a turquoise wave lifts from our throat and is drawn into Avienne's forehead. A pulse sent from aurynx to gnosic orb. A memory. A message from friends left behind, lost in darkness.

A rosy wave of comfort returns to us from Avienne. She turns to Damon. "May I have a few moments with her?" she says.

Damon leans over to kiss our forehead. As he departs, he's almost aware of how the room swirls with color, thrums with unspoken notes and tones.

You've been with the Migrant, Meridia. Avienne's verdant longing says she wishes she could have accompanied us on our journey. *But it wasn't for me to see. It was for you.*

We didn't know to do anything but go where the Migrant led us. So we went.

You did well, child. I feared for you, but you've come back.

They need our help, Eldmother.

Who? Ah, you must tell me.

And so we show Avienne the children, the three Sisters of Saint Odilia, the explosions, the earthquake, the grim caverns. *Who are they, Eldmother? Why did the Migrant take us there?*

The Migrant has made you a witness, Meridia, a witness to something important.

Important? But they feel like such simple, ordinary people. And yet we know they're not. There's nothing ordinary at all about Naomi and Amergin. Nothing ordinary about how they came to be wandering so long in that oppressive darkness.

The Migrant will make it clear to you in time, Meridia. You have to trust that.

We're sure she's right. It's hard for us to think about that kind of trust.

It's hard for us to think.

It gets a bit better as the days pass. We try to reintegrate with life around us, but our mind feels like a burst dam, our awareness spilling out, flowing first one way, then another. They tell us we were gone only a few days. It seemed longer. Everyone treats us timidly, as if they're afraid we might slip away again. As if our journey with the Migrant has made us into something extraordinary. We know we did nothing to merit such reverence.

We miss Naomi and Amergin and Sister Berta and the rest almost as much as we missed Damon and Mother while we were away.

Mother tempts us with the tastiest foods, but we eat mostly out of obligation. It's necessary to eat in order to regain our strength, to nourish the nens of us. Mother tells us this every day. We wonder what peanut butter tastes like.

Father is back. He left his brother and Lambert Quint, declining to accompany them to Fayredell. He thought we might need him.

We recover strength and reclaim our daily routine, but everyone still wants to take care of us. We're hardly ever alone. Mother stays most of the morning. Father comes after midday. Our eldmother Avienne also comes frequently. She didn't come yesterday; Bekanz told us she wasn't feeling well.

Zara visits, too, and Vidvana. We're not certain yet how much to tell them all about what we've seen. Damon, of course, is here from early evening to morning and several times during the day.

Sometimes when Mother is here our mind wanders back to Temur, back to the life we shared there, back to a time when we knew next to nothing about being Melfar. We knew about being Shoon, about being relegated to near invisibility by Mundani who demeaned everything about us—our appearance as well as what they called our superstitious beliefs and practices. Mother tried to protect us. We still don't understand why Father left.

He's here now, though, and he's the only one who understands how much we crave our time alone. Except we don't want to be alone so much when he's here. We want him to explain things to us.

He's arrived near day's end. We offer tea and questions.

How does it happen, Father? They felt so real to us and yet we were still aware of Damon, aware of Mother. And of you while you were with Lambert Quint.

You were experiencing the awareness of the Migrant, Meridia. The Migrant is everywhere and can be in the past and now all at the same time.

We ponder that. We feel the truth of it, though we don't understand it.

We ask the other thing that's been worrying our mind. Or at least the start of the thing.

Why were those children sent away by their parents, Father? We saw how tenderly the Sisters of Saint Odilia cared for the children, but where were the children's own parents? Other than Amergin, whose mother was Sister Berta, all of the children had been sent away. We would never do that. Damon would never do that. *How could any parent want to be apart from their children?*

We look into Father's eyes and see the upwelling of memory and regret. And so we ask: "Why did you leave us, Father?"

"I didn't mean to," he says. *I thought I'd only be gone a few days.*

We reclaim a vague memory of Father picking us up, hugging us, hugging Mother. There were kisses, too, and yes, the bright promise, casually given, to be home soon.

Do you really want to know this story, Meridia?

Yes, Father. Tell us.

He reminds us of the promise he made to his own father to find the Mica Benison whose song was Calling the Rains. Someone had told him—it was Brân who told him—that the stone might be in Brightlea. Brân shared with Father a story he'd heard from a Melfar man who passed through Brightlea while Brân was still living there. Father doesn't know who the Melfar man was who told the story. *It was not a very promising lead, but I'd grown desperate.*

The man told Brân, and then Brân told Father, about a vision he'd experienced on his way to Brightlea from Túl. The man had carried with him two waifs. One was an Old Turquoise and the other was a very small fragment of what was then called the Old Mica. In his vision—a dream, perhaps—this man pertanged a very large waif of mica buried beneath the paving stones around a fountain in the Brightlea Temple. He saw the temple awash with rain.

Brightlea is where Father was going on the day he left us. He thought he'd be back in only a few days. A six at most. He set up camp outside Brightlea, watching the temple to learn the habits of its patrons and caretakers. He made a plan.

He shows us how, on a moonless night, secure in his ability to pertange his way through the dark, he climbed over a low section of the temple wall and made his way to the fountain. Humming a protection cloak around himself to shield his activity, he began digging into the perimeter of the fountain. We see him working, prying up stones, one after another. He found nothing. In his disappointment, he let his attentiveness to the protection cloak falter as he departed. There were only two kinren guards on duty, but they were strong men and more than a match for Father.

Oh, Father. We never knew! Did Mother know?

Eventually she found out. There was nothing she could do.

When the guards saw what Father had done, he was accused of vandalism and theft, though he'd tried to put everything back as he found it and he was carrying away nothing from the temple other than the dirt and grime on his tools and his person. There were no official charges or proceedings. He was Melfar, a Shoon accused by Mundani. *At least they let me live,* Father says. Instead of getting rid of him right there and then, they sent him to a place on the seacoast down near Markham. "It was called Swarthpol."

You told us when we were on our way to Selbourne that you'd been on the seacoast before. Is that where it was? "Swarthpol?" The name of the place feels strange to us. The word has no verberations. No colors, only darkness. *What sort of place was it?* We wonder why he didn't use his Melfar gifts to escape.

My waifs were left behind, hidden at the place outside Brightlea where I'd camped. I had only the songs. He tries to show me how, at this place called Swarthpol, his songs had no power. *I don't know why it was like that, Meridia. But for almost two entire meeds I felt as if I was not even Melfar.* Father goes silent, as if he's thinking things that he can't verberate. Or remembering things he doesn't want to know and refuses to share. He's not certain that he ever recovered his full Melfar abilities.

But you escaped. You did come back. Not to us, not to his partner Maddie and their daughter, but back out into the world beyond Swarthpol.

Yes, although that was by accident. There was a storm and a flood. In trying to survive the flood, I somehow found myself beyond the reach of that place. He went back to Brightlea and found his waifs where he'd left them.

He doesn't want to say anything more, but we see how he still wasn't himself. For several returns after leaving Swarthpol he wasn't himself. Even after recovering his waifs, he was not fully Melfar. We don't understand how such a thing is possible. Father can't explain it either. He went to Beniford and lived there for a while with his mother Avienne and his brother twin Brân.

We think he passed through Temur on his way.

Yes, I went to see Maddie. I wanted so much to see you as well, but I couldn't come into the town. In the eyes of Mundani, I was an escaped criminal. He thought he was protecting us.

Father lingers now, as if this conversation has made him hesitant to leave us. We assure him that Damon will be home soon, so at last he goes. We know that wasn't what he was worried about. But how can he make up for so many returns of abandonment?

We wonder what stories might account for Naomi being sent away. Or Lasaro. What happened to Lasaro?

Knowing why Father left us for so long fills a gap in us. A troublesome blankness, an emptiness. We'd felt during much of that time as if Father simply didn't exist. In a way, we were right.

17.

⚍

"Tell us about your work, Damon. Tell us about your pictures." We want to learn about what we may have missed during our absence.

"I've had some success." Damon retrieves a box from a shelf by the door and from it he draws out a few sheets of thick paper. Photographs. He selects one and holds it up for us to see.

"Oh, Damon. It's beautiful!" In fact the image is streaky and the colors flicker oddly, but the scene it depicts is indeed beautiful. "It's Selbourne, isn't it? It's the pool where Father found the Mica Benison. How did you do it?" We know that Damon didn't take his bulky camera to the island. And yet this image of the deep tidal pool and the people surrounding it is exactly as we remember it, exactly as it was on the day of our discovery.

"I'm not really sure, Meri. I mean, I know what I did, but I'm not at all sure how it works." He describes the procedure, how he coats the photographic plates with an emulsion containing, in addition to some customary chemicals, a substance exuded by the luminous snails he brought back from Selbourne. "And I put the plates in front of Zara or Abél or Avienne and, well, they sing to them. And as they sing... I told you I don't really understand. Zara suggested that I try adding one of the substances that's used in crafting Benisons."

"Ecphorite?"

"That's it. Ecphorite. I'm still working on getting the right proportions of everything. My photos aren't as clear as the ones Fannan made."

"But who knows how long Fannan had been working on the process?" We know it was a long time. We know he was killed and most of his work destroyed in the Great Fires. "Your work is wonderful, Damon." We hand the picture back and lean around his shoulder to see what images the other papers might contain. They show scenes we don't find familiar.

"My snails aren't doing well," Damon says. He draws our attention to the glass box in the corner where he keeps them. Is it only because it's daylight that we can't detect their glow? The slime-covered stones they feed on look dull as well. "I've been thinking I may need to go back over to Aldbeck and collect some more."

"They'd be happier in a bigger community." We aren't sure why we say that, but we feel certain that it's true. We should sing to them more. They like it when we sing to them. "When will you go?"

"It's not urgent. I'll stay here with you for now."

We're grateful for that. We don't want to hold him back from his work, but we're still trying to catch up to the life that continued while we were gone. It still feels like everything moves far faster than we do.

Damon and Zara and Vidvana work every day on the *Book of All Time*, often with help from Father or Avienne or others who have stories to sing. Vidvana writes down the songs, translating the images into words, often in verse. Zara stores away the songs in her memory. She knows so many.

The book they're compiling is a topic of conversation all over New Beniford. We hear the talk, though we hardly ever leave the house.

The rumor of a descendant of Zibal Palinj is also discussed, though in quieter, tersely urgent tones. People mention the approaching Binder, that time of capricious Mundani activity. Father says they also talk about what little they know of our journey. They're curious to learn more. Father thinks our stories need to be told, ought to be included in the *Book of All Time*.

We're not sure about that.

We tell him that, at night, we still dream of the people we met in the company of the Migrant. *Are the dreams real?* we ask. We're not at all certain what we mean by "real," but Father understands. *We feel so drawn to these people. We want to help them.*

They're as real as they can be, Meridia. But I'm not sure they need any help. What you saw was all in the past. It's already happened. He tries to show us that, for the Migrant, past and now are not different.

We know. It's why traveling with the Migrant is so unsettling.

I could teach you the Song of the Canopy of Time, Father says. *With that song and a waif of the Turquoise Benison that holds it, you might be able to travel with the Migrant more securely.* He places a fragment of Turquoise into our hand. It's a small thing, but it floods us with nostalgia.

We'd be able to return when we wanted? To come and go at will? Yes, Father. Please teach us the Canopy of Time.

We sense Father hesitate over the idea of coming and going at will. He's cautioning us not to be too willful. Something about simply touching into the colors that will bring us back. Trusting the tones and rhythms of home.

Every day now, we sit together, singing the Song of the Canopy of Time. We like sitting with Father beside us, singing with his voice resonating in our ears as well as our orb. His physical presence is an anchor.

The Canopy of Time has a great many verses. Father says he doesn't know all of them; the ones he does know leave us filled with the scent of vast forests, the songs of birds, and visions of Melfar in joyous celebration. We find nothing about deep caverns and frightened children.

When we sing it, Father, we always start with the vision of Amos Quint's chamber of mirrors. That was where the Migrant first showed us what we now believe to have been the distant past of that place. Of our people? *Do you think that's okay?*

Abél tries to verberate confidence, but it's perforated with uncertainty. He thinks that what we first witnessed in Quint's cavern is indeed related to the other caverns we witnessed more recently. But his uncertainty contains the uneasy emptiness of Swarthpol.

18.

Mother asked us about Gerd again this morning. We reassured her that her friend is well. She and Gerd are more than friends, of course. Almost like partners, though never pledged.

We hope we spoke truth. Surely Gerd is well. We promise ourself to check on Gerd as soon as Mother leaves.

Gerd is with the Quints' old kinren guard, Roqu. They've been training again. Training to fight. The work is rigorous, but we sense how gratitude and confidence overwhelm their exhaustion and their assorted aches and pains. The women and men are grateful for the increasing self assurance they have as they move about Fayredell. The few who encounter the need to put the training into practice report back to Roqu.

"It was amazing, Roqu. I did as you taught us and as he collapsed, I was able to punch the weapon out of his hand and escape." The woman holds up the weapon, her trophy of the encounter. "Will you teach us how to use weapons, too?"

"Weapons are not my strong point," Roqu says. "But I know someone who could give you such training." His eyes seek out Gerd. "Do you have such weapons?"

"We have some," she says. "We could get more. But I'm averse to the kind of violence such weapons invite. I like your ways better, Roqu."

Gerd knows that whenever weapons are involved, things can get quickly out of control, with much ensuing bloodshed. And death. Not so long ago she had sought such outcomes with determination, desiring to maim her adversaries so thoroughly that they could not seek restoration, could not become Revelant and lay claim to the Melfar-like abilities that entails. Or at least the prestige of claiming the status.

Today a small group has come together to learn how to take captives. Roqu shows them how to attack quickly and stealthily and how to apply pressure to the sides of the neck sufficient to cause the individual to lose consciousness. Gerd remembers her bloody attack on the guard at the Blanton Clauster. She could have left him dazed, disoriented. Instead she'd left him dead. But she'd also left him unworthy to become Revelant.

"Shifra, come at Fergus from behind," Roqu says. "And Fergus, it's okay to try and defend yourself. Only don't anticipate too much. Wait until you hear her or feel her touch."

Shifra obeys so suddenly that such cautionary words to Fergus prove to have been unnecessary. She jumps on his back with his neck firmly grasped by one arm, her legs wrapped around his lower body. He struggles briefly and then goes limp. Shifra lowers him onto the ground, holding his two arms behind him so that they could be easily bound. She lays him on his side as his legs twitch.

"Okay, now give him some space to wake up," Roqu says. He assures them that the boy will only be out for a very short spell. "He'll be fine."

Gerd comes forward and squats down near her son, ready to offer reassurance as he regains consciousness.

She knows Shifra let go quickly. There's no damage. Nevertheless, there's a look of concern on her face.

Fergus' eyes fly open as he jerks to one side. "That was...strange," he says. "I thought I was back in New Beniford and I saw Jalu flying through the air like a bird and he took me by the hand and I flew with him."

"That was me, alright." Jalu laughs. "You were so open, so vulnerable, I couldn't help but tease you a little."

"That was impressive." The voice comes from over by the doorway.

Roqu startles. Could that be the voice of his old Sidayen master? He turns slowly toward the Mundani man who spoke. He looks older than Roqu remembers him, more frail, his wispy hair thinner and grayer. What should he call Lambert Quint now? Roqu no longer serves anyone or anything but the cause. And what is the old Prophet's son doing here anyway? Ann Landry is there with him. Roqu's eyes fall on the Melfar man standing next to Lambert, and he thinks he might be the one who brought the body of Keira Landry of Quint back to Fayredell. But, no, that Melfar man's hair was straw-colored while this one's hair is darker. Roqu's mind reels.

"Is this the one you were looking for?" Gerd asks, smiling broadly as she strides forward to welcome Brân and his two companions to her training room.

Brân nods and offers a hand in greeting to the Mundani woman, who towers over him. "This is Lambert Quint, our friend. Lambert, this is Gerd Finch."

Gerd extends her hand toward Lambert. Such a bold move would have been unthinkable only a few short stints ago—a mere woman taking the initiative to offer her hand to a Sidayen. And not just any Sidayen. This is the son of the Prophet Amos Quint. But Gerd knows Amos Quint. And she knows he would take no offense at her audacity.

Lambert brushes her fingers in the customary gesture. "I'm pleased to meet you, Gerd." His eyes testify to the truth of his words.

Ann Landry is clearly happy to be with Fergus and Jalu again. Fergus, fully recovered from his episode, offers Ann a shy embrace. The three young people excuse themselves and go in search of something to eat. A few of the gathered women and other kinrens bob in habitual deference as they depart from the unexpected presence of the Sidayen Lambert Quint, son of the Prophet. Soon there is no one left in the room with Lambert but Gerd and Brân. Gerd wonders what the gossip will be like around everyone's supper tables. What will be said of the return of Lambert Quint?

Gerd examines her own expectations. What had she thought might be achieved by finding Lambert again, by extracting him from his solitude?

We wonder about that, too. Lambert is not a prophet. At least, he's never been acclaimed as one. What makes someone a Mundani prophet anyway? We should ask Father about that. Or we could ask Amos Quint.

Gerd knows that many men are uncomfortable under the leadership of a woman. Would they prefer Lambert Quint? Men in her own company accommodate well to Gerd's leadership, but others question her every move, informing her about things when she knows far more about the situation than they do.

"I'm impressed with what you've been able to accomplish here." Lambert's eyes meet Gerd's and she can tell he means what he says. Or wants to. His eyes are unusually gentle for a Sidayen. Unusually deep.

"We've accomplished little thus far." Gerd folds her arms and lowers her eyes to gaze at her bare feet. Why should she be so modest? "But we have plans."

"Then you must tell me how I can help," Lambert says. "All I know is that the Palinjians must not be allowed to regroup. Brân's brother told me about their search for a purported descendant of Zibal Palinj."

"What? I've heard nothing about that."

Brân relays what he's learned about the plotting of the Palinjians holding forth at the Blanton Clauster, about their insistence that this Palinj, if they can find him, could become their new leader. Maybe even in time for the celebration of the Binder and the start of a new passage.

His name is Elvrid. He runs a bookshop.

How do we know this? He doesn't go by the name of Palinj and never has. Gerd doesn't hear us, but we pertange her steely resolve not to let such an eventuality deter her.

"All of this makes it even more important that we find an alternative to the old ways," Lambert says. "In the past stints I've had ample time to wallow in regret over what I now see as the error of Sidayen authority and superiority. Whatever we achieved we were only able to do because of our shameless subjugation of kinrens and especially women. And Melfar, of course. But regret isn't enough. Somehow we have to find a way to set things right."

Gerd's eyes bore into Lambert, searching his heart and finding it open and genuine. "Let's share a meal together," she says.

19.

Father says we shouldn't worry about Amergin and Naomi, that they don't need our help. But we think of them often. Surely they must have escaped from the caverns, but how?

Today Father sang a disturbing verse from the Canopy of Time about the outbreak of nacreous fever during the Amethyst Return of the Old Jade Meed. It occurred in the same return as the burning of the great forest of Cödweg. All of that was nearly sixty returns past. Five meeds. Abél and Brân's father Mica and their uncle Fannan died in the Great Fires, but Father wasn't thinking about that. As he sang, we sensed his preoccupation with things that weren't in the song. Or were they? When a song is composed of images, it's sometimes hard to know what's part of the song and what's added by the singer. Father was pondering the effects of the fever outbreak on Amos Quint. Amos lost family to the fever.

Leaving Abél, we take a side path, a path that leads to Amos Quint's cabin at the edge of New Beniford. Or maybe it's a bit beyond the edge. Amos Quint is there, seated on a stool under the shade of a young linden tree. He's an imposing figure, the white of his hair contrasting sharply against his dark face with its deeply etched lines. His grizzled brows reach out protectively over eyes that still sparkle with life. He looks up as we approach and gestures wordlessly to another stool set nearby. It's almost as if he was expecting us.

We exchange greetings and Amos offers tea from a jug at his side. We ask him about the fever.

"Yes," he says. "The nacreous fever was hard on many families. It was in the passage 609 that it started, though it didn't reach Fayredell until early in the following passage. It took my son Rahmond. He was Lambert's older brother." He doesn't say it, but we know that Rahmond was the one who had all the signs of following in his father's path. He was expected to become a prophet.

"Amos," we say, "what is a prophet?"

He laughs that deep rumbling laugh. It's irresistible and we laugh, too, although we don't feel amused.

"A very good question, Meridia." His eyes search the branches overhead, following a skittish sandy pip and its brief snatches of song. He places his hands on his knees and stretches his shoulders. "The people say—the Mundani people, that is—that a prophet is someone who is in close communication with the Creator. Some think that gives a prophet some of the powers of the Creator. The Restorer. The Migrant, as Melfar say."

Are those really all the same? Maybe. Maybe not. Amos thinks people expect too much of a prophet. Or too little? He thinks being labelled a prophet is not necessarily a good thing. Not anything to be sought.

"Something like a Calumet, then?"

"Hmm. In a way, yes. At least as far as I understand it. I think a Calumet is someone who is in close communication with the Migrant. Is that right?"

"That's how we understand it," we say. "But when we asked about it, the first thing we were told was that a Calumet is a peace-bringer." That was what Emba told us when we visited her and her partner Orban in Woodclasp. Emba was the first Melfar woman we ever met. Avienne was the next. Avienne, our Calumet. Our eldmother.

Amos Quint nods thoughtfully, twisting a strand of his beard. "That would make the designation of a Calumet more about what a Calumet does. I'm not sure Mundani prophets are expected to do anything in particular, other than make pronouncements about the will of the Creator." There's a barely audible grunt of disapproval. "There's certainly no expectation of peacemaking. No desire for it, I'm afraid."

"Do you think maybe your son Lambert can become the Mundani's new prophet?"

The old man's face clouds as his brows converge. His thoughts darken. "That's for the people to decide. Many are ready to acclaim as prophet anyone who will tell them what they want to hear." He thinks that is not something Lambert would do. He says no more on the subject, inquiring instead about Damon's progress in making the photographs. We talk about that.

By the time we leave Amos Quint, our belly is rumbling with hunger. We go to the community table and fill a plate with more food than we used to eat in two meals. We sit down next to Mother. She picks at her food as we talk. She asks about Gerd again, as she always does, so I tell her what I've learned. After lunch, Mother goes her way and we return to our cabin. We lie down for a rest with the notes of the Old Granite's Song of Firm Resolve resonating in our mind. We drift toward sleep, still thinking of Gerd.

The women who escaped from the Markham Clauster reassured Gerd that only a few Palinjians remain there. The Markham Clauster is where Gerd is headed now, accompanied by Fergus, Jalu, Daedal, and Roqu. And Teagan, who best knows the way.

Gerd has devised a plan for Jalu to distract the occupants of the Clauster with illusions so that she and Roqu can grab one of the men and carry him away. The closer they get to Markham, the faster their hearts beat in anticipation of this first audacious act to be intentionally undertaken by their group. Their cause. They trust that Jalu's canopy will hide them from view as they travel.

Why do we think Gerd looks different?

Gerd tries not to be overconfident. The reports of Palinjian atrocities may have diminished in number, but any incidents reported remain shocking in the extreme. At first, they'd only tortured Chanters and other Melfar sympathizers in order to intimidate them. Now they seem to be doing it for the sheer pleasure of watching them suffer. Palinjians have become erratic and volatile. Some reports even have them terrorizing their own people who attempt to return quietly to ordinary pursuits of farming and crafting and shopkeeping. Gerd wonders if perhaps they're competing with one another for influence and leadership. If so, they must believe that the most brutal will triumph.

We wonder if such monstrous acts could possibly be construed as the acts of a potential prophet. Or have they given up on the notion of prophets altogether? They're still searching for that alleged descendant of Zibal Palinj. They'll look for booksellers in all the towns. There aren't that many. We turn back to Gerd and her company.

It's Gerd's hair that's different. She's cut her hair short. All of the Mundani there have short hair. Short like Melfar have always worn theirs.

Gesturing toward the pale daytime moon, Teagan indicates how long it will be before they reach Markham. "There's a shelter I know of that's not far from the Clauster," she says.

"Good. We can rest there while Roqu and Jalu move closer to take the measure of the place and see how many men are present," Gerd says.

"Only men now," Teagan says with a grin. "They have to empty their own buckets." Teagan knows several of the women who fled the Markham Clauster in the immediate aftermath of what Palinjians now call the Blanton Slaughter.

Gerd has nagging doubts about the efficacy of the plan they're about to implement. When she'd shared it with Lambert, he had tepidly agreed it was worth a try. With no clear leader to depose, what can they do but move forward to try and turn the Palinjians one by one? Weaken them before they can find this descendant of Zibal Palinj. If such a person exists.

Oh, he does, Gerd. And the Palinjians think they know where he is.

Lambert had offered to accompany Gerd, but she demurred, telling him he was more important to the cause in Fayredell. In truth, she was afraid that he would be a liability. Everyone else was now trained and practiced in skills of defense and attack. Lambert was barely recovering from the privations of several stints of seclusion and, furthermore, not exactly what anyone would call a young man. Even in his youth, he'd never commanded a reputation as a fighter.

While they wait for Jalu and Roqu to return with their report, Teagan plies them with stories of atrocities committed by the Palinjians at Markham. "Just because she spilled some wine," Teagan says. "For that they say she was bound and whipped. That was when they began making their plan to escape, although theirs was not nearly so bold as that of the Blanton women." Her eyes narrow as she slaps at the ground with one end of her loosened sash. "One day I would like to meet this Madeline Einkorn."

"As would I," Daedel says. "Where is she now? You say you've met her, haven't you Gerd?"

Gerd's cheeks warm with the thought of Maddie. "She was my closest friend when I lived at Blanton and I was with her in New Beniford recently, too. With her and her daughter Meridia. Now there's a woman you should all meet someday as well."

"She's the half-Melfar who helped find Amos Quint on Selbourne, right?" Teagan says. "That was quite a feat, too. Why isn't she here helping us in our cause?"

"She's pregnant, Teagan. I thought I told you all that. Meridia is pregnant with Melfar twins."

"Of course. I remember now. Well, a pregnant woman is of little use to the cause." Teagan's face screws into a deep scowl as she re-ties her sash.

Gerd starts to respond, wanting to say there are many different ways of contributing to the cause, but she remains silent.

When Jalu and Roqu return, they're brimming with optimism. "Only three men there now," Roqu says. "And two equids, tied up near the back gate of the enclosure."

"Perfect," Gerd says. "We'll rest here until sunset and let you two take some food and drink. Then we'll move out."

20.

We wake from our nap feeling restless and dejected. We think we ought to get up, but we can't think why. Teagan is right about the uselessness of a pregnant woman. We're surprised at our residual flash of anger toward Malaki for putting us in this condition. Unwillingly, we taste again the rage we felt then. It was rape, and Malaki deserved the full force of our anger; we're not sorry he died in the Palinjian assault on Old Beniford. He was our brother-cousin, Brân's own son, though he hadn't known that when we met. No excuse. Damon's willingness to be the father of these fatherless nens sustains us now. Might that change once they're born? How will he feel—a beautifully dark Mundani man cradling two odd-looking iridescent Melfar nens? We think again about how Father left us. He never meant to. Life is so uncertain.

Barely more than a tide ago, at the Great Turning, we'd felt so sure that our world was changing at last, healing the deep division between Melfar and Mundani. When we all raised our voices together in the Song of All Songs, we believed change was possible. Now, as Gerd's fears about rising competition and violence among Mundani echo in our orb and hearts, we're not so sure. What might happen if the Palinjians are able to claim a new leader? Gerd thinks Lambert Quint might still play a role in leading Mundani away from Palinjian dominance, though she seems no more optimistic than Amos is about the prospect of Lambert being hailed as a prophet.

We're curious to know more about this man we've not yet met face to face.

Where is he now?

We look for him in Fayredell.

Lambert wears the common garb of a kinren as he walks the paths and lanes of the town. The clothes hang loose on his thin form. His face is gaunt, his long plait of graying hair decidedly off-center. He walks with slow, quiet steps, head down. No one seems to recognize him.

He's uncertain what to do with himself. He admires Gerd's sense of purpose. She's an able leader of the kinren uprising. Perhaps there's no actual rising yet, but he can see that it's building.

Maybe it's his morose mood that shrouds his countenance, making him invisible even to people who may once have known him.

He wanders aimlessly, entering shops. Buying things at random because he can, impulsively picking up whatever draws his hand. The purchases will account for his wandering.

The town feels quieter than he remembers it. Quieter than it ought to be. People walk with hesitancy, not greeting one another. Not meeting one another's gaze. These days, they're uncertain about where anyone's loyalties lie.

Something bright flashes in another shop window and Lambert enters. He makes another purchase.

Lambert is lost among his thoughts, swimming in the past. Treading water. He remembers being a child in his father's house. His older brother Rahmond was always his father's favorite, the one destined to assume leadership of the House of Quint. And after Amos was proclaimed Prophet, people watched Rahmond, thinking that he, too, might someday rise to fill that role, thinking he'd already begun to show signs of being favored by the Creator. Lambert, on the other hand, was his mother's pet. He loved the stories she told, the songs she sang, the gentle way she combed his hair and tended his small injuries. She was the one who walked with him in the gardens, teaching him the names of trees and flowers, the habits of birds and butterflies. There was a game they played, catching sunbeams with her mirror. Lambert recalls her laugh.

And then before Lambert reached his age of destiny, the fever swept through the town. Such a strange fever, with its oozing blisters that glowed green and blue in the dark. It took Rahmond. Amos grew sullen and distant with mourning. Sometimes Lambert would find his father staring at him with disappointment, even disgust, as if to say, *Why did the fever take Rahmond and not this weakling Lambert?* His mother Nahla died soon after. It was many passages before Lambert knew that her death wasn't due to the fever, as people said, but rather to her grief. Her grief and the comfort she tried to extract from the jimweed flowers in the garden.

When the fever threatened again in 655, Lambert had been terrified. But again, he never fell ill. Instead, it took his only son. It was Lambert himself who had sent the young man to Benbridge on an errand before he'd heard that there was nacreous fever there. He was left with only his daughter, Keira, and his loyal wife, Fia.

Lambert enters another shop. He thinks it smells vaguely of perfume. He notices a calendar, one of the kinds with movable pegs. Is it set correctly? Is the Binder so close at hand? He makes another purchase and moves on.

He never should have consented for Keira to marry Rolang Landry. But how was Lambert to know that Rolang would turn away from the Quints and take up with Zibal Palinj? And now Keira is dead, too, at the hands of Warreth Pherson, the very worst of the Palinjians. After Keira's murder, even Fia went away, returning to her natal home in Woodclasp. She died there soon after. Now Lambert is left with no family but Ann, his daughter's daughter. And of course, his father Amos, who insists on being a hermit.

The sack slung over Lambert's shoulder grows heavy with his purchases, forcing him to turn homeward, toward the little shed on the old Quint property where he now resides. Built of stone, it was the only building that survived the conflagration that consumed the Quint estate. The old house had been an imposing structure, built entirely of precious wood, harvested long ago from the forests that used to blanket the land. Lambert could have laid claim to the Landry property after Rolang Landry's death, but he doesn't want it. He'd sold his own house, exchanging it for freedom. He no longer has any desire for fine houses or furnishings. He feels guilty about the contents of his heavy sack.

When he reaches the shelter, he sets the sack on the bed and reaches inside. He has no idea what kinds of useless trinkets he may have purchased.

The objects he draws out from the sack cause him to draw back in astonishment. Mirrors. So many mirrors of all kinds. Round mirrors and square ones. Some in ornate frames, some with handles. And Lambert begins to laugh as an idea takes form in his mind. His father built a chamber of mirrors on Selbourne, and amid its reflections he gained congress with the Creator, which Melfar call the Migrant. Could he do something similar here? Here in this decrepit stone shed?

He could. And he will.

21.

～

"I've brought you some lunch, Mer." Mother sets the tray down on the wobbly table next to the door. It's well past midday, and she doesn't remember that we already ate lunch together at the community table. We were sitting side by side. We'd shared our worries about Avienne, who has taken to her bed with some unnamed illness. We think maybe we should be concerned about Mother, too.

Mother is fretting about Gerd, asking again if there's been any word of her.

"She has her work in Fayredell. They're grateful for her guidance there," we say. We don't mention the foray to Markham.

Mother's been more forgetful lately. The strain of our illness was hard on her. We think she also feels discomfort at being Mundani here in New Beniford among so many Melfar. She yearns for Gerd.

We feel the ache in Mother's heart, how she's torn between wanting to be with us and wanting to be with Gerd. Is this how she felt when Father left? For now, she stays with us here in New Beniford. We're grateful for her attentiveness, though it's sometimes misguided and burdensome. The nens kick with delight in her presence.

Maybe we understand a bit better now how Maddie's mind can refuse to cooperate, taking its leave capriciously. It used to do this in Temur before she went away for the last time. Before she died. Before the Migrant restored her and we eventually found her again in Shad-ham, where she had settled into a new life with Gerd. That was before the terrible thing she did in Blanton.

Mother is haunted by that. So often when we think of her, we find her mulling over those events, interrogating herself as to whether there might have been another way for her and the other women to escape the clutches of the Palinjians without leaving all six of their leaders dead. She'll drive herself mad if she doesn't find some way to make peace with it all.

Our mind wanders, too, like Mother's mind, but from different causes.

Mother leaves, promising to bring us something sweet to go with our lunch. She probably won't.

For Mother's sake, we go looking for Gerd again. Well, not just for Mother. Gerd is engaged in important work.

Near Markham, Gerd and her company have put their plan into motion. In the back of Gerd's mind there's a nugget of worry about Mother. She's also fretting over her son Fergus.

Fergus perches in a tree where he can peer over the Clauster walls through the dense foliage. There are three men there, as Roqu and Jalu reported. Fergus watches and listens. The sound comes so suddenly he almost loses his grip on the branches. There's no sound quite so terrifying as the hiss and snarl of an angry zaki and that is what Jalu has conjured. The men below sit up straighter at the sound, their eyes bulging, hearts racing. They bound to their feet at the very real whinnying of equids. Fergus can't see the equids from his vantage point until they explode through the gate, which Roqu has opened for them. The men are running, swearing, casting about for the illusory danger of a wild zaki, shouting for the equids to halt. Fergus knows what comes next: Jalu will see to it that the three men head out in three different directions so that Gerd and Roqu can subdue one of the men while the others capture one of the equids. Then they'll all make their way back to the shelter.

Fergus' task is to quickly search the temporarily abandoned Clauster for whatever appears useful to the cause, whatever he can carry away. He shimmies down a tree branch and onto the top of the wall, then bounds inside. He's impressed by his increased agility, amused by his reflexive nervousness caused by the conjured zaki. A sudden sound—a voice—halts him in his tracks. Is this another of Jalu's tricks? He turns toward the voice and sees a young boy aged no more than ten or eleven passages. The boy's dark skin is patched with scars, but his black hair is thick and glossy.

"Who's there?" the child says. "Nix? Kai? Are you there? Please answer me. I thought I heard a zaki while I was sleeping." The boy seems on the verge of tears as he stumbles across the courtyard, nearly running into a pile of fireblocks.

The boy is blind, Fergus thinks. "Oh, shit," he mumbles. What should he do? He could try to leave before the boy becomes aware of his presence. Or he could sneak around him, robbing the place unseen and then leaving the child to his fate.

And then the boy is facing directly toward Fergus. "Who's there?" he says again. "I don't understand what's going on."

"Your friends had to leave suddenly," Fergus says, feeling equal parts chagrined and inspired. "They sent me to take you to safety."

"Do I know you? I don't recognize your voice."

"I'm Fergus. A friend of Kai's." Fergus remembers one of the names the boy called out. "Recently arrived from Fayredell."

"Oh. I guess that's okay then. Let me take your arm. I see nothing, you know."

"Yes, Kai told me." Fergus is amused at how right a lie can feel. He guides the boy toward the gate, where Jalu waits for them, eyes wide.

Jalu signals silence and so Fergus doesn't speak to him. He's grateful for whatever Melfar tricks Jalu might be able to generate to offer protection as he conducts the blind boy back to their shelter.

"How did you and Kai meet?" the boy asks. "I don't recall him ever mentioning your name. Fergus, right?"

"Well, it was a long time ago. And a long story. Probably better he should tell you about it when we meet up." Fergus sends Jalu an urgent look.

Jalu signals to him again. Fergus thinks he's saying to keep the boy talking, distracted so that he doesn't notice too much about the direction they're taking or the sounds of another person walking nearby.

"Kai didn't tell me about how you lost your sight. How did that happen?"

Jalu rolls his eyes as if to say, *Anything but that, Fergus!*

But the boy merely sighs deeply and launches into a story that sounds like something he's told many times before. A story he finds tedious. "It happened in an outbreak of the nacreous fever. My mother had just birthed me, and she'd had a hard time of it, being a woman of rather advanced age. So when the fever came around Benbridge—that was where we were living, of course— she was weak and had no resistance to the fever. We both got very ill. She didn't survive, but I lived and even though I lost my sight, they all said it was a miracle that I lived at all." The boy pauses. "Would you mind slowing down a bit? This path doesn't feel familiar, and my feet are going uncertain."

Fergus slows his pace.

"Thank you. I'm surprised you hadn't heard that story. If not from Kai, then from someone else. Where is your House based? In Fayredell? And where are you taking me?"

"No," Fergus says. "I'm not from Fayredell." He ignores the boy's last question. "My House is a rather unimportant one, I'm afraid. In Blanton."

"You didn't tell me your full name."

Again Fergus raises his eyebrows, appealing to Jalu. Jalu shrugs as if to say, *Just tell him the truth.* Fergus sees that they're approaching the shelter where Gerd and the rest are gathering. "Fergus Finch," he says. He's always used his mother's last name. His father has been gone too long to be of any significance.

"I don't know that House."

"And what's your House?" Fergus says. He can see the shelter now. Gerd stands in the doorway, her eyes full of questions as Fergus and Jalu approach with this unexpected child in tow.

Gerd looks well. We must remember to tell Mother.

The boy stops dead in his tracks and shakes Fergus' hand away from his elbow. "Who are you?" he says. "If you don't know my House, then you don't know who I am. And maybe Kai is not your friend."

Fergus takes the boy firmly by one arm and Jalu grasps the other as Gerd steps forward. "Perhaps you should introduce yourself then, boy. I'm Gerd Finch."

The boy pulls himself up to his full height, which is barely past Jalu's shoulder. "I'm Saami," he says. "Saami Pherson."

"Bless the Creator," Roqu says. "This must be Warreth's little brother. You've brought in the last of the Phersons, Fergus."

22.

～

"She's asking for you, Meridia."

We stand up at once, ready to go. In this moment, nothing could be more important than responding to the wishes of our eldmother. Avienne is ill and Bekanz has been at her bedside day and night. "Is she worse?" we ask as we follow the healer down the path that leads to Avienne's tiny house.

"No, not at all." *In fact she's better. Her fever has broken and she ate a bit of breakfast.* Bekanz's images ride on a pulse of amethyst light.

We respond with a shower of flower-yellow gratitude.

We're enveloped in a faint but clearly pertangible rosy glow as soon as we enter Avienne's room. The old woman is propped up in her bed next to an open window. Sunlight in all its colors floods into her room.

Ah, my child. I'm sorry I haven't been to visit you. They wouldn't let me out of the house these past few days. Wouldn't even let me have visitors. I'm glad Abél is spending time with you. The Canopy of Time is important for you to know when you travel with the Migrant.

Bekanz leaves us alone with Avienne, cautioning us not to try the old woman's strength too greatly. *She's still in a delicate state.*

Avienne sits up straighter, trying not to appear delicate. She wants to know more about our experiences in the dark caverns.

We try to tell her, but the obscurity of that deep place has become hard for us to penetrate. The colors and sounds we experienced in the company of the Migrant grow hazy and difficult to convey.

Avienne is fascinated all the same. *How odd that they seem to have Melfar gifts and yet are not Melfar. Their appearance is altogether strange.*

We look again at Amergin and the rest, seen through Naomi's eyes in spite of the darkness of the caverns where we left them. Our impression of Naomi is less clear, but we imagine she has the same brown skin as most of the rest of them. We feel the smoothness of her hair, the contours of her face. Amergin finds her beautiful.

We try to convey to Avienne some sense of what we experienced right before we awakened, that heart connection with Amergin and Naomi. *Sometimes I wonder if these might be our eldpeople.*

Avienne draws in a deep breath and smiles. *Something more for the book then.* She's thinking about how Melfar songs have so frequently been misinterpreted and even twisted into unintended meanings by Mundani. She begins humming softly and I know the tune at once. *Even the Song of All Songs isn't enough. We need the book.*

We sing together for a while, each taking a different part. Her voice trembles but never misses a note, every color vivid and clear.

The Migrant favors you, Meridia.

That's what Father tells us. But we think perhaps it's the nens that are favored.

Either way, it's clear that you're being entrusted with something that the Migrant wants us to know. You will be the scribe of this story.

Oh, Eldmother, we can't even write. We couldn't put the story down in any kind of words.

Vidvana and Zara can help you with that. And perhaps you and Damon can make pictures. She thinks that the pictures for the book are as important as the words. *What songs have you heard in your travels?*

We hadn't thought of that. Were there songs? In a sudden rush, we hear them. Disparate notes and tones coalesce into an impression of a tune, a cadence, then a harmony. *Yes, maybe we did hear songs. Maybe Damon can make pictures of them.*

Avienne nods rhythmically and taps her fingers on the edge of her blanket. Does she hear it, too?

Damon needs to go to Aldbeck for more snails, we say.

Then he must go. Soon, I think. I wish you could go with him, but for the sake of the nens, you will stay here.

We think of the Quartz bead that hangs on a string around our neck, an exact match for the one we gifted to Damon on the day of our partnering. *And also for your sake, Eldmother.* We didn't mean to say that. We want to be hopeful. Our sigh resonates like a hammer striking darkest obsidian.

I'm well, child. Regardless of what happens. Even when I'm ill, I'm well. Her eyes glitter mischievously. Avienne encourages us to continue working with the Old Turquoise waif and its Song of the Canopy of Time. *My son is wise and will teach you well. You know the waif he gave you comes from a larger piece that was given to me by my own mother.*

We didn't know. Father hadn't said. But it might explain why we always want to have our Jade waif nearby when we work with the Turquoise. It was through the Jade that we first encountered Avienne, long before we met her face to face in Old Beniford.

Avienne begins to hum the Turquoise song and our waif vibrates softly in the pouch that always hangs at our side. A woman appears next to Avienne's bed and at first we think it must be Bekanz, come back to scold us for keeping the old woman up for so long. But then we see that Avienne is not old at all. She's a young mother who has just given birth to two sons. It's the woman standing next to her who is old. She cradles one of the newborns in her arms, verberating protection and love.

Who is she, Eldmother?

She was my mother. Her name was Meridia, like you. Your father gave you her name.

A door opens in our mind. We'd never understood that name; it's unheard of among Mundani. When Mother tried to teach us to write it, the writing always looked wrong. Why had Mother never told us that it was Father who named us? Father who gave us his own eldmother's name? What else has Mother still not told us? Her mind was so broken for so long, maybe she forgot. We wonder if she remembers now.

We won't ask her about it. Instead, we'll ask Father.

We go to Father as soon as Bekanz sends us away from Avienne, leaving her to healing rest.

"I'm not certain Maddie ever knew that was my eldmother's name," Father says.

We think he's trying to excuse her, but we let it pass.

Father tells us that our eldmother Meridia was born during a time when the Melfar of different regions were becoming isolated from one another, content to dwell apart, each group within its respective forest home. Her own mother was from Cödweg, but her father was from Serani. *As Calumet, she was able to bring our people together in a more meaningful way, teaching us how important it is for us to work together.*

She was Calumet?

Yes, Meridia, as was her mother before her. She was born during the Old Turquoise Meed.

The Canopy of Time.

She became adept with that song. She even added a few verses to it that were shown to her by the Migrant themselves. It was through that song that she began to stitch us all together again as one people. When you were born, I thought about how you also were someone born of two peoples. In your case Melfar and Mundani. You wear her name well.

Show us more of her song, Father.

23.

━━📖━━

There's a particular verse of the Canopy of Time that softens the near boundaries between past and present, making them more pliable. We use it to go back to Gerd and her company, back to yesterday, curious to learn what happened to them after their capture of the Pherson boy. Saami? Yes, Saami Pherson. And a young man whose name we don't recall.

"Why did you choose to follow the Palinjians, Nix?" Fergus says.

Nix is his name. He's the one they took on purpose in the raid on the Markham Clauster. Saami was extra.

Fergus holds onto Nix's arm to steady him as they travel back to Fayredell. The young man has stumbled more than once; he feels off balance with his wrists bound behind his back. Fergus thinks Nix couldn't be much past his own age of sixteen passages. The boy Saami sits astride the stolen equid.

Nix had never thought of it as a choice before. It was simply what he'd done, following in the path his friends were taking. "Power," he says. "Palinjians are Revelants and Revelants have power." The arrogance in his voice belies his captive state.

We think there's a hint of fear there, too. Becoming Revelant means confronting death and then, through force of will, through "yoking the Restorer," coming back. That's what they believe. Such willful behavior is abhorrent to Melfar. It's an insult to taunt the Migrant in such a way.

Fergus presses Nix further. "Are you Revelant?"

"Not yet. But they promised on my next birth anniversary they'd guide me through the ceremony. They'll do that for me and then I'll be Revelant, too."

They walk on, twenty paces or more, in silence.

"Did you ever know a boy named Hagan?" Fergus asks.

We see that Hagan is the young man the Migrant showed to us in that dreadful suicide ritual at the Blanton Clauster. Hagan had been given the opportunity to become Revelant alongside Rolang Landry. He'd failed.

Nix doesn't answer. He did know Hagan and his face goes dark and sullen as he remembers his friend. Hagan was barely two passages his senior.

"You know what happened to him, right?" Fergus says.

"He was weak." In all the passages they'd been friends, Nix had never thought of Hagan as weak. He hates himself for saying it now. But what other explanation is there? Hagan had been unable to yoke the Restorer.

"And you think you'd be strong?"

"Of course I would be." Nix intended to sound confident, but his voice comes out high-pitched and thin.

"They tossed Hagan's body into the fire like it was nothing. You know that. And you know full well that he wasn't a weak man." Fergus speaks quietly. "It's not right to insult the Creator with those willful ceremonies, trying to coerce him into bringing you back to life."

"And what about the six leaders at the Blanton Clauster?" Jalu joins the conversation that threatens to become an interrogation. "Were they weak, too?"

"That was a massacre. A slaughter. That was different." That's what Nix has been told, but when he says the words himself, they don't sound convincing.

"How was it different? Their bodies were intact," Fergus says. "They should've been restored, right? They knew how to do it, since all of them were already at least once Revelant."

"It was a trick. An evil Shoon trick." Nix glares at Jalu.

"There were no Shoons at the Blanton Clauster." Fergus recoils from the word, glancing at Jalu. But he has to use it. Nix has likely never heard the word Melfar.

"Well, the sully women who were there were Chanters. They knew Shoon tricks. But now we've finally got rid of Shoons." He directs an annoyed frown toward Jalu. "Next we get rid of Chanters. That's what we have to do now." Nix shrugs off Fergus' hand and spits into the dirt, splattering dust onto his own foot.

Fergus lets Nix walk on without assistance. "Hmm. You seem to be saying that Shoons and women are more powerful than Revelants."

Nix wheels around to face Fergus. "No! You shut up with that talk. You're one of them and you're a sully liar!" His eyes search frantically for a means of escape. His captors are only Fergus and Roqu, along with three women and a Shoon. There aren't even supposed to be any Shoons anymore. Where did this one come from? He's infuriated that he, the son of a Sidayen, could be taken and held by such a sully lot. And not only him. They have Saami Pherson, too. He thinks that if he could reach the equid Saami is riding, the two of them might escape. But how can he hope to mount an equid with his hands tied behind him?

The whole group has stopped now.

"Let's rest for a while and drink some water," Gerd says. She pulls a bag of roasted qaji nuts from her pocket and hands them to Fergus.

Fergus ties Nix's feet together with a length of rope. After checking to see that the knot is secure, he releases the boy's hands and offers him some water and the bag of nuts.

Nix rubs his wrists and accepts the water, drinking in great gulps. Reluctantly, he takes a few of the nuts. He chews slowly, as he studies his captors. They haven't beaten him even once and now they're sharing their food with him. He sneers but keeps chewing.

Daedal sits down across from Nix and offers him a piece of dried meat. "You remember Rio?" she says.

"I know the man." Nix is wary.

"Rio is my cousin. He's with us," Daedal says.

Nix scans the company again.

"No, not *here* with us," Daedal chuckles amiably. "*With* us."

"What? No. He wouldn't. Rio was as committed a Palinjian as any I've ever known. He'd never betray us."

"No betrayal. We found you quite easily without his help. We'd never press Rio to do anything that would hurt those he cares about. But he's helped us in other ways. You'll be able to talk with him when we reach Fayredell."

An angry petulance dulls Nix's eyes. "Not sure I want to talk to the likes of him if he's turned on us."

"That's up to you," Daedal says. "I'm only saying he'll be there."

24.

≈

You'll have to write that yourself, Meridia, Abél says. He agrees with Avienne that the story of Amergin and Naomi should be part of the *Book of All Time*. He also thinks we should add verses to the Canopy of Time about their experiences.

We don't know how to do such things, Father.

Let the Migrant do it through you. Breathe with your mind. Listen deeply for the songs of the places and times you visit with the Migrant.

We try to do as he suggests. Every day we try. We listen. We call to mind our walks in Amos Quint's caverns, cautiously humming the tunes we've heard. We try to remember.

We recall Naomi and Amergin. We sing their names. We hear their names echo through the caverns, cascading along its walls.

We feel Naomi's breath, shallow and desperate in a terrifying place that feels like being born.

One by one they emerge from the narrow passage into a space that feels almost bright, and not simply because it's no longer the absolute blackness in which they've been entombed for so long. There's a wide slit overhead where they can see blue sky. The stench of bats is nauseating, but hopeful.

"Amergin!" The voice is clear now. "Naomi! Sister Maggie!"

Naomi looks up into the window, blinking against the dazzling brightness. A figure takes shape at the edge of the opening. "Sancho!" Her cry is a joyous sob of relief.

"Sancho?" Amergin's face is tilted skyward, too, his sightless gaze drawn toward warmth and the sound of his friend's voice.

Above them there's a ripple of laughter and Sancho shouts again. "They're alive! My friends are here. I told you they'd make it!"

"Who is he talking to?" Amergin murmurs into Naomi's ear, clutching her hand in his.

"Is it really Sancho?" Sister Berta considers the possibility of hallucinations after so much time, so much stress, so much deprivation and darkness.

There's a rising babble of surprise as they clump together, blinking up at the opening, desperately wanting to believe. Several more heads appear in the sky window.

"Everybody, quiet!" Sister Maggie's voice is thin and weak as she gestures her charges into silence. "Sancho," she calls, her voice fractured by emotion. "Is it really you? Who's there with you?"

"It's me," he says. "My friends are going to help you out."

A moment later there are ropes snaking down through the slit. Three ropes, each with large knots that Naomi knows are intended to be hand holds, foot supports. Sister Maggie begins organizing the little group, trying to focus, trying to decide who should go first. She insists she'll go last. She's about to tell Sister Antonia to go first and try to explain to whoever is up there that they'll need baskets to extract the smaller children, when all at once baskets appear. Two baskets, each one large enough to hold a child. The Sisters help Alfrin and Alondra into the baskets.

After Balbina and Frida and Lourdes have been pulled out, Naomi and Amergin and Cruz take hold of the ropes and begin their ascent.

Naomi's hands are weak, and she wraps the rope around her wasted arms and legs, calling up all her remaining strength as the rope is pulled ever closer to the enticing warmth and brightness above. The freshness. She closes her eyes, murmuring prayers. And then she feels her body dragged onto something soft and fragrant. She opens her eyes to brilliant green and begins to sob as she caresses the grass, feeling the earth's surface alive beneath her arms and legs, nothing but open sky above.

Strangers gaze down at her. Brown-skinned men and women rasping out whispered words that Naomi doesn't understand. And yet she does understand. They're offering friendship and sustenance, sharing in the joy of their escape.

Sancho embraces Amergin and guides him to Naomi. The three of them sit side-by-side, arms around one another. The smiling strangers hand out cups of fresh water and some kind of food held on plates crafted from leaves. Naomi doesn't know this food, but the smell is appealing. She eats a few mouthfuls, watching as the three Sisters emerge and are also welcomed and fed.

"Who's here with you, Sancho?" Amergin says. His hands twitch with the desire to explore the contours of the unseen faces.

Naomi listens for the answer, stifling her horror at the bedraggled appearance of her subterranean companions, knowing that she looks no better than they. Dirty, pale skin patched with oozing red. Emaciated limbs. Matted hair thinly covering scabby heads.

"They're people from a town near here," Sancho says. "They've lived around here forever and know these caverns well. It's where they sheltered when the bombs fell. It's where they found me."

"Why do they speak so strangely?" Naomi says.

"It's their own language. I'm learning some of it."

"But their voices sound so odd."

"They say they haven't always sounded this way. They think it's the dust from the bombs that damaged their voices. But some of them can communicate like we do. Like you and Amergin."

"I knew you'd made it." Amergin had tried so hard to rationalize that feeling away. But he knew. He just hadn't said. He knew it had to be Sancho guiding them to safety.

"Did you actually swim through the passage into another cave?" Naomi shudders, trying to imagine what that would feel like.

"I found the passage when I was fishing," Sancho says. "Every day I went a little farther into it. I counted, so I'd know when to turn back. I kept getting..." He pauses and glances toward one of the strangers. "Well, I got flashes of color and I kept hearing something like music from farther ahead. You know how it is sometimes. And then one day I knew I had to try to go through. I barely made it. Quispe here pulled me out and squeezed the water out of me so I could breathe again."

Quispe nods toward Sancho and smiles. He's a short, sturdy man with thick black hair and gentle eyes. He squats next to Sister Maggie Marie, feeding her some of the soft, sweet food with a wooden spoon. The Sister stares at him, dazed, tearful. Hungry. Overcome with gratitude.

Naomi thinks how miraculous it is that all of them made it out alive. *Not all*, she reminds herself, thinking of poor Dolores whose skull was crushed in the earthquake. And no one knows what happened to Lasaro. They'd searched all through the rubble but hadn't found his body.

Lasaro is another story, Meridia.

We take a deep breath and exhale, verberating the simple notes of the verse that brings us home.

25.

≈

The more we work with the Canopy of Time, the easier it is for us to know what our friends are up to. To keep tabs on Gerd for Mother. And for ourselves.

We find Gerd in her quarters at the old Landry place in Fayredell. She spends most of her time there, working with the assorted kinrens who are as determined as she is to resist the Palinjians. The Landry property fell to Ann after her father Rolang's death and Ann has turned it over to Gerd and the Chanters who gather around her to use as they will. The place is well appointed, with a central staircase made of wood and towering bookcases, all of them empty. The Landry place is comfortable, but Gerd can't call it home. Gerd's home used to be in Blanton, with her son Fergus and her beloved Maddie. But Fergus is grown now, and Maddie lives in New Beniford.

Today we pertange not only what Gerd is doing, but clearly see those around her as well. We see how Daedal and Shifra have taken Saami Pherson into their care.

Saami was always an angry child. Motherless and blind since nenhood, he was closely managed so that he wouldn't come to harm. But he knows that he was also hidden away, always a disappointment to his family. Now he has the run of the Landry place and its surrounding gardens. At first, he searched for a way out, but soon his curiosity fastened on the scents of the myriad plants, the shapes and textures of different leaves and the sounds they made in the breeze, as well as the companionable sounds of other people as they went about their business, occasionally stopping to greet him in friendly tones.

He learns to recognize the new voices and becomes adept at distinguishing the songs of different birds. Nobody seems to mind his boundless questions. He's drawn to Shifra, who patiently describes things to him in all the detail he desires and places things into his hands so that he can experience them.

Ann Landry, who has taken to calling herself Ann breth Keira, spends time with Saami almost every day. She finds him a good listener.

"Tell me again about the trees," Saami says. He has one hand on the trunk of a small tree that Ann calls a firebush. She describes the profusion of fragrant red flowers the tree bears in eleventh stint, which she says Melfar call Blossomtide. Saami likes the sound of that.

"There used to be great forests all the way from the other side of Blanton, down past Brightlea and around to Benbridge and then up the slopes of the western mountains. The Melfar—you know, Shoons—gave their songs to the trees, and the trees helped keep the songs alive, passing them from one Melfar community to another. So it was a real problem for them when the forests burned. They lost touch with a lot of their songs and stories. They lost touch with each other."

"I don't understand how trees can learn songs."

"I'm not sure how that's done either," Ann says, "but I've seen how Melfar put songs into their stone monuments, their Benisons. It's really quite remarkable." She reaches into her pocket and pulls out a small, roundish white stone. She reaches for Saami's hand and places the stone into it.

"What's this?"

"It's a waif. It carries the song of their newest Benison, the New Marble. They call it the Song of All Songs."

"I don't hear anything," Saami says. But his hand jerks suddenly and he inclines an ear toward the stone.

"I know. The most I've ever gotten from it is... Well, sometimes I feel a little prickling when I hold it in my hand and sing some of the song. But I can tell you I saw much more than that when they raised the New Marble Benison. The song is so beautiful." Ann hears it now in her mind and the stone shimmers and shivers.

Saami closes his hand tightly around the stone. "Maybe," he says. He opens his hand again and holds it toward Ann so she can take the stone back.

"Anyway," Ann says. "I've been thinking about what Abél and Brân told me about how forests can carry the songs, and I've decided that what I want to do as my contribution to all of this will be to plant trees. To help bring back the forests so that maybe they can learn the new songs." Ann's face glows with the prospect and although Saami can't see that, he hears it in her voice.

"I like trees," Saami says. "Maybe I could help you."

"Maybe you will," Ann says.

"Maybe I could help, too."

Ann turns to see who spoke. It's a woman she doesn't recognize. She's short for Mundani, with curly hair plaited into two rough braids. The ends of the braids bear evidence of a purplish dye. Ann can't tell how old the woman is. Her eyes and smile are youthful, but there are creases around her eyes and strands of white in her hair.

"Sorry for eavesdropping." The woman holds out her hand. "We haven't met. I'm Rita. Rita Harper. I've always loved trees. The fires that came through when I was a girl made me cry. So if there's anything I can do to help put the forests back, well, I think I'd like that."

We'd almost forgotten about Rita Harper. Crispin Harper was her husband. Rita tried to give us shelter on our way to Fayredell when we were still searching for a fellow called Chapling, who turned out to be Brân. Damon was with us then. We recall how fondly Rita spoke of her trees as she guided us back to the guest room, trying to offer us safety. It was her husband Crispin who abducted Damon. Crispin is dead now.

It makes us happy to see Rita finding her own way, to see Saami settling in and making friends. We wonder what happened to the other young man Gerd and her company brought back from Markham. Our awareness shifts away from Rita and Saami and Ann, searching for Nix.

If Saami was initially annoyed at his relocation, Nix was furious. He was given his own quarters, which he thought of as a prison cell. The room was comfortably furnished, but it had only one small window and the door was securely fastened from the outside. He mostly sat in the corner, refusing the chair, staring out the window, shrouding himself with a mantle of insolence. And loneliness. But every day Rio or Fergus or Jalu came to spend time with him. They didn't interrogate him so much as simply engage him in conversation. They readily answered his questions about Chanters and Melfar. Sometimes Nix thought he was the clever one, gleaning valuable information about the ways of the enemy, but every time one of the three young men left, he realized that he had probably said more about himself and the Palinjians than he'd intended.

Sometimes all three came at the same time, and it wasn't long before Nix was laughing at their jokes and freely reciprocating their stories with some of his own. Nix is a good storyteller.

This is one of those days. Rio has even managed to bring in a small flask of wine for them to share.

After the laughter subsides pursuant to a particularly hilarious story from Rio, Nix looks from one to the other of the three young men. "What do you intend to do with me?" he says.

"Do with you? Nothing, Nix," Fergus says.

"Are you going to let me go?"

"Nix, you've been free to go for the past six. The door is unlocked. No one is holding you here."

Nix stands up and glances toward the door. He glowers at Rio and Fergus and Jalu. He walks to the door and opens it. Then he sits back down and reaches for the wine flask.

"Well done, brother," Rio says.

We chuckle quietly to ourselves as we tuck the Old Turquoise away.

26.

꧄

We know even before we hear the ululations. We knew when we left Avienne's bedside last night that our precious eldmother would not open her eyes to another sunrise. There had been a flickering iridescence embracing her, a scramble of tinkling bells fumbling toward a tune that we couldn't yet discern.

Bring me my stones, Meridia. The verberations from the old woman's aurynx had been fragile but clear.

There were only a few waifs left in Avienne's cache. She'd already gifted most of them to one or the other of her two sons or to Zara. We took the stones out and placed them in Avienne's upturned hand where it rested weakly against her chest.

Avienne didn't look at them as she spoke, her eyes fixed on something far away. *Take the Amethyst, child. Take the Song of Hope.*

We knew this to be a waif of the same Benison that had connected Abél to Amos Quint, the one we carried over the mountains for him. The one Abél gave back to the old Prophet. We know its song.

Take the Jade.

We recalled how we first saw Avienne in the shimmering verberations of an Old Jade through its Song of the Calumet.

No, Meridia. This is an Ancient Jade. Its song is Pacification. Abél knows. He can teach you. Now take the Granite.

We hesitated. We knew how the Preterit Granite's Song of Regret had been distorted into a Song of Revenge by the Palinjians. We'd seen how the stone was used in their heinous suicide ceremonies in which they sought to become Revelant.

This is not a Preterit. This is an Old Granite. Its song is Firm Resolve. I think you'll need it in the coming days.

We held the three stones in our hand—Hope, Pacification, Firm Resolve.

Only one stone remained in Avienne's hand. Her trembling fingers closed around it. *This one is mine and will go with me to the pyre. Promise me that.*

The tears we'd held back overflowed then, streaming down our cheeks. We knew this stone to be the Old Obsidian, with its Song of Embracing Death. *We promise, Eldmother. But surely it won't be soon. Bekanz knows strong medicine.*

Avienne's eyes sought something beyond time or place as the flickering colors around her grew brighter. *Attend to the Migrant, Meridia. Listen. Breathe with your mind.*

We listened as the tinkling bells began to meld, forming into a pattern, a melodious chorus.

We hear that same tune now, clearer, with voices of other instruments joining the symphony as the ululations rise, leaping from house to house as the news is known.

Avienne, the great Melfar Calumet, has died.

27

We're too broken, too desolate to hold our mind in place. Still lying in bed, we cling to Damon as he tries to offer comfort. He speaks, but words are not what we need, only the warm solidness of his body, the raw sympathy of his open heart.

Childlike, we reach for Mother, but she's not yet awake. She doesn't know.

We turn toward Father and rest with him for a moment, engulfed in our conjoined misery and loss. But his memories of Avienne have taken him far away, into a childhood in which we did not exist. Brân is his companion there.

Fragmented, we reach out, finding others who share our sorrow. There are so many.

"What is it, Jalu?" Fergus is alarmed to find his friend huddled in a corner of the refectory, sobbing uncontrollably.

"She's gone, Fergus." His eyes are red-rimmed with grief.

Fergus knows at once who he means. When Brân left two days before, he'd told them what to expect. He'd left so that he could be with his mother again before her death. Fergus sits heavily and places a hand on Jalu's shoulder. He doesn't question how Jalu knows this. He trusts his Melfar friend on such matters.

Shredded by our own misery, we continue wandering, finding comfort in a community grieving the loss of

Avienne. Trying to understand what we feel as we experience their feelings.

Gerd sits alone in the walled garden behind the Landry estate, humming a few broken notes of the Song of All Songs. She wipes away a stray tear. The moon is barely a sliver overhead as the breeze wafts a scent of firebush blossoms. She wonders how the death of the Melfar Calumet will change things. She's lonely and longs for home.

"Gerd?"

"Yes, over here." She recognizes Lambert Quint's voice.

"Is that part of the Song of All Songs that I heard you humming?"

Gerd nods in the darkness. "Yes," she says. "Do you know it?"

Lambert approaches and sits cross-legged on the ground nearby. He reaches inside his jacket and pulls out a white stone. "No. But this stone—it's called a waif, right? This stone was... well, it seemed like it was vibrating a bit, so I thought that might be why." He raises the stone in his open palm toward the scant moonlight. It's the stone Brân gave him when they came to extract him from his retreat in the Northern Lowlands. "I really don't understand how all of this works."

"We have a lot to learn," Gerd says. "Even those of us who have called ourselves Chanters. We thought we knew so much, but it turns out we have a great deal more to learn from our Melfar friends."

They both grieve for Avienne. Everything they say is tinged with her, yet neither is willing to speak her name.

We start to leave Gerd, to follow the trail of sorrow else-where. But then I hear Avienne's voice.

Stay, child. These are your people, too. Hear what they have to say.

We stay. We listen.

"Abél tried to tell me what the Song is about, but I'm not sure I understood," Lambert says.

"It's hard to say exactly what it's about. I was there the day the New Marble Benison was raised and at the time I felt like I understood at least a little. It filled my heart with such joy and peace. But I'm Mundani, after all, and we Mundani need words to bind things together. The messages of Melfar songs and colors fade away too quickly for us unless we peg them down with words. Your father, Amos, made words for his part of the Song of All Songs, you know."

"So Abél told me. But he couldn't remember exactly how they went. I guess Melfar have the same problem with words that we have with their music and colors."

In the darkness, Gerd can't see Lambert's face, but she senses his frustration. "I remember a little bit," she says. "A few of the words he repeated many times through the song. He said, 'We are the myriad expres-sions of the singularity of existence. We are one.' I'm sure Vidvana must have written all the words down. She writes everything. Maybe Ann can get you a copy."

"Would you say that again, Gerd? The words my father sang."

Listen, Meridia. Remember this. Whenever you remem-ber me, remember this, too. And we hear Avienne voicing the song that goes with the words Gerd speaks.

"We are the myriad expressions of the singularity of existence. We are one."

Lambert breathes deeply and murmurs the words to himself, vowing to remember them. "We really are, aren't we, Gerd? One, I mean. Not two. Not Melfar and Mundani. Not Sidayen and kinren. Not men and women. Only the varied expressions of the Creator, who is singular. One."

"Melfar don't talk about a Creator. They talk about the Migrant and they say the Migrant has always existed. Exists still in all of us." She pauses, gesturing with upturned hands. "In all times. All places. All at once."

"That part I don't really understand," Lambert says. "How can anything be in all of us, everywhere, through all of time? That just describes... What? Existence? Oh." He chuckles and reaches out to place a hand on Gerd's shoulder. "Well, they may have something there."

A lulark utters the first notes of its dawn song from somewhere across the other side of the fence. Gerd and Lambert go silent, listening. We listen with them.

"What do you think will happen now that Avienne is gone?" Lambert asks. He's not clear what the role of a Calumet is among the Melfar, leaving him unsure what kind of void her passing might leave. He's concerned that such a disruption has occurred so close to the Mundani Binder.

We, too, are unsure. We only know the void in our own hearts. It's deep and broad and we think maybe this is what death feels like.

Or existence.

"Beyond the sadness and mourning, I really can't say." Gerd knows the emptiness left by Avienne's absence, too. "There has always been a Calumet among the Melfar. Zara says that in the past, when they had large communities in all the forests, they often had more than one. I guess we wait and see."

Lambert knits his fingers together in his lap and lifts his face toward the stars. After a while he asks, "Are you sure my father hasn't become Revelant?"

"He says not. I have no reason to think otherwise."

"But, how...?"

"He says it's the time he's spent in his chamber of mirrors, walking with the Migrant."

"Odd, isn't it, that my mother's mirror was the only thing I salvaged from the burned house? I spent so much time looking into it. I kept feeling that it held some kind of answers for my pain and confusion. But I never saw the Migrant there." He thinks of his own nascent chamber of mirrors in the little stone house on the burned-out Quint property.

Is that what he's looking for? Is it possible for him to find the Migrant there?

Gerd pulls a leaf from the bush beside her and holds it between her palms. "I'm not sure the Migrant is anything we see. More like a presence. Like when you know a river is there even when you can't see it." Gerd thinks about how rivers have begun to flow again, carrying the rains from all across the land down to the lakes and the ocean.

"But you can smell the river," Lambert says. "And I can hear its rush and hum from far away."

"Meridia says she hears the Migrant sometimes."

"Really? Does he speak to her?"

"She says they do sometimes."

"Is Meridia a prophet?"

"I suppose you might call her that. She was, after all, the one who brought the Song of All Songs from the Migrant. And she had the vision for the pattern of stones on the face of the New Marble Benison."

"A prophet. A woman prophet. A woman prophet who is half Melfar. Remarkable."

Hot tears stream down our burning cheeks. Our mind consumes itself in confusion. Our hearts ache for our eldmother.

28.

⚜

When it comes our turn, we walk forward to where Avienne's inert body lies on the funeral pyre. We'd never realized how small she'd become. When life still filled her, she seemed so much larger. As large as life itself.

Dazed and uncertain, heavy with the burden of grief, we let our steps measure the cadence of the drumming. A tinkling of bells embroiders the percussive beat with melody. It's joined by velvety mevelhorns and voices in every register. The rainbow colors of the Migrant swirl above the old Calumet's body as flames embrace her. More vivid and mesmerizing than the fire, the swirl embraces us, penetrating our orb, aurynx, and heart, curling deep into our body, flowing in ecstatic waves. The music rises and we're compelled to sing. It's a song without words, but it weaves a tapestry of peace, singing a grand symphony of the power that emanates from peace. Within the song a single word manifests, repeated in every voice: *Calumet. Calumet. Calumet.*

We fall to our knees, weeping for the old Calumet, our precious eldmother Avienne. Heavy with the two nens, we struggle to rise. Hands reach to aid us. Abél has taken our right hand, Brân our left. Their faces, too, are wet with tears.

The word still resounds from the weeping throng: "Calumet. Calumet. Calumet."

29.

"We don't understand, Father. How could anyone possibly think we could become a Calumet?" *We're not even really Melfar. Not purely so.*

"Nevertheless, it's what we all saw." *The Migrant reached out to you, giving you the benediction of light at your orb and aurynx. But in your case—and no doubt because you are also Mundani—at your heart as well.* "The Migrant has chosen you, Meridia."

But we don't even know what it means to be a Calumet. We recall what Emba told us when we were with her in Woodclasp. A peace-bringer. Is that it?

Yes, a peace-bringer. A bestower of the power that can come only from a state of profound peace, life in harmony with itself, in harmony with the Migrant.

How does a Calumet do that? What is peace? The two questions arise simultaneously and our aurynx stutters with the imagery, causing us to cough.

Abél is amused. *Both of those are good questions, Daughter. And you're right: It is hard to say which one comes first.* He settles on the query about peace. Sensing our multiplied awareness, he chooses to continue his explanation in words, verberating carefully as he speaks. "You might say that peace is a state of harmony. Peace doesn't come from all of us in agreement, all singing the same note. Quite the contrary. It can only emerge when our own authentic notes harmonize with one another, voices lifting up and supporting other voices, all of our unique colors and patterns weaving together, blending into a single concordant display."

Our mind stretches almost to breaking with the immensity of such imagery. *Why wouldn't the Migrant choose you or Brân? You have far more knowledge and experience than we do.*

"Our Calumets have always been women. Avienne was profoundly disappointed that she had only sons, though she loved us deeply. Besides, Brân and I are already old men. Avienne tried to cultivate Zara, thinking she might be chosen as the next Calumet. But the Migrant has chosen you."

"What if we don't want to be a Calumet?" *What if we can't do what people expect of us?* Our orb is clouded with doubt and our aurynx sputters uncontrollably. We wave a hand in front of our face and turn to leave.

Breathe with your mind, Daughter. The Migrant will make it all clear to you.

We have three minds now, Father. It's not that easy.

30.

⌒

"I've tarried long enough. I need to return to Selbourne. If there's no one to go with me, then I'll go alone." Amos Quint speaks with calm resolve. He's come to talk with our father and our uncle.

"I'll go with you, Amos." Brân glances at his brother. "Abél needs to stay here for Meridia, but I can go."

We have a flash of memory, of the calm we felt on Selbourne, surrounded by the ebb and flow of the endless waters and for a moment we wish that we, too, could return there.

Amos wonders if two old men can make the journey back over the mountains safely, but all he says is, "Thank you, my friend. How soon can we leave?"

When Damon hears of their plan, he approaches us. "Would you be alright here for a couple of sixes without me?"

We know how concerned Damon has been about our state of minds, especially since we lost Avienne. How concerned he is for the well-being of the three of us. Our oddness confuses him. "Of course you should go with them," we say. "They need your support and you need to find more snails." We know he'll go at least as far as Aldbeck. Maybe on to Selbourne. But we don't ask for details. We trust Damon. "Zara and Vidvana are counting on you to make more pictures for the book," we say. "And for that you need the snails. We'll be fine. You should go."

Damon pulls from the folds of his shirt the quartz bead that he always wears on a sturdy string around his neck. He raises it to his lips and then reaches out to touch the identical one we wear. "We'll still be together, right?"

We nod, smiling. Of course we'll be with him. We try our best to be reassuring. "Bekanz examined us yesterday and says we're all doing well." We rest our hand on our swelling belly. "Three more tides."

"I'll be back long before that, Meri." He doesn't say it, but he's also determined to be back before the Mundani Binder.

We almost say that Mother will care for us in his absence, but we've grown worried about Mother, about her temporary absences. Her blankness. We try to shield Damon from our fears.

We help him pack his necessities and then wish him well as he leaves early the next morning with the two old men, Amos Quint and Brân. We'll count the days until he returns. The nens feel him drawing away from us and our belly grows heavier with his departure.

We go to a small green glen that lies just past the last cabins and gardens of New Beniford. It's a place where we come to find refuge. Humming the Old Jade's Song of the Calumet, we feel the comforting presence of Avienne. Gone but not gone. We take out our Old Turquoise waif and, thinking of Mother, we sing ourselves back in time. Back to Temur.

Meridia is a child again, before we existed as we do now.

She finishes washing the supper dishes, going slow because she knows there will be another reading lesson before bedtime. Another quarrel.

"Let's go outside this evening, Mer," Maddie says. "Ambia says there's to be a full moon tonight."

Meridia is relieved. She follows Maddie out the back door and sits with her on the ground, facing the woods. There are only a few trees left, and even those have more dead branches than live ones. People covet the dead branches for cooking and fight over them when they drop. Meridia's heart falls when she sees that Maddie has brought a book with her.

"I thought we'd read the poem about the moon," Mother says. She opens the book and turns a few pages. She clears her throat and begins to read.

Meridia knows this poem. It paints the glorious solitude of the moon in mellow tones. The generosity of its pale nighttime light. How it persists in its own pattern apart from the sun's rising and setting.

After a few lines Maddie stops. "Come closer and read along with me, Mer."

Meridia shakes her head and picks up the next line, her voice going all singsong as she recites, gazing toward the rising moon. She never looks at the page. Never looks at Mother until the poem is done.

Mother has tears in her eyes. She reaches for Meridia's hand.

We have tears now as we clasp the Turquoise waif to our heart. Meridia and Maddie are so different. Love can still exist in such circumstances. We send a chain of rosy pulses toward Mother.

We don't find her. Where has she gone? Out walking again. There she is. She'll be safe as long as she stays within the protection canopy.

We sing a different verse of the Old Turquoise song and it arranges itself into a vision of Avienne as a young woman. She's with her mother, our elder eldmother Meridia. Colors bounce back and forth between them like bird song.

The two women walk toward us.

They grasp our hands so that we form a circle.

How can you know we're here, Eldmothers?

We are the Migrant now, Meridia. Wherever the Migrant is, wherever they take you, know now that we are with you. I remember what it was like when I carried my two sons. The nearness of the Migrant brought down all the barriers. It's happening with you, too. We're here so you won't need to be afraid.

But we are afraid. We concentrate on the flow of colors circulating around the three...no, five of us. We let go.

There's a clashing and splashing sound.

Ocean.

Ocean stretching forever in every direction.

Floating on the ocean, a boat. An enormous boat. Amos Quint's vessel would be like an ant alongside this boat. It barely rocks as the waves shove against it. People walk along flat pathways on its surface. People of different shades and colors, garbed in strange clothing. Anxious people.

In small rooms below the pathways, other people lie sick and dying.

A man, dark as Mundani but with different features, leans on a railing that surrounds the pathway. He speaks to another such man standing next to him and we struggle to discern his meaning. The words are unfamiliar and the verberations obscure, but their emotions are strong. There's distress. Distrust. They try to reassure one another, but anxiety leaks out between their words.

They're speaking of the past. Remembering how they embarked on this ship and why.

Brân knows why. Is Brân here?

We're tired, grateful as the disturbing vision blurs and fades. We drum with our fingers, fighting against the flashes of still other times and places that threaten to lure us further away. We struggle to fasten on the images Abél is teaching us, the verse of the Canopy of Time that lands us securely back in our own time-space.

We catch the scent of moon laurel and damp earth. A pair of finches chirp brightly, calling to one another. There's a rock beneath our left hip. We hug our swelling torso. *My children, did you see our eldmothers? Do you see how they love us? They'll keep us safe.*

We hope that's true. We try not to think about the boat.

31.

≈

We watch over Damon as he travels. Brief snippets at random moments, to see where he's got to. We allow ourselves longer sojourns over meals and at bedtime. Father watches over Brân and Amos Quint, and sometimes we talk about what we've experienced, reassuring one another that all is well with the travelers.

We're with Damon now as we finish our breakfast of tea and fruit. We feel the nens object every time we lean forward to reach our cup.

It's taken Damon longer than he expected it would to reach Aldbeck. He had to keep a slower pace for the benefit of Amos Quint. Brân is old, but not so old as Amos, and stronger. At first Damon prods Brân for stories as they travel, stories about Brân's childhood when many Melfar towns and villages still existed within the great forests of Cödweg and Cesta and Serani. When those forests still existed, spreading densely across the landscape, trees reaching for the sky, reaching for one another, intertwining below ground. Stories of what happened after Brân's father Mica delegated him the task of bringing Melfar together. He learns that Brân spent most of those passages in Beniford, but going back and forth, out and back again, gathering Melfar together. Not physically at first. Only offering them solace and encouragement and pieces of what was then the New Quartz, with its maps and messages. It was Brân, working with Avienne, who orchestrated the crafting of beads from the Old Carnelian, which held the Song of the Wide Path. It was they who carried the beads out and began gifting them to Chanters to wear wrapped around their wrists. Damon wears such beads, as do Amos and Gerd and Mother and so many more.

"Avienne went with you?" Damon is surprised.

We're not so surprised as he is. We know it's something Avienne would do.

"She never went into the towns," Brân says. "There were places outside the towns where we were able to meet with Chanters. They loved learning the songs from Mother, from the Calumet herself." He tells Damon about a place outside Fayredell where they met often. "The place burned down some time ago. There's nothing left there now but an old shed."

We wonder if that was the place where Ann took us when she rescued us from the Palinjians in Fayredell. We smile as we recall the mottled scarf Ann gave us to replace the one taken from us by the angry Palinjians in the town. The scarf smelled of pickles.

That was the place, Meridia. Your eldmother loved to visit there. It's where she first met Keira.

Keira Landry of Quint, granddaughter of Amos Quint.

"Do people truly believe that Meridia will be the next Calumet?" Damon wants to ask Brân so many questions about that, but he doesn't know where to begin. He doesn't want to sound selfish, though he feels that way sometimes. He never anticipated this when he began to love us.

Amos responds first. "I'm also told that in Fayredell some people are asking if she might be the next Mundani prophet."

We want to tell Damon not to worry, but our own flustered concern clouds our verberations.

"You must have confidence in Meridia, Damon." Brân places a reassuring hand on Damon's shoulder. "Whatever the future holds for her, I've seen her devotion to you and to the nens. Your partnership is strong. And I know your support for her is also strong."

When they reach the higher slopes of the mountains, the path grows steep and the air thins. Conversation is abandoned as the three men save their breath for the climb.

It's the next day when they finally reach Aldbeck; they're exhausted and hungry. The place is exactly as we remember it. The massive tree is there, soughing gently in the wind, surrounded by stone outlines of vanished cottages. Vanished lives. We glimpse once more the village as it once was, with boats and fishermen and happy children.

We stifle the notes of the Old Turquoise song that had begun to deepen that image, focusing instead on the Quartz that ties us to Damon.

We try to tell him how glad we are that the weather is good there. We remember storms. Damon smiles. He knows we're there.

"Meridia!"

The call wrenches us away from Damon and we turn toward the speaker.

"Meridia, it's Maddie. She's wandered off again." Bekanz clasps her hands tightly in front of her aurynx as

if to shape her words, to compose and focus her verberations. She knows words are often necessary for us these
days. They anchor us when Melfar imagery and colors
grow too intense and multifaceted. When we're in too
many places at once.

"She never goes far," we say. But already we see how
far she's gone this time. Out beyond the reach of the protection canopies. Our hand goes to our mouth and our
eyes go frantic. "Where is Father? He can help us find
her."

"I've already told him. He sent me to get you." Bekanz
holds out her hand to assist us. We shake it off and push
out the door ahead of her, already there with Abél as he
searches.

Before we reach Father's cabin, we know.

"What can we do?" we say as we enter. There's a chaotic buzzing in our minds and frenzied kicking in our
womb. Maddie is in trouble.

She's been taken, Meridia. But you know that.

*What are their intentions? Have they recognized her? Do
they know who she is?* An uncontrollable trembling overwhelms us as we recall how much the Palinjians despise
Mother for what she did at the Blanton Clauster. *Do they
know she's the one?*

*Not yet. The farmers who found her are not the worst sort
of Palinjians. But I think others are approaching and will
join them soon, so it may be only a matter of time.*

*Gerd. We have to tell Gerd. She'll find Mother and bring
her back.* Gerd would do anything for Maddie. We can
reach Gerd through Jalu.

Jalu knows at once that something has gone wrong.
Something he needs to tell Gerd. Something urgent,

though he can't tell for sure what it is. The images make little sense to him.

"Gerd!" Jalu knocks loudly on the door to her room. She always takes time apart after midday to rest and meditate and chant. "Gerd!" He knocks again.

The door opens. "What is it, Jalu?" His urgency frightens her almost as much as the vision she just experienced in her meditation, a vision of Maddie inside a strange house.

"I don't know for certain, but Abél and Meridia are asking for your help. It's something to do with Meridia's mother. Or a servant from the Blanton Clauster?"

Gerd groans and her face tenses with pain. "It's Maddie. Come sit with me and tell me everything you've pertanged. Words, please."

In Gerd's presence, the images Father sends become clearer to Jalu.

Gradually Gerd stitches together an understanding of Maddie's predicament. She's being held at a farm well away from New Beniford. "However did she get there?" Gerd sighs in exasperation, but she knows Maddie's tendency to wander. We'd told Gerd how much worse it had been when she lived in Temur. When Maddie became Revelant after she died, her mind came together, became clearer, but it was never fully sound. "Has she been regressing?"

"Yes, that's what Meridia says. Maddie's been wandering more lately. And this time they're telling me she wandered outside the canopies."

"How long will it take us to get to where she is?" Gerd knows she'll go.

Jalu shakes his head. "I'm not good at guessing such things. But I know it's somewhere northwest of Fayredell." He tries showing Gerd the farm and the rough road that leads to its assembly of shabby little buildings. They're in process of being rebuilt.

"No matter. We'll go prepared and trust you to lead us. How many are there with her? Can you tell?"

"I pertange only two steady presences. Two men. But there's tremolo of others who've been there recently."

"Find Roqu for me, Jalu. And Fergus. Tell them what you've told me and that we need to leave at once." Gerd would prefer to leave her son behind in safety, but she knows he would object and there's no time for arguments. Besides, he's become a canny fighter. If it should come to that.

We're relieved to know that Gerd is going to Mother's aid and try to reassure Father. *Gerd will do whatever is necessary to rescue her.*

Father doesn't seem reassured. His eyes are crusted with regret. He sends us away, telling us not to worry. He feels a need to take all the torment on himself.

We worry anyway.

Before nightfall, Gerd and her three companions are equipped and on their way, departing Fayredell by a little-used lane that's overgrown with grasses and weeds. The evening is warm and laden with the memory of morning's rainfall. They walk in silence, single file, with Jalu in front followed by Gerd and her son. Roqu brings up the rear.

After a while, their way is no longer recognizable as a path or trail and Gerd knows they're following a Melfar way. She studies the bushes and rocks, trying to discern what Jalu sees, knowing that what he sees probably isn't there anymore. She has to trust him.

On and on they go as the moon creeps across the sky. Gerd's heart reaches toward Maddie.

Our hearts unite with hers in anxious longing, a fervent wish for Maddie's safety.

We miss Damon.

Why is everyone so far away?

Half of Damon's jars are already filled with the glowing snails and with rocks covered in the luminescent slime they feed on. He and the two old men have reached the beach across from Selbourne and are relieved to find that the tiny boat and the raft are both still there. Brân and Amos Quint embark, using both of the simple vessels, heading for Selbourne. We know only one vessel will return, leaving the other for Amos to use if he ever decides to come back.

Damon remains on the shore. He reaches for the quartz bead around his neck, expecting reassurance, and we try to send him some. We also try to shield him from Mother's predicament. Gerd will help Mother. Damon frowns as he gathers up his own provisions and begins making his way up toward the shelter on the slope of the mountain. Once he reaches it, he turns to look across toward the island. The little boat is safely ashore, and the raft will be soon. All seems well. He's not sure why he feels so unsettled.

We turn away, back toward Mother. Thinking of Mother takes us to Gerd.

Gerd's heart is brittle with emotion. What possessed Maddie to stray outside the safety of the canopy? What was she looking for? Although Gerd inevitably felt lonely without Maddie, she never begrudged Maddie the safety of New Beniford, nor the circle of family she found there. Still, she misses Maddie dreadfully. She misses her thoughtfulness, her ready willingness to share lovely poems and passages from books Gerd was never privileged to encounter. She even misses the odd moments of madness, when Maddie's eyes would dance with a light from some unfathomable source. And she misses the intimacy of the nights they slept together, the warmth of Maddie's body nestled against hers, the gentle touch of her hand.

We should have watched over Mother more diligently. We'd been aware that she was slipping back into her old ways, though we never spoke of it. We wonder now if the madness she hid behind when she was at the Blanton Clauster was only an act or if it was at least in part the old illness trying to reassert itself. It worked to her advantage then, but we're afraid it won't help now.

"Do you think this could be the madwoman they say carried out the Blanton slaughter? This one seems so harmless." The older of the two men in the cottage with Maddie watches her intently. He's had premonitions of elder madness himself. He wonders what it's like.

They haven't bound or restrained Mother in any way. They've only set plates of food and a jug of wine in front of her and she sits contentedly eating and drinking, letting the wine play with her mind.

"That's what they thought about the assassin at Blanton, too," the younger man says. "We'll see what the others have to say when they get here. Herk was there at Blanton."

Our heart leaps into our aurynx. They don't know now, but when this man called Herk arrives, they will know. We want to cry out to Gerd to hurry, to move faster.

"Yes, Herk will know." The older man thinks that if by chance she is the one, her capture could add a note of triumph to the upcoming celebration of the Binder. An opportunity for revenge.

Oh, Gerd. Please hurry.

"Maybe Herk will also have news of the search for the Palinj fellow. Last I heard was that he'd been hiding out in some bookshop."

Jalu picks up his pace. "What is it?" Gerd stares into the moonlit darkness, thinking maybe he's seen something she can't.

"Others are coming. Not here. There, where Maddie is." His breathlessness communicates as much as his words. "We need to get there before they do."

"How much farther?" Gerd glances over her shoulder to make certain that Fergus and Roqu are keeping up.

Jalu offers no answer. He doesn't know.

We do know. But we don't know if Gerd will arrive in time.

We pace. We try to eat something because we know we should. We're exhausted, but we can't wrest our awareness away from Mother. We can sleep tomorrow, after she's safely back home. We take out our Ancient Amber and hum its song, the Song of Turning. We focus on Mother.

A few more paces on, Jalu pulls up short and holds up his hand as he stares from left to right, trying to pertange the unexpected change in Maddie's position.

Gerd doesn't ask. She's grateful for a moment to catch her breath and take a drink of water from her sheath.

Jalu turns with a smile and signals them to resume their trek. They haven't changed course, but they proceed at a less urgent pace.

We give the landscape another slight twist, hoping to send Herk and his two companions further afield. We tuck the Amber away and try to think what to do next. We trust Gerd, but we can't look away. Not now. We have to know. We press the Old Lapis between our palms and whisper the images of its Song of Liberation, our wish that Maddie be free and safe.

We'd forgotten about the nature of Mundani roads. Herk is following such a road and even though he feels strangely disoriented and the moon seems to have shifted its position, he and his companions press ahead. He's unsure of the turning that leads to their destination and searches for a landmark, anything familiar.

"This should be it," he says. The old dead tree has sprouted new growth on a couple of its branches, which almost fooled him. His two companions are weary and even more disoriented than Herk, but they follow without question.

"That's it up ahead." Jalu speaks in a low voice as he points toward a decrepit little building in the distance. There's a single light flickering in the window. Maddie and one of the men are sleeping as the other man stands guard in front of the cabin, wondering why Herk and his company haven't arrived yet. Then a smile creases his face.

Gerd also hears the voices and careless footfalls. She signals to her own company to duck low and keep silent.

She'd been confident of their ability to handle the two men inside the cabin. Five men outmatches them. Her mind searches for a plan. She knows her crew—and especially Maddie—stand a better chance if they can face these men outdoors in the open.

Jalu! We need a zaki. Can you do that? She accompanies her thoughts with gestures, though she knows Jalu doesn't need them. At least the gestures will prepare Fergus and Roqu for what's coming.

The shriek and hiss still come as a shock, raising the hairs on the back of eight necks. Only Jalu and Maddie remain calm. Jalu because he's conjured the creature. Maddie because her mind is slow to process the noise. She rouses from sleep as the man guarding her grabs a weapon and rushes outside to join his companion as the arriving party scatters. One of the men has already been attacked, but not by a zaki.

After Gerd has subdued the first man and Roqu another, Gerd moves against the man coming at her with a raised longblade, sending him head over heels onto his back. Out of the corner of her eye she sees that Fergus and Jalu have knocked another man to the ground. Then she sees Maddie standing in the doorway, calmly watching the mêlée. She yells, "Get back inside!"

Maddie waves to Gerd and offers a bemused smile.

Herk has escaped Roqu's grasp and runs toward Maddie. "She's the one!" he shouts. "Now you pay, sully whore!" He rushes toward her, longblade drawn, and before Gerd can reach him, Maddie collapses on the doorstep, gushing blood.

Four men lie on the ground, unconscious, as Gerd runs screaming toward Herk, grabbing him from behind as he flails with his weapon. She tightens her grip around his neck and jerks. There's a crunching sound and she lets him fall.

Her anger dissolves into grief as she kneels beside Maddie, reaching to cradle the woman's face between hands that suddenly remember gentleness. Maddie's eyes find hers for a fleeting moment and then go blank. "Oh, Maddie! No!" Gerd crouches over her and picks up the frail body, holding Maddie close as the blood from her gaping wound ceases to pulse.

We cry out in anguish as we witness the grayish cloud unite with the swirl of color hovering above Mother and Gerd. Our tears fall unrestrained as our minds and hearts are assaulted by a storm of memories, grasping toward the Mother who bore us, loved us, tortured us with her expectations, her protection. In the end it was our protection that failed. *Oh, Mother! Why?*

We need Damon. Why is Damon so far away?

He's risen suddenly and casts about, certain he's heard something. He's anxious for our safety. He tries to tell himself that it's his own anxiety that's disturbed his thoughts. But he can't shake the feeling that something has gone wrong, and he has no idea what it might be.

We want to show him what happened to Mother but our verberations are too chaotic.

Where are you, Damon? Has he gone to Selbourne? No. He stayed on shore. But where? Our vision of him is fractured by the deep sobs that rack our bodies. We shuffle aside the glimpse of Quint's mirrored chamber that comes with the thought of Selbourne.

Damon doesn't know what to do. He feels an overwhelming compulsion to return to New Beniford at once, but he can't leave without Brân. Surely Brân will return soon. He assesses the state of the waves and sees them lapping far up onto the land. Brân won't come until the tide has gone out again. But if he knows something is wrong, might he risk braving the turbulent waters at high tide?

Damon will wait.

This beach is where he first found the glowing snails. He'll stifle his anxiety splashing about in the waves and filling the rest of his snail jars, making ready to come home. The snails are easier to find in the darkness.

We've never felt so absolutely alone. The violence that took Mother away from us is unbearable and we struggle to banish the images from our orb. We reach for Mother and find only absence. We want to ask Avienne to care for her. Can she do that?

Damon tries desperately to pertange the nature of this crisis. Our despair. He's built a small fire to ward off the damp and mask his scent in case there are predators around. Zakis or patkánies.

Our sobs subside into a steady flow of anguished tears.

Damon watches the firewood as it begins to sigh and sizzle and pop.

There's a crack as a stick breaks and falls.

Fear clutches Damon's heart with sudden intensity, and he stares over his shoulder into the darkness. All at once, he knows. In a flash he's seen Maddie's blood-soaked body lying inert in Gerd's arms and the full weight of our grief engulfs him. He reflects it back, yearning to help, his heart as open and wounded as our own three hearts.

"Meri! Oh, Meri, I'm so sorry." He calls out to us in agonized words that carry potent verberations.

Damon rises as if he would come to us this very moment. He paces backward and forward beside his small fire, alternately staring up at the stars and out toward the shadow of Selbourne.

Brân knows about Mother, too. He's walking with Amos Quint in the chamber of mirrors. There's something different about the chamber now. Why has Quint rearranged the mirrors?

32.

Gerd has brought Mother home. They're building her pyre in a small clearing near where the New Marble Benison stands. We sit alone in our green glen, fingering the obsidian shard we pilfered from Avienne's ashes, a fragment of the waif that accompanied her into the fire. It shattered in the heat. But this splinter of the Old Obsidian, small as it is, still holds a few shining, dusky notes of the Song of Embracing Death.

We don't know the song. We've been afraid to ask for it, but now we think we should. Maybe we have to learn what it means to embrace death. What it's like to merge into the oneness of the Migrant, into their pervasive singularity. Whenever we're in the presence of the Migrant, we hover somewhere between awestruck devotion and petrified terror. It's only when we remember that the Migrant already holds Avienne that we feel somewhat consoled. We try to tell ourselves that Mother is there now, too. Why can't we find her?

We heard Abél singing this morning and we're certain it was the Old Obsidian song. We'd gone to him, intending to pour out our grief, but when we heard his song, we knew his own grief was enough for now. We must bear our own. We'd almost forgotten how much Abél loved Maddie. How much he loves her still. We recall the image we pertanged once of the two of them as young lovers, singing together, and our tears fall again.

We yearn for Damon. He's been gone nearly a six and it could be that long again before he's back. He knows about Mother, but our jumbled verberations offer him no insight. The nens search for their father's voice, his steadiness.

Gerd has gone into seclusion to mourn Maddie in her own way. To plot her way through grief and guilt, to see if she can find a way back out into the world. Gerd wonders if the world really needs her. She doubts herself. She was not even capable of saving the woman she loved. What good is she to anyone else?

We clasp our hands around our belly, embracing our fullness, seeking to shape loneliness into comforting solitude. But our minds are shattered. We find no comfort. Like Gerd, we can't see our way forward. Everything is dark and unsettled.

Mother's funeral is held according to Melfar custom. The fire is lit at dawn, its flames rising with the sun. Gerd joins the assembled company, looking desolate, sitting alone. We sing verses from the Old Obsidian but also from the Old Turquoise, as we're guided to recall the life that has now gone to the Migrant.

We clutch our own Turquoise waif and murmur a poem. It was always Mother's favorite. It made her smile even on bad days.

Today was such a day and Mother has been crying.

"Father isn't coming back, is he?" we say, as we follow the colorful trails left by the flies at the window.

Maddie draws her little daughter into a fierce embrace. "He had to go." Her words overflow with anger and longing.

"The sun will rise another day," we say. It's a line from the poem.

The promise of a smile warms Mother's face as we continue to recite together. "Behind the clouds it finds its way." Her arms hold us more gently.

The funeral fire rises higher as the song changes again. Flames caress Mother's body, erasing it as she becomes only our memories of her.

The next song is the Preterit Granite's Song of Regret. It's another one that Abêl has been trying to teach us, hoping to show us the dangers of letting regret morph into revenge as happened among the Palinjians. He says we must keep singing the song in its original form in order to purify it. We hear his voice now above all the rest, reaching through his own grief, his regret over the many returns he spent apart from Maddie, apart from us.

The ceremony concludes with the Song of All Songs. Everything comes to that these days. It's our anchor of hope, though we know it's not enough. As the song ends, we see Gerd steal away and we follow.

We catch up to her and guide her to the glen, our place of rest and solitude. We sit in silence, leaning against one another.

"I know I have to go back, but I feel so useless. I failed Maddie. I failed her in the worst possible way." Gerd's head is down, her words barely audible.

We reach for her hand. "You can't think like that," we say. We feel the heaviness of Gerd's regret as it threatens to coalesce into fierce lumps, burning chars of vengeful- ness. Wouldn't revenge at least give her motivation to continue her work?

No, Meridia. Revenge only destroys.

We shiver in the resonant silence of the Migrant's voice. "It's okay to feel regret," we say. We're surprised at our certainty. "And sorrow. Sometimes it's like a heavy stone and you want to throw it at someone. To blame someone. To blame yourself." The image feels right, though we're not certain what comes next. "You're needed out there, Gerd. You're a respected leader now."

"But you're the one they're calling a prophet."

"What? No." We toss our head side to side to shake off such a notion. "I'm just a half-Melfar who never learned to read." Or was that only the girl we used to be? The little girl who maybe went up in flames this morning.

"Vidvana says that here they're calling you Calumet."

We draw our shoulders together. There's a sharp pain between our eyes and a tautness in our chest as we struggle to contain our tears. "We're frightened," we say, our throat constricted, our voice barely more than a whisper.

"Yes. We are."

She thinks "we" means Gerd and Meridia. She doesn't fully comprehend who we are these days. We let it go.

Gerd stares off somewhere past the greening branches that shelter this place. "Maybe fear is okay," she says. "Maybe it makes us more...humble. More aware that we're not so different from those who thrust us into leadership. More willing to listen to their needs and concerns. Do you think that could be?"

We do. But we don't say anything yet, letting this notion bubble through our consciousness. "What do you think it will all come to, Gerd?"

"I don't know," she says. "Something better, I hope. Maddie seemed so hopeful about the Song of All Songs and about the book Vidvana and Zara are putting together. With Damon's help." She brushes a tear from her cheek and swallows a sob. "I'm no prophet, Meridia. I only do what must be done. What I see to do from my small window on the world. I know you see more. You'll tell us what you see, won't you?"

Is that what it means to be a Calumet? A prophet? We think about the children, about Naomi and Amergin and the rest. We recall their perilous journey through the caverns. Their stalwart perseverance. "We will," we say. But not yet. Not until we understand more about what it means.

Together, hand in hand, we and Gerd walk back to where the funeral feast has been laid out. We know Gerd will leave as soon as it's over. She'll wrap her grief in memories and store it away in her heart for another day. It's only a few more sixes until the Binder. Gerd is needed. She'll go.

We're still not sure about ourselves.

In the evening as we make ready for bed, we begin humming a muddled tune that's partly Old Turquoise, partly the Quartz melody that links us to Damon.

Damon has never felt more torn, never more alone. He longs to come to us but has no choice other than waiting for Brân to return from Selbourne. Each man must accomplish what he came for, but Damon wonders why Brân is taking so long. He's watched the tide go out and come back again and still Brân hasn't come. Damon keeps reaching toward us. He finds us elusive. His tears fall soft as feathers and disappear into the black beach sand.

Morning comes and we reach for Damon again. He thinks that he's slept at least a little. How else could time have passed so quickly? He forces himself to eat a few mouthfuls and drink some water before picking up his last empty jar and wading out into the waves.

We walk through our day in a daze, not wanting to let go of Damon. Needing Damon. Needing Mother and searching for the piece of us that was Mother, a piece that is now missing. We keep remembering small things. Remembering her mounting joy over the prospect of becoming an eldmother to our nens. Recalling our life in Temur. So much of it was painful, but there were also moments when Mother would come home from a long walk smiling. Why do we think she was meeting Father? Is that possible? Is that who she kept looking for in her long wanderings, the ones that eventually took her away? Was it Gerd she was looking for this time?

Damon's search for snails keeps his mind occupied, and the effort of diving and ducking and swimming helps his body feel calmer. He's not hungry, but he gathers a couple of handfuls of berries from behind the dunes and sits on the beach to eat. He watches Selbourne, out there beyond the surge and swell of the bay.

We watch with him.

He startles, thinking he's felt a shuddering of the earth, seen flashes of something at the edges of his vision. He blinks, looks around, and decides it was his imagination.

It happens again.

It's not your imagination, Damon. We felt it, too. Brân felt it. And Amos.

Brân is walking in the caverns with Naomi and Amergin and Sister Maggie. *Are these the ones you met, Meridia?*

Yes, Uncle. But as we say this, he's already gone, falling further into the chasm that's opened up through Amos Quint's chamber of mirrors, falling into unfathomable time. We're engulfed in uncomprehending wonder.

Damon blinks again. He tells himself that everything appears normal. Except that it doesn't. Whenever he looks away from Selbourne, the image of it in his mind shifts and sparkles. Damon rubs his forehead; he's getting a headache.

The tide has begun to rise again, and he strains to see whether Brân is returning. The raft is still anchored in its place. He stares so hard that his vision blurs and the whole great rock of Selbourne seems to flicker and almost disappear.

Night falls and still Brân hasn't returned. There will be no moon for a long while yet. Damon finally abandons his watch and returns to his hillside shelter.

We stand outside our cabin, breathing in the fragrance of moon laurel. Breathing in the devastating strangeness of Selbourne.

Damon assures himself that Brân will come tomorrow.

He wants to ask us if we know what happened.

We're with you, Damon. We see you. We try to touch him, but our hearts are too troubled.

Damon is restless and lonely. Sleep eludes him.

We, too, lie awake. Drifting.

As the moon finally rises, Damon makes his way back down the hill to the beach. He brings all his gear with him, telling himself that Brân will be there soon and that he must be prepared to leave as soon as he arrives. *I'm coming, Meri.*

Soon the sun sends a tentative gleam across the water, stealing beneath the layer of clouds that had gathered, obscuring the moon, dimming the stars. The tide is out. There's movement on the waves, but it isn't the raft. It's Quint's little round boat. Why would Brân take the boat and leave the raft for Quint? Damon tries to think of reasons, but he finds nothing that satisfies him, nothing that might make him feel less apprehensive.

As the boat approaches, he sees that the occupant is not Brân. It's Amos Quint.

Damon splashes out into the water to assist the old Prophet in bringing the boat to shore. As soon as he's safely disembarked, Damon asks the necessary questions. "Where is Brân? Is he hurt? What's happened?"

Quint glances out toward Selbourne before replying. "Let's sit down for a while and I'll try to answer that."

After the old man has caught his breath and quenched his thirst, he speaks. "Brân and I were in the mirrored chamber," he says.

This much Damon knew. We knew.

"We were chanting together. And then the walls began to quiver and... I think maybe Meridia's told you about some of the things the Migrant showed her in that chamber?"

Damon nods, acknowledging that we have told him about such things.

"The Migrant's presence was strong. As we chanted together, everything began to shake. Well, I felt it shaking. I lost my balance and fell. Maybe I hit my head." He reaches up and touches a lump above his left eyebrow. "Anyway, I saw images of...well, strange boxes with flickering lights and glowing pictures. There were great flashes of white light, brighter than anything I've ever seen. And then I felt... I saw whole regions of land shaking and sliding into the sea. It was altogether strange." He glances over his shoulder toward Selbourne. "Terrifying," he mutters.

"Did Brân see all of this, too?" Damon asks.

"I don't know. When I got to my feet again and looked around for him, he wasn't there. I walked all through the cavern. I called his name many times. Then I searched the other chambers and finally walked all the way around the island. He's gone, Damon. He's not there."

"What? Not there at all? Do you mean to say he... disappeared?"

"So it would seem. Or maybe somehow he left the chamber and fell into the sea." It's clear that Amos finds the latter explanation unconvincing. He wonders if what happened has anything to do with the two mirrors he'd arranged recently so that they faced one another. They were the two mirrors that had been in the chamber before Amos arrived on Selbourne. How long before? That is something Amos doesn't know.

"Should we search? What can I do?" Damon struggles to make sense of what Amos Quint has told him.

"Well, I'll continue searching. But you should go back to New Beniford. Brân told me what happened to

Meridia's mother. I'm very sorry about that. You need to be with Meridia." The old man's knees pop and creak as he stands. "She's important, Damon. Melfar say she's their new Calumet. And Mundani Chanters are calling her a prophet." He passes his hand across his eyes and emits a deep chuckle. "Whatever that is. Anyway, you need to go to her. Look after her and the nens. And your snails. Your work with the pictures for the book will be important, too. Perhaps more important than we know. As for me..." He stretches his back and shoulders and turns toward his boat. "There's one more thing." Amos laces his fingers together and studies their interconnections. "I'm concerned about my son Lambert. Once Meridia is back on her feet, could you ask her to check on him for me? You know, in that way she does?" He reaches into a pocket and hands something to Damon. "And could you ask her to take this to him? It's for his wall of mirrors."

The object is about the size of two fingers and reflects the morning sun. Amos had already asked Brân to do this, but now that Brân is gone, he'll ask us.

He didn't need to ask. We've already seen how Lambert intends to try and follow his father's path toward the Migrant, to walk with the Migrant, and how he's using his wall of mirrors to aid his efforts.

"Of course. I'm sure Meridia will be happy to check on Lambert," Damon says. He places the shard of glass inside his backsack. "And I'm sure she'll be able to get this piece of mirror to him as well."

Amos expresses his thanks. "I need to go back to the island before the tide changes again," he says. "No, no, I'll be okay." When he looks at Damon his eyes are bright under his grizzled brows and there's the hint of a smile on his lips. "And if the old Melfar turns up, I'll send him back to you. Provided he wants to go."

Damon helps Amos back into the boat and stands on the shore watching until he's sure the boat has reached its destination. Then he gathers up his gear and begins his solitary journey home.

33.

The proliferation of our awareness is more pervasive every day. Memories of Mother come unbidden, in disjointed fragments that tear at our hearts. We beg Avienne to guard her, but sometimes we can't even find Avienne. We try to remember who we are. Have we ever known? We're at the mercy of the Migrant. There are moments when we fear the Migrant might tear us apart. Or forge us into something too vast to hold onto.

We focus on Damon, on finding Damon amid all the colors and vibrations. He's safe. We know he's safe. But we're frightened by what happened to Brân.

"Can you tell us what it is, Father?" We stand in the doorway of Abél's cabin, breathing heavily from the short walk, feeling the physical weight of our plurality, using words to focus our verberations. Despite the pull of the Migrant, sometimes we feel so Mundani.

"Come sit down, Meridia." Father's face is lined with concern. "How much longer do you have before the births?"

"A little more than two tides. Although Bekanz says that with twins sometimes they come sooner." We sit with our knees apart, back straight, shoulders back. Making room. Breathing as deeply as we can. "Tell me about Brân." *Did he have an accident? Is that it?*

Abél pushes his shirt sleeves up and stares thoughtfully into the empty cup in front of him. "I don't think it was an accident." *I believe he's gone off with the Migrant for a while. But not like you did, Meridia. Not through his mind and orb. He's...gone.*

"You mean his whole body?" *Gone? Completely? How can that be?* It's what we had pertanged, but we weren't sure we believed it.

Father has no answer. He's never seen anything like it. He'll use words not only for us, but for himself, in order to peg down what he wants to communicate. "You know that when we work through the Migrant to experience a different time-space, sometimes we're no longer pertangible to those around us. Well, I should say that Mundani can't see us. Most Mundani. But other Melfar, and especially those we're close to, can usually pertange where and when we are. As children, Brân and I always knew each other's thoughts. We were never apart." Father stops, shifting in his chair as he rubs his forehead. He continues, choosing his words carefully. "After what I experienced at Swarthpol, our connection was never quite the same. Right now, he feels as absent as I was then. You know he's even more receptive to the Migrant than most Melfar, because of his rebirth." *Like you are, Meridia, because of the lives taking shape within you, the births to come.*

A shiver of fear curls upward from the base of our spine. Could this happen to us as well? We're also thinking about the twinned lives to come. Will they be like Abél and Brân? We're not sure how Brân changed when he became Revelant after his encounter with the Palinjians near Blanton. After the accident that killed him. We'd known him only a short while before that happened. We remember how we pertanged Avienne singing him back into life, singing him back to his unfinished task of gathering Melfar to sing the rains. That task is complete. "What can we do?" we say. *What ought we to do?*

Abél raises his hands, palms up, in a gesture of helplessness. "I'm not sure there's anything we can do, Meridia. I'll keep trying to reach out to him, but I'm not even certain what aspect of the Canopy of Time might have absorbed him." *Or whether he's gone beyond what the Canopy can reach.*

We remember the strange canyons of mirrored towers that we slipped into once through Amos Quint's chamber. There's nothing in the Song of the Canopy of Time about that. Not yet.

"If you think you might be able to reach him, you can reach out, too. The Migrant has already taken you into times none of us had seen before. But be careful, Meridia. Remember what you've learned about how to return."

He's reminding us of the verse that facilitates that. But surely Brân knows that, too. If he wanted to come back, wouldn't he do it? Or maybe because of the manner in which he's gone to wherever he is... maybe it doesn't work. We've only used the verse a couple of times. It worked then. The eldmothers have said they will guard us. They and the Migrant are one now. Wherever and whenever Brân has landed, surely the eldmothers will guard him, too.

After we've rested a while and drunk a cup of tea, we leave Father. Walking home feels like a journey.

Damon is on his way home, too.

He approaches the mountain pass, breathless. His legs ache and the burden of his snails and rocks and sea water grows heavier with every step. He'll be home tomorrow.

We hold our Quartz bead a little longer, cradled between our palms, and then tuck it away, drawing out the Old Turquoise instead.

We hesitate, uncertain how to proceed. We're still thinking about Brân, lost somewhere in time. Curiosity overwhelms fear as we breathe deeply. We steady ourselves and try to recall the sparse notes of incipient song that came with our vision of a vast ocean and a great ship.

Why do we think that's where Brân has gone?

We find the deep notes of the ocean's vastness, the pulsing slap of waves. We hear the exotic tones and inflections in the voices of the people. But there's no music in their muddled thoughts, the worries they toss back and forth.

Then we pertange him. It's Brân. He seems so young! He nods toward us, because wherever this is, whenever it is, he pertanges us, too. *Go carefully, Meridia. I'll help you find what we need to know.*

We send a golden pulse of gratitude. Relief? We linger, mystified by the sounds of an incomprehensible language, disturbed by the distress emanating from these peoples' hearts.

A breeze riffles the grasses along the shore. We focus on the rhythmic thrumming of waves. The sound of our fingers drumming on the table.

And then we're back, sitting in our own house, holding a Turquoise waif. Our hearts beat wildly and our hands tremble, but we're back. Brân is okay, or at least he seems to be. The emotions of the people where he is are so strong. We're sure that Brân went there intentionally. Or at least willingly. He said he'd help us find what we need to know. We send a pulse of gratitude to Brân, but he's beyond our reach.

34.

Damon is exhausted by the time he reaches New Beniford. The weight of his mission has been almost too much. We hold him in our arms, craving the solidness of him, emanating sun-yellow bursts of gratitude for his safe return, carried on sobs of relief.

"Dear Meri, you shouldn't have had to bear this alone. I should've been here with you."

"We're never apart, Damon." We say this, but we also know how desperately we missed the physical presence of him, how fractured and tenuous our linkage has been. "Gerd tried to save her you know." And we offer Damon the details he's missing about Maddie's wandering and about Gerd's urgent expedition.

"It must have broken Gerd's heart," he says, "as it did yours." He knows what Maddie meant to Gerd. He knows how conflicted I've always been about Mother.

"We and Gerd helped each other through the funeral," we say, unsure whether that expresses what we mean to say. "We only hope Mother understood that after everything, we forgave her." Our eyes overflow with sadness as we lean into Damon's nourishing presence. We cling to one another in silence.

"So it's true," we say at last. "You left Brân behind?"

"I had no choice," Damon says, sounding slightly defensive. "He was gone."

"Father says the Migrant took him." We don't say he went willingly.

"That's what Amos Quint thinks, too. I don't understand how that can be possible. I keep thinking it's more likely that he wandered away and perished in the ocean."

"No, he's with the Migrant. We saw him. He's well."

"Ah. Well, that's good to know." Damon marvels for a moment at how he's come to accept such statements. He pulls us closer and caresses our hair, tangled as it is from neglect.

We devour his touch. "You got what you needed?"

"I hope so. It felt like too much over the mountain pass, but I think it will be enough. Have the boys returned from the Northern Lowlands with the salt?"

"Yes. And we've done our best to take care of the snails you left here. We're worried about them."

"What worries? I know they were running short on food."

"Billbugs. They keep swarming around the edges of the tanks."

"That's not surprising. Billbugs always feed on slime. As long as they aren't getting into the water, the snails should be okay. I don't think billbugs would lay eggs in the saltwater. I'll check on the snails and pour some of the pure seawater I brought into their tanks. They'll probably like that."

"There are more billbugs than usual. Probably because of the rains."

"Have you had any word from Lambert, Meridia? Amos said he was worried about him and wanted me to ask you to check on him."

We know. We just haven't done it. We drift these days and unless we make conscious efforts we never know where we're going to end up. Or when. We miss

Amergin and Naomi. "The last we knew, Lambert was planning to stay apart for a while inside the Quint property in Fayredell."

"Isn't that place pretty much a ruin these days?"

"It is. But there's a stone shed on the property that he finds agreeable." We almost mention the mirrors he bought at the shops all over Fayredell. The ones he's hung on the walls of the shed. The mirrors he's gazing into right now.

"Oh, that reminds me," Damon says. He picks up his pack and takes something out of a side pocket. He offers it to me in an open palm.

We know what it is.

"It's a piece of one of Amos Quint's mirrors," Damon says. "He wants you to give it to Lambert."

We reach for the shard. We stop, our hand hovering above Damon's palm. We pull our hand back, cradling it protectively against our chest. "It looks like glass," we say. "But it doesn't feel like glass." A strand of the shard yanked at our very being. A fiber of sound, at once high-pitched and gravelly deep. It's gone now.

"What do you mean?"

We don't know how to explain it, so we shake our head. We tell Damon to put the shard in the little basket on the corner table. We promise that we'll find someone to take the fragment to Lambert.

"I think Amos wanted you to take it," Damon says.

"Oh. Well, in that case, it could be a while before he gets it."

35.

≈

All this loss is changing us. Who we're becoming is still unclear. We get occasional reassuring glimpses of Avienne, but Mother remains elusive. And wherever Brân is, he doesn't seem to want or need our company.

We watch Damon's snails with casual fascination. They seem livelier. Can we say that about these torpid creatures? We're convinced they dance when we sing to them. The fresh slime is making them glow more brightly. But the billbugs are growing even more pesky, especially in the evening when the luminous slime is perhaps most alluring to them. We've covered the tanks with mesh cloth, but the bugs still find a way in. They cluster right above the water line.

Damon is kept busy working on photographs for the book. It's only nights and mornings that he's all ours. Mornings are especially precious, when his mind has been quieted by sleep. Evenings his work comes home with him.

"There's so much of our history I knew so little about, Meri. Well, I knew next to nothing about Melfar history, of course. But even episodes of Mundani history are far more complicated than we wanted to believe."

"Tell us," we say. We know he's consumed with the images and stories that Zara or Father sang into his plates that day, accompanied by Vidvana's lines of poetry. Talking about it for a while unburdens him and helps him sleep. Besides, we like the images he conjures in our minds with his words. He's promised to show us more of his prints soon.

"Today we printed images of the terrible drought in the 270's of the Mundani record. Even worse than what we've known recently. Zara says it happened during a Preterit Turquoise Meed that had a Song of the Sun. She sang some of it for our picture."

We hear a fragment of the song. It shows a dreadfully parched and barren landscape. And conflict. There was conflict among Melfar and it was that conflict more than the song itself that inflicted drought across the land.

"But listen to this," Damon says. "In Mundani passage...I think Vidvana said it was 279... the Melfar of Túl created a Benison mid-meed and gifted it with a song that brought rain to the Cesta region. Nowhere else. Only there. And in Cesta, it flooded. Then a few returns later, at the start of an Amethyst Meed, two Benisons were erected."

"Two? Both for the same meed?"

"Zara says it's the only time this ever happened. Anyway, one was in Lindmor, which was as it should have been according to the customary rotation. It held a Song of the Migrant. The other was in Túl and had a Song of the Forest."

"Really? A Song of the Migrant? We've never heard anyone mention that one." We're trying to imagine what it might have been like. A few notes drift just beyond our grasp.

"Zara described it to us as a song of accepting natural cause and effect. She didn't seem to know much about it. Mostly we talked about the Song of the Forest. Zara said that one was intended to protect Tùl and the region of Cesta. Their own forest."

We try to recall if we've ever met anyone from Tùl. It's always seemed so remote.

"Now, do you remember when Razak Pherson was born?" Damon grins with anticipation.

We don't remember and aren't at all sure what this has to do with a separate Benison erected by the Tùl Melfar. We do know that Razak Pherson was born a long time ago and that he was supposedly a rebirth of the great Mundani Prophet Razak Caloyer. And didn't Razak Pherson live a very long time, becoming several times Revelant? We'd rather hear more about the Song of the Migrant, but Damon has already left it behind.

"Razak Pherson was born in the passage 282," he says. "In Benbridge, which, at the time, lay at the northwestern edge of the southern forest of Cesta. Vidvana says that all this conflict between the Melfar of Túl and the other Melfar was directly responsible for Razak Pherson's emergence as Prophet."

We're trying to follow his story. We focus. "How did that happen?" we ask.

"In Mundani Passage 287, a Melfar Calumet called Iria traveled to Cesta to try and make peace with Túl. She knew that Túl had become isolated due at least in part to their troubles with the Mundani around Benbridge. Iria sensed the potential of young Razak Pherson as someone who might help foster peace for both peoples. She was the one who healed him, and she was the one who caused the florapple fruit to be dropped into his hand. You remember that story, don't you? It became an important part of the legend of his greatness. Oh, Meri, the Mundani owe so much to Melfar!"

Maybe we do recall that story. We hear it in Gerd's voice as she read it to us in Mother's cottage in Shadham. It told how a bird brought a florapple to the deathly ill child and how he was healed. And how his healing brought rains to the land. The Mundani tale never mentions the intervention of a Melfar Calumet. The Mundani never knew.

The next day, after Damon goes off to work, his stories continue to swirl 'round and 'round in our minds. Our little cabin feels small and oppressive. We need space.

Outdoors, we breathe more deeply.

We're drawn toward the stream that's begun to flow near our cabin and when we get there, we take off our sandals and walk right out into the water. It's cold. The splash and movement of the water call up images of walking on the beach at Selbourne.

No, this is a different beach. The water stretches endlessly into the distance.

There's a ship.

Brân is there. People inside the ship are dying. They've already come through a time of horrific death and intolerable suffering and it isn't over. The image tears at our heart, our vital nexus.

We step out of the stream, leaving the unhappy image behind. "Be well, Brân," we whisper. *Go carefully.* Recalling his promise to find out what we need to know about these strange people, we send a pulse of gratitude. We don't know if he received it. Loneliness grabs at our hearts again.

We wander on toward the spot that Vidvana calls "Meridia's temple." It's only a small glen of sheltered greenness. We come when we need to think. No one else comes here unless we invite them. We settle on the stool we brought recently; we'd begun to find the ground uncomfortable and getting up almost impossible.

We empty our collection of stones onto a cloth spread across our lap. Taking up one waif after another, we invite each song to course through our bodies. We pause for a moment, holding the Turquoise, and catch a brief glimpse of Amergin and Naomi. They escaped from the caverns, but what happened after that? We touch the Amethyst and send what hope we can.

We're drawn into the green stones, the Ancient Jade with its Song of Pacification and the Old Jade with its Song of the Calumet. The latter brings us almost to tears, remembering our beloved eldmother, recalling the chant that entreated us to take up the task ourselves. If only we could believe ourselves capable of such a task. We sit with one waif in each hand, listening.

The call of a bird distracts us. It sounds like a pilgrim finch, singing a tale of where it's been. It was a pilgrim finch that took us to the Blanton Clauster, showing us the terrible ritual of the Palinjians as they invited death so that they could seek renewal and the Melfar-like abilities it conveyed. Only sometimes it didn't. And sometimes renewal didn't come at all.

Without willing it, we're there again, in Blanton, inside the Clauster where Mother was once held.

An overwhelming stench emanates from beneath the piles of stones dotting the Clauster's grounds. The piles are smothered in great bunches of withered flowers and herbs to no avail. The incense burning in every corner only serves to make the air heavier and harder to breathe. There's only one man here, sitting in a corner, his face swathed protectively as he stares at the rotting remains of his deceased leaders.

Where is everyone?

At the outskirts of Temur, a group of six Palinjians stride purposefully in the direction of Blanton, pushing along a reluctant companion.

"No," he moans, as he stumbles yet again. "I'm not who you think I am."

But he knows he is exactly who they think he is. His mother told him on her deathbed only four passages ago. He's been denying it ever since and has vowed to take the secret to his pyre. "My name is Elvrid Conif," he mumbles. "I sell books in Temur."

Our heart flutters fearfully. This is the one they've been searching for, the man whom Palinjians are convinced is the son of their great Prophet Zibal Palinj. Their false prophet.

We gaze through a turquoise veil, curious to learn more about this Elvrid Conif.

Elvrid has lived in Temur all his life. Our heart knows the perils of a child growing up with only their mother, being nobody. At least this man is Mundani. At least he's a man. We try to recall if we ever visited his shop. It was near the center of town. On a side street.

Elvrid Conif looks up from his book to acknowledge, with a nod and a grunt, a stranger's entry into his shop. The place is only open a short while each day. Only long enough to handle sufficient business for Elvrid Conif to keep from starving. He loves the shop, but he hates the business. People annoy him, especially the arrogant Sidayens who invariably want him to print lavishly decorated books of lies claiming to be the history of their Houses. Elvrid has no House. Or at least he thought he had none until the terrible truth his mother told him with her dying breath. Was it the truth? He's torn between wanting to believe it was a lie and refusing to call his mother a liar.

"I'm searching for a book, and I'm told that you might know something about it," the stranger says.

Elvrid puts down his own book, wrenching his mind away from the world within it, and stands, his head tilted submissively. "I'll help you if I can," he says. "We have the best collection of books in the region." It's what his mother always said.

"So I've heard. The book I'm looking for is the history of the House of Palinj."

Elvrid's left hand trembles and heat rises in his cheeks. He steadies his hand by placing it on top of the closed book. He takes a deep breath. "No," he says. "I'm afraid that's not something we have." He tries not to think of how the gold leaf from the covers of that book had glistened in the ashes after the flames died.

"And yet I'm told it's something you might have information about," the stranger says. "Something your mother may have known about. Didn't she live in Benbridge before inheriting this shop from her deceased father?"

Sweat prickles in Elvrid's armpits as he struggles to control his breathing. He says nothing, but his eyes stutter as two more men enter the shop.

The first man continues speaking. "And didn't she move here in the passage 612, the very passage in which you were born?" All three strangers face Elvrid, feet planted, arms crossed over their chests.

All of this is true but Elvrid shakes his head in denial. "I'm sorry I can't help you," he says. His mind reels in mounting desperation. "My shop should have closed already, so I'll have to ask you to leave. Maybe the bookshop in Benbridge will have what you seek." Elvrid tries to calculate whether he can reach the door to the back room and secure it before these men—these Palinjians—attack him. Then where would he go?

Elvrid's eyes close and his arms drop to his sides as the men move forward. He offers no physical resistance, but his mind clamps down hard around his secret. He won't say it. He will never say it.

But we know. We know that the Palinjians have found the only son of Zibal Palinj and that they mean to use him for their own ends.

We rise too quickly and are overcome with dizziness. We reach for a tree to steady us. We have to get Father to warn Gerd. We'd do it ourselves, but we're finding such communication unreliable these days. The more plural we become, the harder it is to focus on a single message. We make our way toward Abél's cabin.

He's engrossed in weaving a basket, one big enough to hold a nen. He intends to make two. He asks us something, but his verberations are broken into pops of disparate colors by our anxiety. We'll have to use words.

"It's the Palinjians. We have to warn Gerd."

"Warn her of what, Daughter? Here, sit down and catch your breath. I can see that you're upset. Take a moment to collect yourselves."

He's beginning to understand. We welcome the rosy waves that caress our shoulders. We settle and take a few breaths, seeking words that can convey what we need to verberate. "The Palinjians are holding a man from Temur. His name is Elvrid Conif. But they say he's rightfully Elvrid Palinj."

"So they found him. And they're convinced he's in the line of the old false prophet? Well, this could be an interesting development."

"They say he's Zibal Palinj's own son. By a young woman he knew in Benbridge."

Abél pushes his unfinished basket aside and turns toward us. "What manner of man is this Elvrid?"

"He had a bookshop and printing business." We concentrate, trying our best to show Father what we've pertanged, focusing on the man Elvrid. We think he and Father could have been friends.

Father's face goes strange for a moment. "He had a shop where he printed books of poetry for Chanters."

"Did he?" We knew about the shop. We didn't know about the poetry, only that he hated printing the self-aggrandizing histories of the Sidayens' Houses. "Is it true? He did that?"

"Yes. And that makes this development all the more interesting. We definitely need to tell Gerd. I'll let Jalu know, and he'll pass it on to her." He's thinking about the fact that we're now little more than a six from the Binder.

We're sorry we're not able to do such things ourselves right now, Father. Not reliably. "You see how it is. Things come to us easily enough, but we have difficulty making ourselves known to others or verberating clearly." *How much worse do you think it will get before our nens are born?* We catch our breath with the sudden thought of separation.

"I can't say, Meridia. That's between you and the Migrant. I'm sorry your eldmother won't be here to guide you through your pregnancy. She would know such things."

We do know, Meridia. Stay steady.

We walk back down the path that leads to our cabin, wandering toward the gardens, thinking to pick a few fresh vegetables. Our awareness strays toward Gerd and Jalu.

At first Jalu thinks it's only a bizarre notion that came into his head. But as it becomes clearer and more detailed, he knows that it's coming from Abél. He goes in search of Gerd.

She's in the old packing shed, where the sour smell of sweat from combat training has at last overwhelmed the scent of pickles from the old Landry business that once occupied the space. Jalu waits near the door while they finish their training session. He thinks Ann is becoming scary good at these skills. Jalu knows he needs to get in more practice himself, but he has other skills that are in greater demand.

As soon as Roqu signals dismissal, Gerd strides toward Jalu with a stern look. "I've told you before not to disturb our sessions. Concentration is essential." She mops a cloth across her face and then rests it across her shoulder, waiting.

"I'm sorry, Gerd, but this seemed important."

"Okay, then. Out with it."

Jalu's eyes dart about anxiously.

"Ah. Okay, then. Somewhere private. Follow me."

They walk a few paces down the hallway and enter a small storeroom. Gerd closes the door behind them.

"I have news from Abél." Jalu furrows his brow, searching for the right words that can express what he's learned through images and tones. "The Palinjians in Blanton have taken a prisoner. They claim he's the son of Zibal Palinj."

"So they found him! Where?"

"In Temur. But he denies being Palinj. He's always gone by Elvrid Conif."

"How can they be certain he is Palinj? Didn't old Zibal take a vow of celibacy after his wife died? Never mind. Sidayens have never been very good at that sort of thing." Gerd takes the damp cloth from her shoulder and wipes the back of her neck, still surprised at the absence of her customary braid. "Do we know what manner of man he is?"

"He ran a bookshop in Temur. He also printed books there. Maybe some poetry books for Chanters. That's what Abél thinks."

Gerd chuckles. "Well, that could make for an interesting situation."

"Anyway, that's all I know. It's what Abél wanted me to tell you."

36.

Once when we were living in Temur, a pair of echo thrushes built a nest in the eaves of our house. We watched every day as the mother thrush sat on her eggs and her mate flew back and forth, feeding her worms and bits of scavenged fruit. We feel like that these days, as life goes on all around us and we feel less and less a part of it.

Gerd and her associates are in a quandary over what to do about Elvrid Conif. Damon continues his work every day with Vidvana and Zara, composing the *Book of All Time*. We're wishing we had something useful to do. Something more than brooding nens and flying backward and forward with the Migrant. We feel powerless, useless. It's only when we're learning songs with Father that we feel some sense of purpose.

Our irritation is interrupted by a remembered promise.

Lambert. We promised to keep an eye on Lambert Quint for Amos. Our glance flits briefly toward the basket containing the mirror shard. We close our eyes tightly, focusing on Lambert.

His shed is tidier and sturdier than when we last pertanged it. Fallen stones have been replaced and the mortar between all the stones restored and strengthened. The place is bigger. There's an extension at the back, still unfinished.

The interior is clean and surprisingly bright. Sunlight streams in through openings between wall and roof. The light is reflected and reflected in the mirrors Lambert has mounted along one wall. This room may not be as submersive as Amos Quint's chamber of mirrors on Selbourne, but it's clear what Lambert Quint is trying to achieve.

He's humming a tune, and we recognize it as a fragment of the Song of All Songs. He adds words: "We are the myriad expressions of the singularity of existence. We are one." Lambert's heart radiates colors as he voices the words his Father put to the song. Chanting them is his practice.

We retreat from Lambert's presence, carrying with us an admiration for his sense of purpose. Amos Quint will be pleased.

Our irritation at our own lack of purpose resurges. A deep sigh dissolves our sense of being anything at all as we disintegrate outward, touching this and that, none of it of any importance whatsoever. Our attention lands on a drab little bird outside the window. It sings and we pause to listen. Our hearts recoil as we recognize the song of the pilgrim finch.

Follow the bird.

We don't want to. We know where it will take us.

The bird sings a few notes from one of the Palinjian anthems. Maybe the one about revenge? The one that is a twisted misinterpretation of the Preterit Granite's Song of Regret. It's what we heard in their suicide ritual.

The air in the courtyard of the Blanton Clauster crackles with crimson anger. And fear. Or is that the fire? They've built a huge pyre in the center of the courtyard where a corpse has just caught fire. A second corpse. The bones of the first one still smolder. The day is still, windless, and smoke hangs heavy over the men gathered there. The smoke is rank with the scent of roasting meat. Rancid, rotten meat.

"Look at them, curse you! These are the ones the sully women slaughtered. These were all revered Revelants, your father's devoted disciples. Watch! They died for you!"

"My name is Elvrid Conif," the man murmurs as he stares skyward through the smoke that is making his eyes water uncontrollably. "I am Elvrid Conif. I sell books in Temur."

We're sure the corpse waiting next to enter the fire is that of Crispin Harper. The face is covered in mold, its features eaten away by maggots. After all, it's been nearly three tides since his death. But we're sure that's the same cross-patterned shirt he wore that day when we and Damon first encountered him at the little bothy outside Fayredell. He still wore it when his men killed Damon.

Are these the men Maddie killed? Jalu has joined us. He's never seen such sadly decomposed bodies before.

We try to tell him that Mother didn't kill them. That they killed themselves. *She only prevented their Renewal.*

Jalu acknowledges our presence, wondering how we seem to be both vague and pervasive at the same time. Transparent. Vibrant. Here and there. We do our best.

We recognize one of the men who was in the party that wreaked the Palinjians' revenge on Mother. He was the only one who escaped Gerd's rage that morning. He's still nursing a broken arm and a wounded ego. And a thirst for revenge.

The man who speaks is Halvor, his eyes aimed like blades at the man in the center of their group, the man who refuses to look back at him. "No longer. You're not Conif any longer. No more hiding behind your mother's name. It's time to live the truth and the truth is that you are Palinj. Elvrid Palinj, sired by the great Prophet himself (may he rest in peace) then stolen away and held in secret by the sully whore you call your mother. But the time has come for that secret to be revealed. Now you will claim your rightful House and galvanize your father's followers into claiming our glorious revenge."

Tears flow down Elvrid's cheeks as he continues to mutter. "My name is Elvrid Conif. I sell books in Temur." And more quietly, "My mother was a good woman."

"Leave him be, Halvor," another man says. "He'll come around. Why would anyone fail to claim the glory of the House of Palinj? He may need a little time to get used to it. Time to get to know us and to learn the truth about his exalted father and our plans to restore Palinjian power and glory."

"He talks like a sully poltroon." Halvor's voice oozes disgust. "How could the likes of Zibal Palinj have sired a wimple-clinger such as this?"

"Maybe if he went through the ritual and became Revelant..."

"This one? He'd never be able to yoke the Restorer. He's got the will of a shama nestling."

Jalu has a different opinion of Elvrid's will. With a surge of amethyst light, we assure him that we agree with his assessment. In his refusal to bend to his harassers, Elvrid is as stubborn and strong-willed as a young equid.

A man who has been sitting quietly at the margins of the group speaks up. "He may come around, Halvor, or he may not. Maybe it doesn't matter. Maybe we only need to spread the word that a son of Zibal Palinj has come to us. We can make of him whatever we like in the minds of the people. We'll tell them Elvrid Palinj has gone into retreat to prepare to lead our resurgence. We could even announce a great presentation for the Binder. People will believe it because they'll want to."

Halvor's face contorts into a vicious smile. "You may be right, Naviq. We can clothe the nestling in the plumage of a corona hawk and make him a leader whether he ashing well likes it or not."

Murmurs of approval greet Halvor's adoption of Naviq's proposal. Elvrid's red-rimmed eyes grow wide with comprehension and fear.

You have to warn Gerd, Jalu. Gerd will know what to do about this. Whether Jalu pertanged our request or simply knew what to do, we can't tell and it doesn't matter.

"They should know better than to try their hand at Melfar trickery," Jalu says, speaking aloud to Gerd.

"What do you mean?" Gerd shuffles her feet, impatient. He's caught up with her in the hallway.

Jalu explains what he's seen and heard. As Gerd listens, she shifts from one foot to the other and back again.

"That doesn't seem like much of a plan, does it?" she says. "But people are expecting something for the Binder. This might motivate the return of some of the Palinjians who've gone back to their farms and shops. Do

196

you think this Elvrid fellow will be able to continue resisting their persuasion?"

"Maybe. I know that he's firmly resolved not to acknowledge Zibal Palinj as his father. But knowing so little about what manner of man he is..."

"Do you think he really is Palinj's son?"

"He might be."

We think Elvrid himself believes it. He doesn't want to believe it, but it's what his mother told him, and she'd never lied to him before. She'd only refused to name his father, refused right up until her final moments.

Gerd is already planning how to address this new development. "As I see it," she says, "We have two possible courses of action. For one thing, we can counter their attempts to spread lies. With the assistance of Melfar, that is. But the other thing we can do is to physically take Elvrid away from them."

"Another abduction?"

"Perhaps," Gerd says. "Yes, we may have to do that."

37.

We tell Damon what we've learned, feeling a flush of pride at having something important to speak of, followed by angry shame. We're turning into nothing more than a gossip, talking of others' activities while having none of our own.

Damon is as disturbed as we are by the plot taking shape at the Blanton Clauster. We'd hoped that the Palinjians would disperse back into their farms and shops and let the zealots burn themselves out quarreling with one another. We'd hoped that this Binder could pass without incident.

"This Elvrid fellow sounds dangerous," Damon says. "Well, not dangerous in himself. Only dangerous in what he might be made to represent for the Palinjians."

We're strolling with Damon along one of the easy paths among the vegetable gardens at the margins of our community. Our arm is linked through his.

"The Mundani farms are doing so well," we say. "It would be a shame for them to abandon them now." But they will. And crops will be lost. Burned?

Damon slows our pace. "I'm trying to remember what Vidvana was telling us the other day about Zibal Palinj's family. I know she said that he was married. And his wife died. Died in childbirth, I believe, along with the child." He looks at us and a brief shadow of fear flickers behind his eyes.

We lean toward him and squeeze his hand, trying to offer reassurance. *We're doing well and Bekanz is the best midwife we could ask for.* "How did Zibal Palinj become who he was?" Our question is awkward, but Damon knows what we mean.

"He was born a long time after Razak Pherson's death and in all that time there'd been no prophet with anything more than a local reputation." Damon's brow furrows as he tries to remember what he's learned from Zara and Vidvana. "Things were not going well for either Mundani or Melfar."

"How long? How bad was it?"

"I don't recall how long exactly. Less than two hundred passages after Razak Pherson died, but close to that. Most Melfar were keeping to their separate forests at that time and they weren't in constant touch with one another. They'd retreated after the Mundani down around Benbridge tried to turn Melfar into near slaves, forcing them to labor in their workshops and fields."

"That didn't work out so well." We mumble the words, calling to mind the Song of Liberation of the Old Lapis, the song that led us to Maddie's cabin in Shadham. The song came with a bird who also guided us until we lost him in the journey over the mountains toward Selbourne.

"Mundani at that time had no leader to unify them all and they followed whatever House was prominent in their region. Like the Quints in the Fayredell area. Although eventually Amos Quint was recognized more widely."

"And Razak Pherson left no descendants?"

"He did, but they were never recognized as prophets. Not until Warreth Pherson, although Warreth's actual connections to Razak have always been a bit vague." Damon's fringed brows gather into a deeper frown. "I can only tell you what Vidvana has told me."

"Okay. So what was it that led Mundani to call Zibal Palinj a prophet?"

"Zibal's mother and brother had died in what Vidvana thinks may have been a local outbreak of the nacreous fever. Zibal was married by this time, though he had no children. Anyway, one day when Zibal was out and about in Benbridge, a terrible storm came up, blowing in from the sea, and Zibal was struck by lightning."

There was such a wind that day. Crashing thunder. It was one of those dry storms that never resolves into rain.

The young man is frightened, exhausted as he battles the wind, trying to reach home and safety. He stops for a moment and leans against the high wooden tower that used to mark the center of Benbridge. At that exact moment, a bolt of fireseed strikes the tower, racing through it and into the body of Zibal Palinj, tossing him out into the street. There he lies, unconscious. Not breathing. Heart stilled into death.

There he is discovered by a nearby shopkeeper. "He's dead!" the man calls out as others gather to gawk.

The wooden tower has caught fire and a gust of wind blows a billow of smoke over the body of Zibal Palinj, who suddenly convulses, coughing and jerking, and then trembling violently as his eyes open wide.

Damon is still speaking. "Of course, Zibal was hailed as Revelant and it wasn't long before some people were also calling him Prophet. Are you okay, Mer? You look pale."

Zibal was an arrogant man and did not object to the adulation. He claimed it was his own destiny stone, an Obsidian, which he'd had in his pocket that day, that accounted for his miraculous renewal. He later inherited the destiny stones of his father and grandfather—a Granite and an Amber. All of these he had sewn into a sash along with lumps of metal from his father's forge.

"Meri?"

"We're okay. Only... It must have been a frightening experience." We still see the lightning, the fire, but we also see the hulking, dangerous man Zibal Palinj became, the man we saw in the image evoked by the percussive music of Malaki's waif of the Old Obsidian.

"Palinj always wore that sash slung across his broad chest in the Sidayen fashion," Damon says. He's remembering the image he and Zara imprinted on a photograph.

We silence that disturbing image.

"What do you think Gerd will do about this son of Zibal Palinj?" Damon says.

"She may be planning something," we say, "but we're not sure what it is." We only know that she's determined to take the man known as Elvrid Conif away from the Palinjians, regardless of whether or not he is truly Elvrid Palinj, son of the false prophet.

We're still thinking about Gerd as we prepare for bed, as we settle next to Damon, as we yield to sleep.

Gerd isn't planning. They're on their way.

It's the same group as the one that attempted to rescue Maddie—Gerd, Roqu, Fergus, and Jalu—but this time with the addition of Daedal. Gerd had felt premonitions of misfortune and thought it better to enlarge the group. Daedal volunteered.

The night is cool and blessedly dark as they make their way toward the Blanton Clauster. They arrive just before daybreak.

Gerd reviews their plan. "Once Fergus has made it over the wall, we'll wait for him to throw the signal flag to indicate everything is safe for our approach. We'll move into position beside the gate and wait for Fergus to unlock it. Jalu will be ready to unleash a zaki if we need a distraction." That trick had worked well at Markham, though not so well in the attempt to rescue Maddie.

They huddle in the darkness, watching as Fergus climbs up the crumbling wall, somehow finding handholds and footholds that manage to support his weight. He seems glued to the wall like a rock lizard. At last he reaches the top and peers into the courtyard of the Clauster. Then he disappears from view.

They wait. Gerd wanted to send Roqu rather than her own son, but Fergus and Daedal argued that someone lighter and more agile would be more successful. The longer they wait, the more Gerd wishes she had insisted on sending Roqu. Gerd is about to decide that they should send Roqu over the wall to see what became of Fergus, when a stick adorned with a scrap of blue cloth comes sailing over the wall.

Gerd breathes a little easier as she and Roqu and Daedal advance toward the closed gate, which Fergus should open momentarily.

Suddenly the morning is rent by a clamor of shrieks and growls. "Run!" Fergus cries out as he bursts through the gate, followed by a pack of patkánies that snarl and snap at his legs and hands and lunge for his face. Gerd retreats a few paces and then she and the others turn, knives and longblades drawn, and begin slashing at the beasts. There are four of them, each one almost twice the size of the cavoutis they're related to. But whereas cavoutis have meaty hindquarters with almost delicate forelegs, these creatures are muscled from nose to rump, with teeth and jaws well adapted to their predatory pursuits. When three patkánies lie whimpering and helpless on the ground, Roqu shouts, "I've got this one. Go! Run!" And they run. Gerd stops and turns when she hears Roqu scream in pain. But then she hears the death shriek of the last patkány followed by the labored, uneven steps of Roqu running as best he can to join them.

The men from the Clauster, roused from sleep, are already in pursuit.

No one in Gerd's group has escaped injury and it's only Jalu's ability to generate a canopy of protection that saves them from their pursuers. Jalu is uncertain about how effective the canopy might be in concealing the trail of blood they leave behind. He follows last in line and occasionally adds to his canopy of protection a few muttered lines of the Ancient Amber's Song of Turning, twisting the landscape just enough to throw the Mundani off course. At last Jalu guides them to a sheltered spot well away from any road. Here they can catch their breath and tend their wounds.

Gerd is dismayed at the abject failure of their mission. "This is all my fault," she says. "I should've taken more time to plan, more time to consult and prepare. I was too eager."

"We all wanted to act quickly," Daedal says. "None of us wanted to give them the chance to win Elvrid over to their schemes. We all came willingly, Gerd."

The wounds that bleed most profusely are bound up with leaves Jalu collected along the way and strips of cloth from whatever articles of clothing can be spared.

"It wasn't a total loss, Mother," Fergus says, grimacing with pain. His injuries are the most severe, especially his shredded left hand that one of the creatures had seemed determined to consume for breakfast.

"No, I think it was worse than that," Gerd says. "Now they know our intentions and they'll be more watchful."

"But now Elvrid knows, too. I spoke with him. That's why I took so long throwing out the signal flag."

"You spoke with him? What did he say?" Gerd looks into her son's eyes, avoiding the sight of his devastated hand. Her own wounds are superficial.

"He would've come away with us, but he was locked inside a shed." Fergus winces and cries out as Jalu tightens the binding on his hand. After a couple of quivering breaths, he continues. "Elvrid is desperate to get away. He seems a timid sort, though. He says they never let him leave the shed. But twice a day they bring him food and empty his bucket."

Gerd's mind is racing. "So he's willing. That's good. If we watch, we can go for him when the kinren comes to bring his meals. I wish we had some way to let him know when we return to get him out."

"I told him to listen for the call of a thrushawk, repeated three times." Fergus blushes. That's the signal he and Ann have been using to arrange their private meetings. It was all he could think of in the heat of the moment inside the Clauster.

"Excellent!" Gerd's pride momentarily overwhelms her concern for her son's injuries. "Now that their pack of patkánies is out of commission, we may stand a chance. Well, once we get everyone patched up." She hopes there aren't more patkánies caged somewhere at the clauster.

"I'm sorry about the patkánies," Jalu says. "You know they're the only creatures that Melfar can't pertange. For some reason, they're invisible to us. We have to see or hear or smell them in the same way Mundani do."

We wonder if the Palinjians at the Blanton Clauster knew that. Of course they did. Why else would they risk keeping such vicious creatures inside their walls?

Gerd thinks that the reason she can't see Jalu anymore has something to do with the protection canopy he continues generating to hide them from the pursuing Palinjians.

That's part of it. But mostly it's the fact that Jalu has headed back to the Blanton Clauster to see if he can extract Elvrid from his prison while his Palinjian guards are out of the way. He didn't ask Gerd for permission because he doubted that she'd give it. As soon as he's sure that Gerd and her crew are safe, he abandons the protection canopy and, holding a small waif of the Old Turquoise, he sings the only verse he knows of the Canopy of Time. It's a verse that shifts things by only a short time, but it enables him to arrive back at the Blanton Clauster mere moments after he left it.

He picks his way among the still quivering corpses of patkánies in front of the gate. In their rush to pursue the interlopers, the Palinjians have left the gate unlocked. Confident that he can't be perceived by Mundani because of the shift in time-space, Jalu walks boldly through the gate, searching for the shed Fergus described as Elvrid's place of imprisonment. He's uncertain how to deal with the fact that Elvrid also won't be able to perceive him. Not directly anyway. Jalu has little experience with the Canopy of Time and he isn't sure exactly what to expect.

He stands in the center of the courtyard, humming and watching in the early morning light. Soon a kinren comes from behind the main building, carrying a basket. He sets the basket on the ground next to a shed and takes a key from his pocket to unfasten the chain that secures the shed's door. What was the signal Fergus told Elvrid to expect? A thrushawk. What does a thrushawk sound like? Three times? Jalu does his best. Can they even hear it? The kinren glances skyward at the second call. With the third he glances toward Jalu, frowning. Quickly, Jalu resumes humming the Canopy of Time.

The kinren has the door open now. Elvrid sits on the cot, eyes wide. He heard the hawk's call, too, but is uncertain what he should do about it. He stares at the doorway, expecting someone else to enter. The kinren sets the basket on the floor and moves toward the corner to retrieve the waste bucket. Elvrid closes his eyes for an instant and then pulls from under the thin blankets a slat he's worked free from the cot's frame. As the kinren bends over to pick up the bucket, Elvrid brings the wood down across the back of the man's head with all the force he can muster. It isn't a lot, but the man is stunned sufficiently for Elvrid to administer a second blow and then a third. The kinren slumps to the floor.

Jalu stands in the doorway, unseen. "Come, Elvrid! Let's go!"

Elvrid stands frozen in place, staring at the wood in his hand, then at the unconscious kinren.

"He's not dead. We need to go!" Jalu remembers that the kinren seemed almost to perceive him when he made the hawk cry. He calls again, reaching his hand toward Elvrid. On the third cry, Elvrid runs toward him and Jalu grabs his hand.

"I don't know who you are or how you're here. I can feel your hand, but I can't see you. Just get me away from here!"

Holding hands, Jalu and Elvrid flee.

Once they're well away from the Clauster, Jalu stops singing the Canopy of Time.

Elvrid stares in disbelief at the young Melfar he now sees in front of him. "Is it safe? Aren't they following us? Who...? How...?" Elvrid can't find the words.

Jalu begins to chuckle. "I can't believe we pulled it off! I've never done that before." Now that he's abandoned the Canopy of Time, Jalu begins to feel his wounds. One of the patkánies left a deep bite on his right calf. The right ankle hurts, too. He vaguely remembers kicking the animal, sending it flying with bits of his own flesh hanging from its jaws. "I'm Jalu," he says. "I'm a friend of Fergus. He's the one who spoke to you earlier." How much earlier that was, Jalu is no longer sure.

"Elvrid," Elvrid says. "Well, you know that. This is all very confusing. Where are we going?"

They're going to Fayredell. We're relieved that Elvrid Conif is out of the clutches of the Palinjians. We're uncertain what might happen next.

38.

≈

Bekanz says it's no hotter than usual for a late Fruit-tide. Twelfth Stint. She says it's the advancing pregnancy that makes us sweat and grow short of breath with even simple activities. Today Bekanz is coming to examine us. We've completed the seventh tide of this exceptional state of being. We crowd one another more all the time.

Bekanz should have been here by now. We waft a sandy apology toward Abél. He's expecting us. We've been working with a Quartz song, the Ancient Quartz Song of Reconciliation.

"Meri, you're here!" It's Damon.

Of course we're here. Doesn't he remember that Bekanz is coming?

"Bekanz isn't coming," he says. "She wanted me to tell you."

"Why?" There's an uncomfortable buzzing in our gnosic orb. We've missed something. There's something wrong and we should have known. We were so involved with Gerd's plight.

"People are falling ill, Meri. An outbreak of some kind of fever. Bekanz thinks it's beginning to look like it might be nacreous fever."

"What? There haven't been any cases of that in almost a meed." We search Meridia's memories for information about nacreous fever. There weren't very many cases of it in Temur. "Wasn't it right before the last big fires?"

"That's what I remember," Damon says.

"How would such an illness get here? Hardly anyone comes in or out of New Beniford." Then we recall the boys who traveled to the Northern Lowlands to bring back salt for Damon's snail tanks. And of course Damon himself, recently returned from the coast. People came for Avienne's funeral, but that was a full tide back. No one except Gerd and Jalu came from outside for Mother's funeral.

"Bekanz says you should stay in. Until we know more about this illness and how it's spreading. Stay away from other people."

Damon still stands in the doorway.

"But we could help. We'll need healers." We feel eager now to claim that designation. Back in Temur, we used to discount our abilities as nothing out of the ordinary. Now we know otherwise.

"Talk to Bekanz about that. She said she'll come this evening, after she's had time to thoroughly cleanse herself from tending the sick." Damon turns halfway and leans against the door frame. "Will you be okay until then? You know I'd stay with you, but..."

"We understand. We'll be okay." Our eyes mist over as we force a smile.

We exchange a few more words with Damon. Golden orbs. Rosy caresses from a distance. We watch him walk away. We'd intended to tell him about Gerd's latest exploit, but that will have to wait.

Our day rearranges itself. Bekanz won't come until evening. Abél knows we aren't coming to him and he knows why.

Use your solitude, Meridia. Lay your waifs out and let the Migrant guide you.

We're not sure how Father expects this to work, but we're willing to try. At least it's something to do.

We lay the stones out on the table in a line. There are so many of them now. We feel a need for order, and so we arrange them according to when we acquired them.

First, there's the New Jade. Well, it's "Old Jade" now, since the start of the New Marble at the Great Turning that pushed everything back. The Old Jade is the one Damon got from Brân. It's the one with the Song of the Calumet that introduced us to Avienne and began revealing to us the deep world of Melfar. We listen for a moment to its song; a tear forms for Avienne. We brush the tear away and move on.

Next we lay down the Old Lapis with its Song of Liberation. This is the waif we discovered on our way to find Damon and Maddie. The one that provided release from our unbearable rage at what Malaki did. We pause for only a moment, remembering the rape, acknowledging the fragments of anger that still cleave to the memory of how our growing twins came to be. They're Damon's twins now. Damon's and Meridia's. Malaki is dead. We thank the Old Lapis song for helping us get through that difficult time. We extend gratitude as well for Amergin and Naomi's liberation from the deep darkness that they endured for so long.

We position the waif of the Old Quartz next to the Lapis. This stone had no Benison, no song, but each waif contained maps and other links so that Melfar from all the dispersed settlements could reach one another. We remember how this waif guided us on our way to Woodclasp when we'd barely begun to be us. It was in Woodclasp that Emba first pertanged our pregnancy.

Emba, partner of Orban and elder sister of Bekanz. Emba, too, is now dead. One hand goes to our heart, searching for the other piece of Quartz, the bead that signifies our partnership with Damon, our enduring link, the growing map of our shared life.

A Mica waif comes next, but we push it aside to make space for a Turquoise. We have two waifs of the Old Turquoise and sometimes we forget that this one came first. This is the one we found long ago, the one we gave to Mother, the one we took back again when we pilfered her little collection of stones in Shadham. Maybe it should've been placed even before the Old Jade. No matter. We had no idea what a waif was until we came across the Old Jade.

We grasp the waif of the Ancient Mica, recalling the journey over the mountains with Brân and Abél and Damon. Finding the Ancient Mica (which, at the time, was still known as the Old Mica) was the task Abél's own father assigned to him as the old man lay dying, his body nearly destroyed by the Great Fires. His name was Mica. Avienne's partner Mica. Our eldfather Mica. We carried a much larger piece of the Mica Benison across the waters from Selbourne and over the mountains to New Beniford. We helped rewrite its song of Calling the Rains. That song is sung every day now and has brought healing rains to all the dry places. Our waif sheds a few shimmering notes of its song into the palm of our hand. A gentle spark of fireseed follows the stone as we place it on the table next to the Quartz, a reminder of the destructive storms held by the original Benison.

The Ancient Amber was a gift from Abél. It contains the Song of Turning and we've used it only twice. Once

to keep Damon safe when he was returning to New Beniford from Temur, diverting his Palinjian pursuers. The
second time was not so successful. We tried to use it to
protect Mother.

Pulses of turquoise light draw us into the memory of
Maddie. We tried so hard to be a good daughter, but
there was so much we didn't understand. So much that
Mother didn't understand. Things about Melfar and
Mundani and how they're different. How Meridia was
different. We tried and we're sure Mother did, too. We
remember the last time we were able to bring her home
to Temur from her confused wanderings. And we recall
how we kept searching for her the next time she wandered away. She went so far that time, to the place where
she died and was brought back by the Migrant, where
she was discovered by Gerd and nursed back to health.

We brush away a tear and turn to the larger waif of
the Old Turquoise, the one Abél gave us. "Dear Father."
The whispered words sound almost like *eldfather*. Soon
Abél will be that. We caress the stone and let the notes
of its song seep into our awareness. Reluctantly, we will
the visions away and look to the last four waifs.

The New Marble comes next, with its Song of All
Songs, the song we brought fresh from the Migrant.
We're still mystified about how that happened, awed by
the fact that it happened to us, humbled by the profound
effect the song is having on our people. Even Mundani
people like Amos Quint and Vidvana and Damon tell us
that the Song of All Songs is a powerful force. We keep
feeling the need to act, but that song, the most important
thing we've done, came with no intention whatsoever on
our part. We close our eyes for a moment, searching

again for that sense of oneness with the Migrant. But it's not something we can will into existence.

The last three waifs are the ones Avienne gave us shortly before her death. There's an Old Amethyst, with its Song of Hope; an Ancient Jade carrying the Song of Pacification; and an Old Granite. Its song is the Song of Firm Resolve.

We place our hands on the table, one at each end of our line of stones.

We listen.

We breathe with our minds.

There's a jumble of tones and glimmers of shifting colors as our awareness wanders among our waifs, touching first one and then another. One pattern surges to the fore. Not louder than any other, but clearer. More insistent.

We begin to vocalize a few of the notes. It's the Song of the Calumet. And yet it feels different this time. We're drawn toward something deeper inside it. A hint of another song we can't quite grasp. We let the song carry us. We hear its notes trill like a lulark until they're joined by a deep, slow harmony, a fuller sound, almost Mundani in its resonance.

We see Avienne, so young and lithe as she dances, swathed in all the colors. Her companion follows her dance haltingly, as if she doesn't know the steps. They sing and the dance becomes more graceful, more confident, more conjoined.

Who is she, Eldmother? Who dances with you?

Avienne spins once and then spins her partner to face us.

It's Meridia!

But not Avienne's mother Meridia. It's us.

The vision shatters and the notes of the song break apart. Tears course down our face, tears the color of these notes, the notes of a new song. The new song of a new Calumet.

We sit in silence, staring at the line of waifs, at the glistening tendrils still emanating from the Old Jade. A glow emanates from our face and from every cell of our being as well. We will learn this song. We will learn the dance, although at the moment our conjoined bodies feel too heavy for dancing.

Maybe we can become the Calumet the people desire. The Calumet they require. After all, isn't a healer already a peace-bringer of a sort? Healing the rifts that tore our two peoples apart, healing the wounds of history—this is another step along the path.

We gather up the stones and place them back inside our pouch, lingering over the Jade, relishing the last sparks of its song.

Another memory rises, unbidden by any waif.

We recall how Brân showed us the fires that burned Cödweg. It was after Gerd read to us the Story of Razak. Why do we remember this now? There was a song that the people were singing around the Obsidian Benison that wasn't the Benison's Song of Embracing Death. We try to focus our attention on the memory. It was a simpler song. A healing song. Brân said that Cödweg had burned during a time of widespread fevers and the Melfar were singing a healing song meant to soothe the fevers that were afflicting the people. We listen intently. We hum the song softly as its pale blue notes trace a spiral pattern.

Maybe this is something we can do now. We can sing healing.

Be the healer now, Meridia. It will teach you how to be the Calumet.

We send the song spiraling out across New Beniford, letting it spill over whoever needs it. We sing it again and again, sensing not one but three voices, singing in healing unison.

39.

꩜

Our throat grows dry with thirst and singing.

"We should have some lunch." We say the words aloud and push the chair noisily away from the table. Speaking ordinary words pleases us. We like hearing and feeling the vibrations of our voice. Spoken words break song into something simpler, settling us more firmly into our physical bodies and surroundings. We're Mundani, after all, as well as Melfar.

We find some nutbread and dried meat. We fetch the jar from the doorway where the tea has been brewing in the sunshine. We spot some ripe sunberries. We take a small basket with us.

There are more berries under that tarbush.

"Meridia!"

We turn to see who's speaking and we're surprised at how far we've wandered from the house. We have a nice full basket of berries. "Good day, Zara!"

Yes, yes. "Fine day." *But what are you doing way over there? Didn't Damon tell you that you need to stay indoors?* Zara's golden curls quiver with concern and she brushes a few wisps away from her eyes.

We were only picking some berries. She can see that. We'd forgotten that we were supposed to stay in. Because of the illness. Maybe Zara knows more about that. We offer her some berries.

They do look lovely and ripe.

Inside the house we find two bowls and divide the berries. We give one bowl to Zara. She refuses to come inside.

"Until we know more about this illness, Bekanz says we need to keep our distance," she says, using words to make absolutely certain we understand.

"What are the symptoms?" The berries are deliciously sweet and juicy. *How many have come down with it, do you know?*

Bekanz says that fever and a rash seem to be the most consistent symptoms. So far, it's only five people who have fallen ill.

In a community this small, five seems like a lot. *Can you show me the rash?* We're trying to remember what Meridia knows about the preparation of unguents for skin rashes.

You'll have to ask Bekanz about that. I'm a historian, not a healer.

Then tell us what you know about other outbreaks of fevers with rash.

"That I can do." Zara licks the sweet berry juice from her fingers. She'll use words. This is about both Melfar and Mundani. "The first outbreak we have record of occurred in the Lapis Return of the Old Jade Meed."

"Which would have been..." We still have trouble making sense of all the Melfar meeds and returns. We grew up learning only about Mundani passages. Those never made much sense either.

"Mundani passage 608 or 609, I believe. That outbreak started around Woodclasp and spread rapidly into Blanton and Fayredell. A great many people died and eventually all the major towns were affected. There were a few small outbreaks of fever in later returns that some people think were also the nacreous fever, but nothing to rival that initial episode."

"Have there been any outbreaks in recent returns?" Why are we thinking of fires?

Yes, that was also the time of the Great Fires. "It's said that the fever outbreak in Benbridge in the Mica Return of the Old Amber Meed—that would be Mundani passage 655—was very similar. It came and went and didn't spread to other towns." Zara sets her bowl inside the door. *Maybe this is nacreous fever, but it could be something completely different. I'm sure Bekanz will figure it out.* The lavender wave of hopefulness she tries to radiate is weighted down with clumps of sandy doubt.

Zara lingers next to the door. The sun shining through her mass of curls highlights the silver strands around her face. There are more lines around her amber eyes than we'd remembered. She has vertical lines at the center of her forehead, too, etched by worry.

Did Bekanz tell you when she would be coming around to check on us?

"Probably not until after supper." Zara is distracted. There's something she wants to say but doesn't want to say.

"You miss Avienne as much as we do, don't you?" we say. *No, you miss her even more. You knew Avienne most of your life.*

Of course I miss her. I used to spend time with her every day. Every day for so many returns. She taught me everything I know.

You were to be the next Calumet. If we'd stayed where we were, you would have been Calumet. "We're sorry, Zara."

Maybe you should be the Calumet anyway, regardless of what people are saying.

Zara shakes her head vigorously. *No, Meridia. The Migrant has chosen you. And you are the Calumet we need. You're the one who can unite us. You hold both worlds, both Melfar and Mundani.*

But we still know so little. You were trained. You were educated.

Avienne was a wonderful teacher, Meridia, but the Migrant is teaching you. The Migrant and your father, Abél. And me if you'll have me. There's a sudden burst of colors like a clear sunrise, and a smile shines through the mist in her eyes.

"Oh, Zara, yes." *There's so much of Avienne in you. If you'd be willing to share that with us...* The light linking Zara and us shimmers with promise.

Nothing would please me more.

Then come whenever you have time, we say. *If Bekanz wants us to stay in for a while, you'll know where to find us.*

We watch Zara leave, her steps buoyant along the path, Avienne drifting in her wake.

Our collection of stones still lies on the table. They pulse and glow. Across the room, the tank containing Damon's snails glows, too. The tank is fairly swarming with buzzing billbugs and we go to adjust the covering, shooing the bugs away. We look closely at the ring of luminous sludge along the edges of the tank. It looks as if the glass is being etched away where the slime is thickest. Is there really a pattern there? We light a bundle of beegrass, hoping the bugs will find somewhere else to hover.

The day drags on. We sing the healing song again, but our colors grow weak as we struggle to pertange the nature of this illness that has invaded our community. We nap. We eat another simple meal, alone.

The sun is moments from disappearing behind the mountains when Bekanz finally arrives. Her shoulders slump with tiredness. She smells of soap and her pale orange hair clings in dark, damp wisps around her face.

"I'm sorry it took me so long, Meridia," Bekanz says. "How are you holding up?"

She comes inside and takes a seat at the table across from us. Despite her weariness, her green-gold eyes sparkle with affectionate concern.

"We're doing well." *But we're full of questions about this new illness. Can you tell us about that first? What symptoms are you seeing?*

Of course you'd want to know that. You're a healer like me. She shows us the symptoms as she explains in words. "The first indication seems to be a mildly itchy rash." It comes as ashen gray patches on Mundani, more reddish on Melfar. Then, as these swell up and begin to raise into blisters, the fever comes. *The most recent case is my sister's partner.*

Orban? Oh, how is he doing?

"I'm treating his rash." *No blisters yet. No fever.* She's hoping the rash won't develop into the luminous oozing sores of nacreous fever.

"Zara told us that the first outbreak of nacreous fever began in Woodclasp, around 608 or 609."

Of course you knew that's what I fear about this illness. "That's right. I was born soon after it had burned itself out there." *After the fires. Mundani think their fires are what stopped the fever, but that isn't true. My mother and her brother derived a medicine from some plants found deep in the forest and it was the medicine that was curing people.* Bekanz is hoping to find some of those plants in the patch of forest that still stands in the mountains north of New Beniford. She wants to go search for them. *But I can't leave my patients. Well, I guess I'm not even certain yet that this is nacreous fever. We should be prepared.*

It seems likely. What is the plant that was used? We know a few plants for curing fevers and some for soothing rashes.

She shows me a plant that looks a little like mistdrop. "Mother called it furtivine." *It's hard to locate because it grows from underneath the roots of large trees. The shoots it sends up are as fine as a cat's whisker.*

We're sure we've never seen such a plant. *What can we do to help?*

You can stay well, Meridia. The community needs you to stay healthy.

That prickles. It sounds too passive. We don't mention the healing song. It suddenly seems feeble in the face of something as potentially calamitous as nacreous fever. We desperately want to do more.

Bekanz pertanges our displeasure. *If we can find the plants, I'm sure you could help process the medicine. I can show you how it's done, and you can work here in your house. Although, if you know any healing songs, I'm certain that—coming from you—those would be a help, too.*

Is she trying to placate us? *How will you find the plants? Maybe we could go up into the forest to search. We'd be well away from town.* We know her answer to that before she says it.

No. We need you here. "Now, let's take a look at you and the nens. How are you feeling?"

We're feeling frustrated. "Fine," we say. "A little dizzy sometimes and out of breath, but all-in-all we're doing fine." Just when we'd begun to feel that our role as healer might ease us more confidently toward becoming the Calumet people desire, we find that we're prevented from hands-on action as a healer. It is frustrating.

Bekanz palpates our torso, tracing the outlines of our nens. She listens to all our heartbeats with her conical device. *Your feet look a little swollen,* she says, as she begins to massage them. "Are you eating well? Drinking enough water?" She reminds us of the special tea she wants us to drink every morning and evening.

We report on what we've consumed today and Bekanz seems satisfied. *Will Damon be allowed to be with us here?* We'd been afraid to ask; he's usually home by this time of day.

Yes, but I've instructed him that he must wash his whole body and put on clean clothes before coming inside. And I've told him to keep on the lookout for signs of the rash. On both of you. "We still don't know how this disease is being passed on." *We never figured out the mechanism of infection of nacreous fever. So we have to be careful about everything.*

She doesn't have to say it, but we know that if either Damon or we develop a rash we'll be isolated separately. We desperately hope that doesn't happen.

We stand in the doorway and bid farewell to Bekanz. There's splashing coming from the little shed in the back of the cabin. Damon is home. Has he had supper yet? What can we give him for his supper? He'll want tea first. We prepare that.

Damon comes in looking as scrubbed and tired as Bekanz did. We send rosy waves of welcome and approach tentatively, not knowing whether embraces are permissible.

They are. We rest for a moment in the reassuring strength of Damon's arms, our ear against his heart. We offer tea.

"I ate some supper at the workshop, but tea would be nice," he says.

We pour two glasses of tea and he sits while we get the comb and untangle his wet hair, restoring the plait before we join him at the table. What was it we intended to talk with Damon about? So much has happened. Gerd. We have to tell him about Gerd.

Damon listens attentively as we describe what we pertanged of Gerd's bungled attempt to rescue Elvrid Conif from the grasp of the Palinjians at Blanton, how Jalu was able to get him into their care.

"Were any of the injuries serious?" Damon asks.

"Fergus was the worst. His left hand had a number of broken bones and severed tendons." We massage our own left hand as we speak. "We doubt he'll ever be able to use it again."

"That sounds awful. Are they safe now?"

"We think so. They've reached Fayredell." Elvrid is grateful for the rescue.

We're still thinking about Gerd and Elvrid as we prepare for bed.

They're resting now. Gerd will know what to do next. We hope Gerd will know. Elvrid seems to be a good man. We're glad that he's out of the clutches of the Palinjians. But he's also a liability. The Palinjians will stop at nothing to get him back.

Bring them here. The thought comes to us in Avienne's voice, wafting like a breeze through tall grass.

Elvrid? Elvrid and...?

Elvrid and the boy Saami.

40.

Do you think that would be wise, Father? We think about the safety afforded by New Beniford's protection canopies, but also about the uncertainty posed by the fever outbreak for anyone brought in from outside.

Abél was aware of Gerd's futile assault and Jalu's subsequent extraction of Elvrid. He's come here to our cabin to discuss what should happen next, to talk about Avienne's advice regarding Elvrid and Saami. It's early morning and it's clear that Father has been as restless as we were. His eyelids droop. We step outdoors, offering tea, hoping not to awaken Damon.

Father readily agrees that it would be unwise to continue keeping Elvrid and Saami in Fayredell. *The Palinjians are consumed with rage, still ravenous for revenge. Even Maddie's death was not enough to satisfy them. And the Binder begins in less than a six. Who knows what they might do to get their prisoner back? And while the Palinjians have shown no indication of being concerned about the fate of poor Saami Pherson, if they can't have a Palinj, they might decide to settle for a Pherson, albeit an underage and blind Pherson. Even a dead one, as long as they can keep him from being used against them.*

We shudder, thinking of the dangers that may lie ahead. Still we hesitate. *What if we bring Elvrid and Saami here and they get sick? There's so much we don't know yet about this disease.* "Bekanz says she knows a medicine for nacreous fever, if she can find the plant the medicine comes from."

Father says nothing. He looks older these days, his golden cheeks wilting gray above his silvered beard. He's still mourning the loss of his mother, our precious eldmother Avienne, and the burdens that passed to him with her death.

Burdens that passed also to us.

Father's grief intensified with Maddie's death. Although they'd lived apart for many returns, Mother was the only partner he ever had. And now he's left without his brother twin as well. Abél has always relied on Brân as his confidant. Brân isn't dead, of course, only lost somewhere, traveling with the Migrant. We're all the family Father has left.

Maybe we can find somewhere else to keep Elvrid and Saami safe until we know more, we say. At least until we find the medicine.

Abél's sigh is a dull gray, tinged with purple, flecked with shimmers of mirror-like brightness. *Consult with Bekanz, Meridia, and see what more she's learning about this fever. I'll convey a message to Jalu for Gerd. We need to know if they think it's even possible to bring Elvrid and Saami here.*

We sip tea, watching Father walk away. Our stool is hard and unsteady, tipping occasionally to one side or the other. We pick up Abél's cup and go back indoors.

"Your father was here early," Damon says. "Is anything wrong?"

"Avienne seems to think we should bring Elvrid Conif here. Along with the young Pherson boy, Saami."

"Avienne? But she's..." Damon chuckles and shakes his head.

"We saw that you brought a package in with you last night," we say. "What is it?"

"Since Bekanz says you shouldn't go out for a while, I brought some work home with me. Something I thought you might help me with. There are some of Fannan's photographs that Zara finds confusing. She wanted you to have a look at them."

"We could try," we say. "Which ones are they?" We try to remember the pictures we saw when Damon pulled them out of the underground vault where they'd been sequestered at Woodclasp.

Damon takes out the package and lays it on the table. Delicately, he unwraps the pictures for us to examine. They seem brighter than they were when Damon and Orban dug them up. How could that be? Or are we now able to pertange more of what they contain?

The photograph on top is one we remember. A group of men and women, Mundani and Melfar together, holding hands as they dance around a great stone. This was the dedication of the Old Lapis. The Benison is deep blue, and I hear its song resonating clear as a rung bell, a song that contains the memory of servitude as well as the aspiration for freedom. Heaviness and flight.

"That one was over a hundred returns ago," we say. Our Lapis waif taught us its song.

Damon lays the photograph aside, revealing another. "This is the one Zara was having trouble with," he says.

At first we see only a picture of a forest. We know it's Cödweg, the great eastern forest that burned in the Old Jade Meed. A partially underground cabin at one edge of the picture comes into focus. It's Fannan's workshop. And here's Fannan. He's inside the forest. Distress is etched in his face. He crouches beside a pond, where the stones around the pond's edge seem to glow. No, they do glow. The same glow as the rocks Damon brought back from Aldbeck. The rocks are swarming with billbugs. Fannan's arms are bare; there are visible sores. Nacreous blisters. More billbugs are gathered at the edges of the blisters.

All at once, our orb is pierced with icy cold realization and our eyes fly wide, as if they would burst from their sockets. "Damon, that's it! That's what happened! That's *how* it happened." Fannan was sorry; his eyes are crusted with sandy regret.

"What?" Damon says. "You know I see nothing but some shimmers of color and the vague figure of a man near what might be a pond."

"It's the billbugs. The billbugs feed on the residue of the luminous slime and they're infected. When they bite us, they infect us, too. That's where the nacreous fever came from. That's why Fannan stopped his research and buried his snails."

"He buried them? On purpose? Are you sure?" Damon's face goes ashen as he looks with horror toward the glass tank in the corner, at the glowing rocks and snails within it, the glowing rim at the edge of the water. The swarm of billbugs. He rises from the table as if to follow Fannan's example.

"Wait, Damon," we say. "Yes, take them away and try harder to keep the billbugs away from them. But don't destroy them. Not yet. They have their purpose." Is this right? Wouldn't it be better to let Damon do as Fannan did? "We've seen some of your new photographs and they're wonderful. Vidvana and Zara say so. And Father. Amos Quint wants you to continue your work, too. Surely we're not meant to sacrifice all the good that could come from your photographs."

Damon looks doubtful. "As you wish," he says, his voice hard and flat. "Why didn't Fannan tell people about what was causing the fever?"

"He was caught in the fires and killed." Or did he die from the fever? He tried to warn people, but the ones he told died, too.

"Well, we know now," Damon says. "I'm going to get a cart and someone to help me take these evil creatures away from here and isolate them as best I can. And I'll warn Bekanz."

We've already warned her.

After Damon goes, we examine our hands and feet, our arms and legs, for evidence of billbug bites. As soon as we pertanged the truth of the billbugs, we began to itch. We find a couple of suspicious-looking bumps but nothing that looks like a rash.

We light a bundle of beegrass and then go outdoors, away from the offending insects. We try to remember what we saw in the photograph, querying every detail. How did the luminous slime spread from Fannan's workshop to the pond in the woods? Has the slime from Damon's work spread as well? We should clean the tanks. Keep them cleaner.

We need to collect more beegrass. We need to burn it in all the houses of New Beniford to keep billbugs away. And we desperately need to find the plants containing the medicine that Bekanz' mother used in curing the nacreous fever in Woodclasp.

We need to talk to Bekanz.

We have to tell Gerd.

41.

≈

Gerd isn't in her room at the Landry place. She's not in the training hall. We find her walking along the street, lost in thought. Worried.

Gerd knows something is wrong. Something more than her second failure to rescue someone from danger. First she failed Maddie, then Elvrid. She's relieved that Jalu was able to get Elvrid to safety, but his success somehow makes her own failure more humiliating. And now Jalu has told her that we want Elvrid to come to New Beniford. And Saami too, for no good reason that Gerd can think of.

The boy has been getting along well in Fayredell. He's much friendlier now. Happier. Gerd suspects he wasn't treated well in Markham, though the boy still doesn't talk much about his life there. He was clearly surprised that here he's allowed to wander freely in the gardens and around the buildings. Gratified that people aren't always grabbing at him, pushing and pulling as if he needed to be shepherded everywhere. He's appreciative that people take time to answer his questions. The boy has a lot of questions. Why disrupt that?

Those concerns would've been enough to plunge Gerd into the sort of flat, dark mood she's experiencing, but she's sure it also has something to do with the fever Jalu says has cropped up in New Beniford. She'll talk to Jalu when she gets back to the Landry house. Maybe he'll know something more.

We want to tell Gerd about the billbugs, but her mind is too intent on her immediate worries.

Gerd's destination is the old Quint property. She wonders why the burned-out ruins of the old house were left to weather away like this. She suspects they've been thoroughly picked over by people looking for treasures or at least small mementos of old Prophet Amos, even though he'd disposed of most of his personal property before the fire. Before his hastily staged death and subsequent flight to Selbourne. Gerd likes Amos Quint and had hoped that he might decide to stay and lead their movement. But he'd insisted on returning to his secluded island. His son Lambert goes silent whenever anyone suggests that he himself might take on the Quint mantle. At least he's moved back into the old homestead. Isn't that some indication of accepting who he is and the potential that implies?

The door of the stone shed stands open, but Gerd stops anyway. "Lambert?" she calls out. "Lambert Quint!"

"Good day, Gerd."

The voice comes from behind her. She turns. Lambert is seated comfortably at the base of the old peppertree that everyone had thought was dead. After the rains began again, it put out new growth and now it plays a leafy shadow across Lambert's shed in the morning sun.

Gerd walks a few paces toward him, suddenly uncertain why she's come. She felt a need for someone to talk to. "Fine day, Lambert," she says.

Lambert makes no move to rise so Gerd settles onto the ground near him.

"It really is a fine day." Lambert looks up into the branches and smiles.

Gerd hadn't noticed, but she has to agree that it is indeed a fine day. The sky is a soft turquoise blue and there's a light breeze, fragrant with the promise of fruit.

Lambert narrows his eyes and looks directly at Gerd. "I expect you're wondering what to do with that Elvrid fellow now that you've got him."

"How did you know about that?"

"My granddaughter comes here frequently. Ann seems to think I need looking after. She's always full of news about what's going on. She says Fergus was hurt in your latest mission. Is he okay?"

"There were quite a few injuries, though Fergus' was the worst. The injury to his left hand is healing, but I doubt the hand will ever be of much use again. It was Jalu who got Elvrid out, you know. My own attempt was ill-conceived and hasty."

"You're concerned about yourself then. Everything turned out alright, didn't it?"

"No thanks to my planning. Or lack of it. Why do I keep doing these things, Lambert? Why can't I learn to be patient? Why can't I learn to take time and plan things out better?"

"It's a fine line, Gerd. If one dithers and worries too much, the opportunity to act can slip away. But, as you say, acting without sufficient forethought can also lead to problems."

"I definitely need to employ a little more forethought. Before I get someone killed. Someone else."

"And I'm the opposite. I sit here day after day, thinking and thinking and doing absolutely nothing."

Why don't you work together? You'd make a good team.

Gerd and Lambert sit looking at one another, unsure where that idea came from, unsure what the other would think of it if it were voiced.

"Abél and Meridia want us to send Elvrid to New Beniford for safekeeping," Gerd says.

The Pherson boy, too, Gerd.

She doesn't quite believe that. She wants to know what Lambert thinks about Elvrid.

Lambert sits up straighter and gives his back a scratch against the rough bark of the peppertree. "I'm not sure that would be a good idea," he says. "Aren't they having an outbreak of some kind of fever in New Beniford right now?"

"That's what we've heard. Although they aren't sure yet what it is or how serious it might be. But it would be a shame if we sent Elvrid there and he got sick."

"On the other hand," Lambert says, "sending him away would relieve your people from having to guard him. I'm sure you're aware that the Binder begins in a few days. Besides, not having him here would leave you freer to carry on with your own operations."

"That's true. Although we don't have any other specific operations planned at the moment. The last two didn't work out the way we'd hoped, you know."

"Your foray to Markham worked out well. What's become of the hostages you took from there?"

"Nix isn't exactly a hostage. Not any longer, anyway. It looks like he's come around to our way of thinking."

"And the young Pherson boy?"

"He seems to like it here. He's too young to think much about politics. He's making friends."

"That's progress, Gerd. You could try something like that again, couldn't you?"

"It's high risk. So many things can go wrong. And the Palinjians are getting wise to our tricks and tactics. We'd have to come up with a whole new kind of plan."

"Ann tells me that the word among the weftreds is strongly supportive of the work you did getting Elvrid out of the clutches of the Palinjians. And yes, they credit you with that even if it was Jalu who actually rescued him. Of course, not everyone believes Elvrid really is Zibal Palinj's son."

"Maybe he isn't. But if they'd been able to convince people that he was, it could've been the impetus they've been looking for to revitalize the Palinjians."

Lambert thinks that Elvrid really is who they say he is, though he can't logically justify that conviction.

Gerd's preoccupation with her own work is making her mind impervious to our efforts to convey to her what we've learned about the illness. But Jalu knows now what it is and what causes it. We'll have to trust that Jalu will warn her.

42.

Damon has taken the tank with its offending luminous slime away and is attempting to secure his snails out of the reach of billbugs. New Beniford is blanketed with the scent of burning beegrass as we do what we can to protect ourselves.

"Would you recognize the plant if you saw it?" we ask.

Bekanz has told us that the medicine her mother formulated to cure nacreous fever came from a plant called furtivine. *I'm sure I would,* she says, *though I've not seen the plant since I was a young girl helping Mother search for it in the interior of Cödweg. I don't even know if it ever grew in Serani.*

All the forests were connected once, we say. "How many are infected now?"

"Three new cases this morning, making twelve all together. One of the new cases is Vidvana."

Our hearts wrench painfully at that news. We love Vidvana like a sister. We try to tell ourselves that every case must be of equal concern to a healer. "Is the ointment we made having any effect?" *Are there any differences in the way the illness is affecting Melfar and Mundani?*

Mundani seem to go down more quickly. Higher fevers. Angrier sores. The ointment allays the itching, but it doesn't prevent the blisters from coming.

Now that we know what causes the sickness, there's no reason why we can't join you in tending to the sick. No, no. We'll deal with Damon. He won't object. Well, he will but then he'll understand. Maybe we could go look for the plant in the forest, too. Furtivine, you say? Teach it to us.

Bekanz shows us the plant: The tendrils of the vine are mere threads, its leaves round and delicate and no bigger than a nen's fingernail. It grows from the underside of tree roots.

Any particular kind of tree?

That part Bekanz doesn't recall clearly. Big trees. Rough bark. Gnarled roots.

Maybe some type of acorn tree?

That could be. She tells me that it's the root of the furtivine that contains the medicine. The root is thick, bulbous. A connected sequence of woody globules growing deep underground. *The deeper they grow, the stronger the medicine.*

And then we hear it. A simple tune. Not melodic, but distinctive, like plucking untuned strings held taught across a bowl. *Is that it?*

Bekanz is smiling. "That's it," she says. *How odd. I hadn't thought about that sound in meeds, but that is definitely the sound of the furtivine.* She shares the sound with us again and I sing it back to her.

"What tune is that?" Damon stands in the doorway, removing his shoes before coming in. "It sounds odd."

"We were talking about the plant that has the medicine for nacreous fever," we say. "We need to go up into the forest and search for it."

Damon isn't sure how this information answers his question. We'll explain it later. He stands behind us and places his hands on our shoulders. We feel the weight of his concern. "I understand the need to search. But not you, Meri. Surely someone else can do this."

We bristle red. We're tired of being protected. We need work. Purpose.

"I wasn't thinking of sending Meridia," Bekanz says. She's pertanged our frustration. "Because we need her help here. Now that we know this illness is only spread by the billbugs, there's no reason why she can't come and help me care for the sick." *Hush, Meridia. Let him consider this.*

Damon's grip on our shoulders loosens. "I'm not sure that's a good idea," he says. But he already knows he'll agree.

43.

~

It feels right to be taking care of the sick again, even though all we can do is give medicine for fevers and treat the rashes and blisters with tinctures and ointments. Bekanz has sent her young apprentice Yuli and two others up into the forest to search for furtivine. They've been gone nearly three days now.

In Fayredell, Jalu has warned Gerd to beware of billbugs, told her that they are the source of the illness in New Beniford. He knows we're doing our best to contain the sickness here, and that they need to burn beegrass in Fayredell. Ever since the rains started up again there seem to be swarms of billbugs everywhere.

We worry about the welfare of our other friends in Fayredell.

Ann slaps at her arms as she makes her way from her home at the old Landry pickle factory to the site of the destroyed Quint House. She's bringing her grandfather a gift. He'd shown her how he was transforming the interior of the old stone shed.

"Why, Grandfather?" Ann had thought the mirrors lining the walls of the shed were quite lovely, but she wasn't sure why he'd gone to the trouble of collecting and hanging them. There were all kinds of mirrors, some large and ornately framed, others simple rectangles or squares or discs. One was a woman's hand mirror, cracked and tarnished. That one had belonged to his own mother, Ann's great-grandmother, Nahla.

"The mirrors make me feel closer to the Creator." That's what Lambert had said to Ann. "Or the Migrant." He didn't think it mattered much what name was used. "My father found them helpful on Selbourne and I found my mother's mirror a comfort during my retreat in the Northern Lowlands. I haven't grown as close to the Migrant as Father has. I'm no prophet. But there are moments when I almost understand what might be possible."

Would the fragment of mirror we hold for him be of any help with that? The shard still rests in the little basket where Damon put it. Amos Quint wants us to deliver it to Lambert, but with the fever outbreak, the possibility of carrying out his wish seems more remote than ever. We recall how this small piece of glass affected us when we tried to take it from Damon's hand—the fibrous pain, the high-pitched squeal that was also a deep growl. It's no ordinary bit of mirror.

Ann lifts the latch on the sagging gate in the fence that still surrounds the ruins of the Quint house. She stands for a moment, thinking about her great-grandfather Amos and what he told her about his solitary sojourn on the island of Selbourne. He's back there now. Amos says we're all connected. All of us are part of the Migrant. Expressions of the Migrant? Ann isn't sure she remembers that correctly. She's not at all clear what it might mean.

Lambert is not under the peppertree where Ann often finds him. Nor is he in the kitchen shed. And then she hears his voice. He's chanting inside his chamber of mirrors. Ann ducks her head to enter the little building and stops inside the door, waiting. She listens to Lambert's words: "We are the myriad expressions of the singularity of existence. We are one." He repeats the words over and over in a resonant singsong as he walks slowly, gazing into his mirrors. Reaching the far end of the room, he turns and, seeing Ann, nods once. He continues chanting and walking until he reaches the little hand mirror. He stops there and, in silence, reaches out to touch the mirror gently, lovingly, as if he's touching his own mother's face. He inhales deeply and turns toward Ann. "I'm happy you've come," he says.

"I like the words, Grandfather," Ann says, "even though I don't understand what they mean."

"They mean precisely what they say, Ann. It's pointless to use more words to explain it. I try to let the words—each one, and then all of them together—open themselves up and show me their meaning. Would you join me for a glass of tea?"

As they sit drinking tea, Ann feels uncertain about the gift she's brought for Lambert. She's afraid he might think it's foolish.

It's a thoughtful gift, Ann. Not foolish at all.

As if she's heard us, Ann reaches inside her bag and draws out a package, something wrapped in a clean blue kerchief and tied with a yellow string. She places it on the table in front of Lambert. She says nothing.

Lambert looks at the package, then up at Ann, a question in his eyes. Of course it's for him. He unfastens the string and lays open the kerchief, revealing a hand mirror, very like the one that already hangs on his wall. But this one is undamaged. The metal handle is polished bright and the image it reflects is clear. It's been well cared for.

"Is this yours?" he says, his eyes brimming with gratitude.

"It was Mother's," Ann says. "I think she'd want you to have it for your wall."

"Oh, my dear Keira," Lambert says, clutching the object in both hands. "She knew, didn't she, Ann? Your mother knew about the power of chanting, but I was too arrogant to listen." He reaches with one hand and grasps Ann's fingers. "Thank you, Ann. Will you come help me find a spot for it?"

We watch a while longer as Lambert Quint and Ann breth Keira walk among the mirrors in Lambert's little sanctuary. They find a spot near the mirror that belonged to Nahla and affix there the mirror that belonged to her granddaughter, Keira Landry of Quint, Lambert's only daughter.

We leave them, our thoughts drifting to our own grandmother Avienne and our great-grandmother Meridia. Our eldmothers.

It's nearly evening and we're expecting Bekanz. She promised to come by. We need to share information with one another about our patients. There are new cases to report.

When we pertange where Bekanz is, we're dismayed. Her apprentice, Yuli, has returned from the forest. She and her companions were unable to locate the medicinal plant we so badly need.

"We found no furtivines," Yuli says, "though we dug around the roots of every acorn tree we could find, and I listened intently for the vine's tune. But what we did find is something terrible." Yuli holds up a rock.

In the dim evening light Bekanz sees what Yuli has discovered and her eyes widen in alarm. The rock is covered in a luminous residue.

The pestilent slime has escaped Damon's snail tanks.

44.

People are falling ill in Fayredell. The knowledge rests like a stone in our hearts. Black despair at having no medicine to send, tinged with crimson fear for the future. We've stopped sending rain, certain that the full ponds and persistent puddles are only breeding more billbugs and more slime.

We've sent people out into the countryside to seek out and destroy the luminous slime wherever they find it. It's spread far more widely than we would have thought possible. Damon is beside himself, caught between guilt and fury.

We try to reassure him. "There's no way you could have known that the snails carried the risk of disease."

"It really doesn't make any sense," he says. "Most things that live in salt water can't survive in fresh water, so how has this slime managed to spread like it has?"

"Have you noticed that it also eats into the glass of your containers?"

"Is that what it's doing? I noticed that the glass still looked dull and a little rough even after I'd cleaned it. How can anything eat glass?"

We have no answer for that, but we can tell that the question itself is eating at Damon. Father says the slime is properly called algae. He says there was a lot of it in Swarthpol.

Father conveys to Gerd what we're learning about the slime. The algae. It's everywhere. We urge Gerd to do as

Avienne requested and send Elvrid Conif and Saami Pherson to New Beniford.

She's considering it. She's had little contact with Elvrid, but she feels the weight of her responsibility to make good decisions. She knows his welfare is important. As she does so often these days, she's consulting Lambert.

"How would you propose to get Elvrid safely to New Beniford?" Lambert asks. "If you should decide to send him." He feels sure she's already acquiesced to this course of action, but she hasn't said, and he doesn't want to presume.

"Jalu has volunteered to escort him. He can provide a canopy of protection as they travel. We have a few other Melfar with us here in Fayredell so Jalu's absence wouldn't leave us without Melfar support."

"I'd like to go, too." Gerd and Lambert hadn't noticed Ann where she sat almost out of sight, in the shadows next to the kitchen shed. She comes closer now and sits down across from Gerd and her grandfather.

"You?" Gerd says. "Why, Ann?"

"I've been wanting to go up into the forests above New Beniford. To learn more about the trees," she says. "To collect seeds and seedlings to plant. Jalu says there's still quite a healthy forest there. It's the last surviving remnant of Serani, the last of the Melfar forests." Ann's face glows with mounting excitement as she speaks. "We really are going to plant new forests, Gerd. New forests for the new songs."

Lambert reaches out and places a hand on Ann's shoulder. "She's found her own work, Gerd. And I think it sounds like excellent work."

Gerd isn't sure she understands, but she sees how enthusiastic Ann is. "If you truly want to, I see no reason why you shouldn't go with Jalu and Elvrid. Abél and Meridia want us to send Saami, too." She shoots a questioning glance toward Lambert. "I was thinking of sending Shifra to help guard Saami on the journey. Would you be willing to take on that responsibility instead, Ann?" Gerd knows she'll need to send another of the Mundani Chanters on the mission, too. Someone to keep tabs on Elvrid. She's not sure she trusts Elvrid. Not completely. Not yet.

"Yes, of course," Ann says. "Saami and I are good friends now. He's interested in trees, too."

We're relieved that Gerd seems to understand what needs to happen. We're happy about Ann's intent to plant new forests, even though that happiness is tainted by a nagging sense of our own lack of purpose. Being called to be Calumet is one thing; knowing how to respond is something else altogether. We recall watching ourselves dance with the eldmothers and tears form as we gaze down at our bulging heaviness.

Our awareness wanders away from Lambert and Gerd and Ann. We look for sick people in Fayredell. There are a lot of sick people. We send our healing song in great blue spirals. Near the center of town, there's a fountain with luminous slime all around its margins.

"Burning these little bundles of grass is not enough!" Halvor is walking past the fountain with two companions who defer to him.

"But Chanters say the beegrass is protection from billbugs. And if billbugs are the source of the illness..."

Halvor stops in the middle of the street and turns to face the other men. "Chanters! What do we care what those sully Shoon-whores say? It's a lot of superstitious poltroonery. We need to recall how this fever was beat back the first time. It wasn't done by lighting little bundles of grass." He spits on the ground. "We need a real fire! The kind of ashing great fire that honors the power of the Creator, our Restorer. It's time to bring back the holy fire of Sidayens to our world! This Binder will once again witness the greater fire of Palinjians!"

Oh, Father! What are these people contemplating?

45.

≈

The first day of the Binder finds Ann and Jalu and their Mundani companion Umbrin well on their way, bringing Elvrid Conif and Saami Pherson to New Beniford. They're protected by the canopies Jalu knows how to use. He tries not to be distracted by Ann's presence, by the way her dark hair brushes the back of her neck or the feminine strength of her tall figure. He tries to remind himself that she could never be interested in a Melfar such as himself when it's clear that Fergus finds her attractive. Jalu sighs through the notes of the canopy and attends to the spots where it had begun to thin from his inattentiveness. Once it's repaired, he scans the countryside around them for signs of danger.

He's aware of our presence. We keep watch, too.

We've seen something, Jalu. Two men nearby.

I pertange them, Meridia.

The two men hurry toward Fayredell. They look back over their shoulders at the cloud of smoke rising from the fire crackling fiercely through the drying brush. So much brush after several tides of healing rains. Drying out now that the rains have stopped. These men know little of the ways of brushfires.

"Ash it, Teff, it's going all wrong!" Naviq is prepared to blame his younger companion. We recognize Naviq as one of Halvor's Palinjian followers.

"I thought it would spread the other way," Teff says. "It's almost like it's following us back to Fayredell." Teff is taller than Naviq, though clearly younger. He's gangly and slightly stooped, as if still unaccustomed to his height. "The wind changed from what it was on our way out here. Maybe it'll change again. Wind is so unpredictable."

Naviq is worried about what Halvor will say if this fire goes wrong, fearful that its main effect may be to consume the crops that stood almost ready for harvest in the fields around Fayredell.

The men change their own course, heading now directly toward Jalu and his little company.

"I smell smoke," Umbrin says.

Jalu smells it, too.

Can you find shelter, Jalu? Father is sending rain to quench the fire.

Jalu is certain the shed he'd already sought out for a brief rest can provide shelter from the rain. He can't tell if the shed is abandoned or not. So many things that were once abandoned have been reoccupied. They'll go there anyway.

"It hasn't rained in sixes," Naviq says. "Ash it all! Why does it have to rain now?" But he and Teff can see the clouds rolling in rapidly from the west and they break into a run toward a shed as the first drops begin to fall.

It's the same shed Jalu is aiming for.

"I know those two." Elvrid speaks in a terse whisper. "They're Halvor's men. They're up to no good."

"They're the ones who set that fire," Jalu says, suddenly certain that this is true.

"What's going on?" Saami shifts nervously from one foot to the other. He senses the presence of the other men, shimmers of something when their anger speaks.

He grips Ann's arm tightly as she moves a step closer to him.

"Is there any other shelter nearby where we could go?" Umbrin rests his hand on the longblade at his side. He's glad he honed its edge last night.

"Nothing I can see," Jalu says. The rain comes down harder. Jalu knows that if the intent is to quench the fire, it won't stop raining for quite a while yet. A plan takes form in his mind and as he explains it to his companions, he hums it into existence. The canopy he crafts doesn't hide them, but it does produce a pale aura of orangey innocence around the group. It also obscures Jalu's appearance, making him look less Melfar, though it can't do anything about his short stature. Umbrin presents the group at the entrance to the shed as hapless, harmless travelers begging for refuge.

"There's room for all of us, I guess," Naviq says. He and Teff move farther back into the shed to make way for the new arrivals.

Jalu has cautioned his companions to keep silent. He's not sure his deception can sustain much direct interaction with the two Palinjians. But as Elvrid watches Naviq and Teff, his anger simmers and he emits occasional snorts of displeasure as he recalls his treatment at their hands in Blanton. When he notices Teff beginning to shiver in the cold dampness of the shed, he can keep silent no longer.

"It's chilly in here," he says. "If only someone had brought materials for starting a fire." His brows converge, almost hiding his narrowed eyes as he stares directly at Naviq.

Jalu tries to signal Elvrid back into silence, but it's too late. Naviq is staring back.

"Elvrid!" Naviq spits out the name like bitter jimweed, and an instant later he's on his feet with his knife drawn as he lunges toward this son of Zibal Palinj.

Umbrin rises and steps in front of Elvrid, reaching for his longblade.

"Wait!" Teff cries. "We want him alive!" Too late. Naviq has already attacked, but it's Umbrin who lies bleeding at his feet.

Elvrid seizes the weapon Umbrin had intended to draw and slashes upward with it, deflecting Naviq's first thrust. Before the man can regain his balance, Elvrid has plunged his weapon into the man's heart.

This is not the first time Ann has seen a man killed. The horror of it is undiminished. She turns to see Teff pinned to the ground with Jalu's short, sturdy arms around his neck. Teff falls slack and silent.

"Is he...?" Ann barely whispers the words.

"No, but he'll be out for a while." Jalu had perceived the man's youth and couldn't bring himself to kill him. Knowing that he could have was frightening enough.

"Ann?" Saami reaches a trembling hand toward Umbrin's lifeless body, trying to touch the foggy cloud streaming up and out of the room. "This one is dead, isn't he?"

Ann puts her arm around Saami's shoulders and draws him closer as she explains as clearly as possible what she witnessed.

"Why do we keep killing one another?" Saami says. He doesn't expect an answer.

At least we now know for sure that Elvrid is on our side.
Jalu verberates this and Ann nods sadly in seeming
acknowledgement.

"Why do we have sides?" Saami says.

46

It's the second day of the Binder. Three more days remain until Full Sun and the beginning of a new Mundani passage. Father reminds us of the danger: *A time out of time when anything can happen.*

There's unrest in Fayredell and Blanton, intensifying as more and more people fall ill from the nacreous fever. People are dying. The Chanters' weftreds try to spread the use of beegrass smoke to dispel billbugs, but the Palinjians push back with their insistence that bigger fires than that are the only thing powerful enough to stop the fever.

Halvor is infuriated by the failure of the brushfire set by Naviq and Teff. He wonders why the two men haven't returned to Fayredell. He tries to accommodate to the idea that they might never return. Are they dead or did they abscond? Halvor is tortured by the uncertainty. His need to burn something smolders.

Jalu and Ann arrive in New Beniford just before sundown, delivering Elvrid and Saami into comparative safety. Ann tells us what happened on the way. We already knew, but we also knew she needed to speak about it, so we listen as she describes how Umbrin was killed trying to protect Elvrid. How Elvrid killed one of the Palinjians while Jalu dealt with the other.

The dead man was Naviq. Teff has gone back to his farm west of Temur.

We hold Ann close and let her cry until her tears are finished.

"Oh, Meridia," she says at last, "we were all so happy when the New Marble Benison was dedicated. I was so hopeful. Now I don't know what's going to happen." She wipes her eyes with the sleeve of her shirt. The muscles in her jaw pulse and her eyes harden. "What I do know is that we'll never solve anything with more killing."

Ann knows a lot for one so young. She reminds us that she's a woman now, with the regular flow of moonblood to prove it. But becoming a woman among Mundani is not much of an achievement. Mundani childhood is a relatively privileged status; Mundani womanhood is not. At least it never has been.

Ann is concerned about Vidvana's health and leaves us to go visit her.

Bekanz arrives and we compare notes on the patients each of us treated during the morning. We share our worries over Orban and Vidvana and a few others whose illness grows worse. We treat the fevers and keep the oozing nacreous blisters cleansed and bandaged. We try to soothe them with unguents. Even with our best care, two people have died here in New Beniford. We fear there will be many more deaths elsewhere.

Are there other medicines we could try? We've tried several and none of them seems to help.

I'm sending Yuli back into the forest one more time to look for furtivine, Bekanz says. She tries to show us something else, but she sees how our present state draws us in many directions at once. She resorts to words. "This time I'm advising her to bring back anything that looks even similar. A related plant might also contain a useful medicine." She sighs and leans back in her chair.

"Would you let Ann go with her?" we say.

"Ann? Won't she be wanting to get back to Fayredell? I'm told she's been tending to her grandfather Lambert and assisting him with his new hall of mirrors."

Ann has her own work as well. We show Bekanz the forests that Ann wants to plant. The seeds and seedlings she intends to collect in the remnants of Serani and distribute all across the regions once occupied by all three great Melfar forests.

Of course she should go with Yuli. Can she be ready to leave tomorrow morning?

47.

≥≤

Today is the final day of the Mundani Binder. We're exhausted from tending patients. Did Damon tell us he'd be home late? Probably. We pour a glass of tea and sit at the table to drink it. We'll find something to eat after we've rested. We don't even have energy enough to scratch the itchy place on our ankle. We sip the refreshing tea and let our minds wander. Our dark mood slips our awareness into the dark caverns where we knew Amergin and Naomi. We almost want to go there.

We think of Ann.

Ann is in the forest with Yuli, but they haven't found any sign of furtivine yet. She's collecting seeds and has stashed tens of seedlings in her pack, carefully wrapped in moist cloths.

"What seeds are you collecting?" Yuli asks.

"Mostly acorn trees. A few arrowpine. Weren't the Melfar forests primarily acorn trees and arrowpine?"

"The acorn trees were some of the biggest trees and arrowpine were tallest, but there were many other kinds of trees. Bekanz says all the trees worked together to carry the songs of the Melfar. All of them are linked under the ground, you know."

Ann hadn't known that. We recall how we'd felt the verberations of songs rising from the ground, from the roots of trees long since destroyed by the Great Fires. Now Ann notices the other trees, smaller trees of many different kinds. She searches and finds some of their seeds and offspring.

A woman we don't know is there with Ann and Yuli. They call her Salma. She's one of the Mundani women who has trained with Gerd in Fayredell.

Gerd.

Gerd is worried that so many people are falling ill. At first she thought it might be an opportunity for the Chanters' weftreds to finally overwhelm the weakened Palinjians. But then she found her own ranks being decimated by illness. She herself has not succumbed to the disease yet, though she's developed an annoying cough and itchy eyes from the constant beegrass smoke.

Smoke.

There's a great deal of smoke in Fayredell today. Not only beegrass smoke. At the center of town Halvor has led the Palinjian faithful in building a great bonfire in celebration of the culmination of the Binder. "Today we burn all our doubts, all our fears," he shouts. "That's it, my friends. More books! More furniture and clothing, anything that ties us to remnants of a groveling past. If your past was mired in puerile hopes for peace, be heartened! Our days are coming! The future belongs to the true followers of the Sidaya, to those faithful to the memory of Zibal Palinj! We've taken our revenge on the Assassin of Blanton and now we celebrate that victory with holy fire!"

Our heart shrinks. They're talking about Mother. We think their cheering sounds half-hearted. Some of the men in attendance don't feel right about celebrating the murder of an old woman.

Halvor had intended to throw in promises about Zibal Palinj's son at this point, but that's no longer possible. The fire grows as more people toss items onto it. Fireblocks are added to ensure that the flames are not snuffed out by the musty books and threadbare cloaks and half-rotted chairs. Halvor continues his exhortation: "This is not the only fire cleansing our path toward the new passage. Even as this fire burns, our faithful are also setting fire to the last of the Shoon forests, those detestable places harboring disease and danger of all kinds. No longer will their sully sickness be unleashed upon us!" Halvor screams more loudly and his eyes bulge. "We will burn them all! At last the forest of Serani will burn!"

Serani!

That's where Ann and Yuli are now, searching for the furtivine. We have to warn them. But they're so far away, so intent on their own activity.

Ann pokes delicately around the root of an acorn tree. It's an enormous root that stretches far across the ground.

"I know I heard something," Yuli says. She isn't certain her two Mundani companions believe her about the sound of the furtivine. She's sure they didn't hear it. But Ann is down on her hands and knees, searching along the length of the root for the wispy vine with its diminutive round leaves that Bekanz described to her before they left New Beniford.

"Could this be it?" Ann says. The plant is barely discernible except for two tiny leaves. The stems are as fine as a cat's whisker.

"Hailjoy!" Yuli's eyes go wide. "I believe you've found it!" She pulls two trowels from her pack and they begin digging as Salma stands watch. Before long Yuli cries out again. "I've found a root bulb!" Soon she and Ann have collected three small sacks full of the root bulbs that promise to be the source of a medicine that will cure the dreaded nacreous fever. They laugh with the sheer joy of their success.

"Are you almost done there?" Salma asks.

There's a tenseness in her tone that pulls Ann away from their celebration. "What's the matter?" Ann says.

"Can't you smell it? Smoke. Hard to know where it's coming from." In this ancient remnant of Serani, the trees still form a dense canopy, making it impossible to see any distance in any direction, even up.

Yuli stands still for a moment, breathing. Then she points. "It's over there," she says. "That's where the fire is. And it's a big one. Yes, we should go." She casts an eye toward another acorn tree with equally extensive roots. Could there be more furtivine there?

Another time. Leave it to grow.

"If the fire is where you say, Yuli, we can't return to New Beniford by the path that got us here. Can you help us find another way back?" Salma holds out her hand to Yuli, inviting her to take the lead.

Yuli looks frightened. Uncertain. "I'll try," she says.

Our minds reel, trying to think what help we might send to help get them safely home. It's so important to get them back soon with their precious cargo of furtivine root bulbs and the medicine they contain. We called up rains for the brushfire. Could that work again? Will it be enough for this fire that seems to be flaring up all over what's left of Serani?

Father, what should we do?

Do you remember the first time you encountered the Old Mica?

We remember. We recall how frightened we were. How the song within the lost Benison felt so fierce, so threatening. Now Father wants us to sing that song. Not the new song of the rededicated Mica Benison. Not the song that waters the land with gentle rains. No, he's asking for the old song. The original song. The one that stormed and flooded and washed away homes and people without mercy.

But what about Ann and Yuli and Salma?

Father is already swept up in the song. We join in.

The sky darkens with thick clouds.

Soon winds howl and shriek, punctuated by explosions of thunder. Fireseed flashes and flashes again, but we discern little through the dense curtains of rain. Cold, harsh rain. Percussive against the forest canopy. Leaves are ripped from branches and branches wrenched from trees, crashing down, severing other branches as they fall. Already the earth beneath their feet grows soft. So much water with no place to go. We remember the ocean. There is no end to the water that can be drawn into this storm.

Ann. Where is Ann?

We have to keep singing.

The fire is diminished but unquenched. Its immense heat battles to push back the rain.

More steam than smoke now. The smell of wet burnt wood and brush.

Salma huddles at the base of a sturdy tree, sheltering Ann and Yuli as best she can under her dripping shawl. All three are soaked through and shivering.

The song grows quieter. We see that Father had collected several others to sing with him. That's how the storm grew to such intensity so quickly.

The winds calm. Rain becomes a gentler, steady shower.

Where are they, Father?

Where they shouldn't be. We'll get them home, but it may take a while.

48.

Today is Full Sun; the Binder has passed. Serani was badly damaged by the Palinjians' fire, but not destroyed.

One more person died of the fever today here in New Beniford, here where we have good care. We can only imagine how many are dying in Fayredell and other towns.

One of the sick in Fayredell is Halvor.

Ann and Salma and Yuli are on their way back. After crossing through the still smoldering lower reaches of the forest, they were stopped by a raging stream and had to wait almost a half day for it to subside. Father didn't want us to know how close they had been to a Palinjian camp, but we saw. We knew that the men in the camp were some of the ones who had set Serani ablaze. Two of the arsonists never returned. Their charred remains lie beneath a blanket of ash. Two more have fallen ill with the fever.

Ann suffers from countless billbug bites, as do Salma and Yuli. A rash has emerged on the backs of Ann's knees and on Salma's neck and Yuli's wrists.

Tomorrow. Father says they should make it back to New Beniford tomorrow.

Will the medicine really work? Does the furtivine from Serani have the same properties as the one Bekanz worked with from Cödweg?

We want to tell Gerd that the medicine will reach them soon.

Gerd.

Most days Gerd goes to Lambert's sanctuary of mirrors to walk with him. But also to talk about the work. About what needs to be done. She keeps trying to feel the presence of this Migrant that Lambert talks about, but she's never been entirely sure what sort of entity the Migrant is. She tries to imagine what such a presence might feel like. Gerd is beset by a simmering anger fed by deep regret over things in the past for which she can't forgive herself.

Last time Gerd visited Lambert, she'd had good news for him, news of Ann's safe arrival in New Beniford in the company of Elvrid and Saami and Jalu. She'd started with that and followed up with the details of their violent encounter along the way.

"At least," Lambert had said, "now we know for certain that Elvrid is on our side. Although of course I'm sorry there had to be loss of life." On both sides. He thinks it balanced out. Lambert seems to think most things balance out eventually. Gerd finds that naïve.

Today Gerd leads with the good news again. "They've found the plant that contains the cure for the nacreous fever," she says. "I'm told Ann was the one who located it."

Lambert feels a surge of pride for his granddaughter's contribution. "How soon will we have the medicine?"

"They're still waiting for Ann and the others to get back to New Beniford. There was a forest fire."

Lambert knows without Gerd telling him: Such a fire was no accident. "So now the sully Palinjians have burned Serani?" He shakes his head in disgust. "We knew they'd do something reckless." Lambert had watched from a safe distance the bonfire the Palinjians built in the heart of Fayredell, hoping that would be the extent of their burning. He'd been heartened by the small crowd and the tepid enthusiasm, but saddened by the abuse of Maddie's memory.

"Fortunately, Abél and Meridia and others were able to call up a rainstorm and put out the fire. It was apparently one ashing great storm. It quenched the fire, but it's slowed down Ann's return to New Beniford. I'm told that they're safe and should be back soon. And then it won't be long before we'll have the medicine."

Lambert nods, staring at the ground. "That will be good. It's hard to think of anything other than the sickness these days."

We see what he means. Sores are spreading across his shoulders beneath his shirt. He doesn't say anything to Gerd about it, only asks her how she's doing.

"I'm fine. I can't say why, but billbugs don't seem to like me very much. They hardly ever bite me. And you?"

Lambert waves his hand. "Don't concern yourself over me," he says. "I'm too obstinate to die any time soon. Tell me about your people."

"Three more sick today. One died last night."

We can't tell who it was. Theirs wasn't the only death in Fayredell.

Lambert takes a deep breath and lifts his eyes skyward. "I'm guessing the Palinjians aren't faring much better."

"Likely not. They're also undoubtedly displeased at the failure of their fires. Especially the one in Serani."

Serani.

Ann and Yuli and Salma are still in Serani. We feel so helpless. What can we do?

"What are we to do?" Gerd says. She stands facing Lambert, head down, arms crossed like an embrace. "We can't keep dwelling on the illness. Now that we know the medicine is coming, I'm confident that the fever will be dealt with soon. We have to begin asking ourselves about what happens afterward. Before this illness struck, I'd begun thinking about something." She looks up at Lambert and takes a deep breath. "I was wondering if maybe it might be time to step into the light. Our weftreds have operated in secret for so long because we were few and frightened. Intimidated as much by the past, by habit, as anything else. But now... Lambert, you know how our numbers have grown. Even with the losses due to the fever, our numbers are large and the Palinjians—the true, committed Palinjians—are few and weak. Surely the failure of their fires will discourage them further."

"What are you suggesting? A public event of some sort?"

"Maybe. What do you think? Could we do it?"

Lambert chuckles, thinking that their short hair and carnelian beads, now worn visibly, have already dispelled much of whatever secrecy Chanters may once have enjoyed. He says nothing, but there's a light in his eyes that wasn't there before.

We hope Gerd is right about this sickness being dealt with soon. As we go about our rounds, tending the sick, we offer assurance to our patients, telling them that the medicine that can cure their illness will be available any day now. *Please don't die, Orban. Please hold on for a few more days.*

Damon has stopped his photographic work for now and sealed his snails away. We try to tell him that this is not his fault, but he feels deep regret all the same. He works every day with the crew that's searching out pools and ponds and streams where the luminous slime has taken hold. He comes back covered in billbug bites. We've worked with Bekanz to try and create a lotion from beegrass extract that people can spread on their exposed skin. So far it doesn't seem to work very well. We try not to think about the rash emerging on our leg. There are no blisters yet. No fever.

One of the patients we call on is young Saami Pherson. He has a host of billbug bites but no evidence of rash. We know that he survived the nacreous fever as a nen and we hope that will cause him to be spared this time.

"Are you sure I don't have a fever?" he says. "I feel so hot."

"Don't worry about the sickness." We try to reassure him, telling him that his previous illness protects him, hoping that's true. "If you feel hot, I'm sure it's only the weather. First Stint. Suntide. It's always hot." We feel hot, too.

"We did just pass Full Sun, didn't we? I almost felt the sun stand still for a moment around midday. They must have had an ashing great celebration in Benbridge. We always did."

We hope they didn't. But Saami isn't talking about forest fires. He's recalling childhood frolics around blazing bonfires. We can't help but think of Amergin as we watch Saami. We wonder what this boy sees. What he might pertange. "Saami, do you have any vision at all?" we ask.

"I can tell the difference between day and night. Between indoors and outdoors." He pauses and turns and appears to stare directly at us. "And sometimes..."

"Sometimes what, Saami?" *You can pertange us, can't you?*

"Sometimes I imagine that I see colors or movements when certain people are around. People like you."

We move a few silent steps away to the left and Saami's sightless eyes follow us. "We met a blind boy recently who was able to see such things," we say. "His name was Amergin."

"Really? Is he here in New Beniford? I'd like to meet him sometime."

"No, he doesn't live here. But we can tell you more about him sometime if you'd like. The last we knew of him he had led a whole group of people out of a deep underground cavern."

"He led them? I thought you said he was blind."

"We think it was because of his blindness that he'd learned to see things that the others couldn't. So when there was no light, nothing to see with the eyes, they trusted him to lead them through the darkness."

Saami is overwhelmed by this news. We shouldn't call it news; it happened so very long ago. We promise to tell him more of the story soon. As we walk out into the searing sunshine, we wonder if perhaps we've said too much already.

It's so hot today. It's making our vision blur.

We think about Naomi and Amergin.

And Lasaro.

What happened to Lasaro?

Lasaro is sick. His stomach heaves again, even though there's nothing more to expel. He sits with his back against the broken wall of what was once Saint Odilia's Home for Children. It's only a pile of rubble now. His head aches and his thoughts are fuzzy. He'd cry, but he has no more tears. He knows he can't stay here any longer. It's so hot. He needs to find somewhere to shelter. He needs food and water.

He needs to go home.

Without thought or intention, he heads toward the exact place where the second bright wave originated, the wave that swallowed his companions deep into the ground and vomited him back up to the surface. He tells himself that they're all dead, buried under the ruins. There's no reason to remain at Saint Odilia's, guarding their grave.

He drags his body along the road with little awareness of anything. He's sick and exhausted but still he moves ahead, step by painful step. It's so hot. He plunges his hands into his pockets, and his fingers close around an object he finds there.

And then everything stops.

His world becomes a dream.

The dream is vague and tinged with turquoise moments where he laughs and plays with friends. But even those moments are heavy with an overweening darkness as he murmurs "I'm sorry, I'm sorry."

That object in his pocket shouldn't be there. Why did he take it? It's so beautiful—a milky translucent thing that glints gold and blue and green when he holds it up to the sun. He sees the colors now and they guide him onward. Toward home.

"I will always love you, m'ijo," the woman says, and Lasaro knows that his mother means it. Her arms stretch toward him as the vehicle carries him away.

Why can't I stay with you? His mind shouts into the growing distance. He knows it's all his own fault. Because he took this thing that's in his pocket. He's sure that's the reason they're sending him away. If he goes back, if he returns it, would they let him stay with his parents?

Where is he, Brân? We know Brân is here, walking beside Lasaro. Or looking over our shoulder. Maybe both.

Lasaro was found by a farmer's wife and brought to a mountain town where they took care of him. The woman is dead now. Most of those who survived the explosions are dead or dying from the poison it left behind. Or their children are. Even those who haven't been conceived yet are already dying.

And Lasaro? Does he survive? We ask the question, but there's no answer.

"There you are, Meri!" Damon is hurrying along the path to catch up to us.

We hadn't expected to see him until supper back at the cabin. Or were we supposed to meet him for lunch? We look toward the sun and see that it's already dropping low in the sky. We try to remember what we had for lunch. Did we have lunch? Saami is right. It's very hot.

"Are you okay, Meri?"

"Fine, Damon. Tired." We don't mention the headache.

Damon takes our hand in both of his. He places one hand on the back of our neck and then on our forehead. "I think you have a fever, Mer."

"No, I'm sure it's the heat. It's been so hot ever since the storm."

The storm.

Where is Ann now?

Tired legs struggle to navigate the debris of broken limbs and branches. Ann clutches the bag stuffed with furtivine roots as if her life depends on it. Perhaps it does. And many other lives as well.

"If we keep going, do you think we can make it before dark?" Salma says.

"I'm not sure." Yuli is tired, too. Near exhaustion, her breath coming in increasingly painful gasps. "We'll be close." Yuli's shorter legs mean she's taken more steps than either of her Mundani companions. But the roots she carries in her own bag make her determined to carry on.

"Will we be close enough to know where we are and finish the journey in the dark?" Salma tries to remember whether there will be a moon tonight, to calculate when it will rise.

"Yes. Yes, we're almost that close now. I've pertanged some trees ahead where I've gone several times to gather mushrooms."

Nothing more is said. Yuli begins to hum something we recognize. It's the Granite Song of Firm Resolve. We hum along with her.

Bekanz hums a different tune.

Why is Bekanz here?

We open our ordinary eyes.

We're lying on our bed; Damon offers us a cup of something with an unpleasant smell. We know that smell. It's fever medicine. Why is Damon giving us fever medicine?

Our head aches and there's a burning, tingling pain in our legs.

Ann's legs are so tired.

We drink the medicine, trying not to gag.

Ann is tired, but still she keeps going.

Like Naomi when she was trapped inside the caverns.

We feel sleepy. We know it's the medicine, but we recall how Naomi felt after so many days and nights deep underground. So little food. Always thirsty. No medicine at all.

Such a joy to emerge at last into the open air, to walk across the earth's surface with only sky overhead, feeling soft grass beneath our feet.

49.

～📖～

"Meridia! Come now. Come back. You need to rest. Rest and let the medicine do its work. We'll go out together soon. When you're well."

Why do you call me Meridia? My name is Naomi. I was only going for a walk. Only a little walk. Why is everyone so worried? Even Amergin pulls at me and tries to tell me things I don't believe. Tries to tell me his name is... Damon? But I know this is Amergin. I've known Amergin more than a dozen years now.

What is a year?

Es un año...doce meses.

Yes, okay, I will lie down. I will rest.

A babble of voices awakens me. An aroma of meat roasting with fragrant herbs. I try to roll over on my side and find the weight of my bulging belly constrains me. I reach out for Amergin.

He lifts my hand to his lips. "Buenos días, querida," he whispers, wishing me good morning, calling me beloved.

"Fine morning," I say. That sounds odd. Amergin doesn't mind. The rosy cloud that envelopes the two of us pulses, releasing tiny bursts into the air.

I remember being underground. Shrouded in a dark, dank space. Hungry and exhausted. I remember comfort offered by brown-skinned people speaking a strange language. I remember liberation.

Like the great blue stone. Like being released from servitude.

I remember being taken to a mountain village and learning how these people had been spared from the worst effects of a nuclear blast by hiding in caverns deep underground.

What is a nuclear blast?

I remember the bright white light, the wind, the rising cloud. Was that it? And then the earthquake.

I understand the speech of these people now, although they use it very little. Their vocal cords were almost destroyed by poisoned air and water after the explosions. But some of them see and hear the same colors and sounds that Amergin and I do. Amergin and most of the other children who were with us. And Sister Antonia. We communicate like that much of the time.

Amergin and I emerge from our house and walk through the dusty street toward the shared space where we take our meals. Everything is shared here. When there are so few people left, it seems pointless to call anything "mine." It's all ours.

Sister Antonia is here. She sends golden waves of welcome and invites us to sit next to her. Across the table are Alfrin and Alondra, almost grown up. It's clear that they'll soon be a couple, too, as Amergin and I are. Frida has taken a partner from among the local residents. Sancho's partner is also local. She's as pregnant as I am. We've been here so long.

The early days were painful. Some got sick from the radiation, but no one died. At first Sister Berta was concerned that there would be no babies. I thought she might be right, as time and again women became pregnant and then lost their babies long before their time. It happened to me twice. But this time I've come further than before. Berta says this time I'll likely come full term. But even that is no assurance. Some of the babies that are born have terrible afflictions. Sister Maggie Marie helps care for such unfortunates, saying her prayers to Saint Odilia. Oddly, the healthiest ones seem to be the few that are born covered in a pale iridescence that soon fades to a soft yellowish brown. Their hair and eyes go yellow, too, as the months pass. Berta says it's due to a recessive gene. Something that was there in the makeup of the local people that perhaps used to be a disability but that under the new circumstances makes them stronger, more resilient. More fit to survive, she says. To survive and reproduce. I asked her if my baby might have such genes. She said it's possible, since Amergin's father was of indigenous stock.

"What about your parents, Naomi?"

I tell her I don't know. "My mother didn't look indigenous. I don't remember my father." There was a photograph. A sturdy man with thick, dark hair and a round face.

I'm not sure I understand about these genes Berta seems to think are so important. I only hope my baby has the right ones. I hope my baby lives this time.

Berta is probing my belly, talking about the baby's size and position.

"Both nens have their little heads pointed downward now, Meridia. That's good news."

Both?

It's Bekanz. There's Damon. Why do they look so worried if there's good news?

We blink a few times and try to think of some words we could say to bridge this chasm between us, between Meridia and Naomi, between Amergin and Damon. "That's good," we say. Our voice has a metallic taste and we hear it echo off an unseen wall. We say it again. "That's good."

"I think she's back," Damon says. "Meridia? How are you feeling?"

"We're good," we say. We pull the muscles of our face into something we hope will be seen as a smile. "Don't worry."

"I've given you some more medicine that will help you rest." That's Bekanz talking again.

"Okay," we say.

Bekanz and Damon walk outside. They speak in quiet voices, but we hear every word.

"Her fever is down, Damon. I think the medicine from the furtivine is beginning to take effect."

We have the medicine now. Hailjoy! We didn't even have the plants this morning. Was it this morning? How long have I been in bed?

"Are you sure it's the fever that's causing this behavior?" Damon's voice is tense with concern. He's remembering what I've told him about Mother. About how she used to lose herself. *Oh, Damon. It's not that.* Our hearts reach toward him.

"Well, no it's not only the fever. Abél says that due to the fact she's carrying Melfar twins—and due to who she is—she's more open to the Migrant. That's not a bad thing." *As long as she doesn't slip into a coma like she did after her accident.* Bekanz doesn't say this to Damon. She doesn't mention what's happened to Brân.

276

Due to the twins. Due to who we are. Those words settle in unwelcome lumps, grinding their way into our understanding.

"What are we hearing from Gerd?" Damon speaks again.

"Only that the medicine is very welcome in Fayredell. Among all but the staunchest Palinjians, that is. Those still distrust it as some evil Shoon trick."

How can it be evil for Mundani to accept gifts from Melfar and see their worth, to feel gratitude instead of hatred?

We're drifting again.

We're with Gerd in Fayredell. She and Lambert are planning an event. They'll call it a Gathering. It will occur on the full moon of Darkening Symmetide. They're enlarging the chamber of mirrors and cleaning up the grounds of the destroyed Quint place. There's discussion of using the castoff stone from other ruined buildings to construct a tower. Lambert has discovered that the old spring at the center of the property only needed a little cleaning to begin flowing again.

We travel to Ann and her friends. They're on their way to plant trees, moving southward through the old reaches of Serani. Starting there. Later they'll travel down toward Cesta. Her little company, Melfar and Mundani together, sing to the seedlings as they place them in the earth. They sing the sweetest notes of the Song of All Songs like a lullaby to the small trees.

We're drawn toward Jalu where he meets with Chanters to teach the Melfar tunes and to learn Mundani words for the old songs. Their voices blend and shimmer and rise into the evening, reaching toward the stars.

"Tell me more about the stars," Amergin says as he draws me closer.

We're lying in the cool grass on a hillside, listening to the quiet sounds of the evening, the peaceful browsing of a cluster of animals nearby. They look like lamins but bigger and with a lot more hair. They look so soft. The blanket I pull up over our legs is woven from their hair. "There are so many stars," I say. I focus my attention on the bright path shimmering directly above us, passing the image to Amergin without words. The facility we developed with such communication in the dark tunnels of the caverns still serves us well in the brighter world above ground. I show him the patterns within the stars in different directions, the pictures we compose from them. He sees the pictures more clearly than I do. "The moon will rise soon," I say, "and then we'll see fewer stars. They're still up there all day long. It's only the brightness of the sun that blocks them out so we don't see them."

"I know," Amergin says. He places a hand on my belly and asks, "How many more weeks?"

"Two weeks, maybe less." The baby stirs and stretches as if it hears us.

Amergin feels the movement. "What if our baby is blind, Omi? You know I was born this way. I could have passed that on to our child."

"There are far worse things than blindness, mi amor." I'm thinking about some of the children for whom Sister Maggie Marie sends up her prayers to Saint Odilia. Giving birth to a blind child is the least of my worries. "You're a wonderful man just as you are," I say. "I'm sure our child will be fine." Of course I'm not really sure. Amergin knows that.

We sleep. We awaken. We go through our days and nights, the baby growing heavier within me, struggling to stretch its limbs, nestling its solid little head more firmly between my legs. Sometimes I feel the beginnings of contractions. It feels like any other muscle contracting. But each time it's unexpected. Not anything I do. Only something that happens.

It's become more intense. That one was painful.

"Should I go for Mother?" Amergin asks, referring to Sister Berta who is, after all, his mother. "Is this it, Omi?"

"Not yet," I say. "Let's wait a while longer. We'll see if they're coming closer together. You can help me do the breathing Berta taught us."

The next one is even stronger, and I grip Amergin's arm too tightly. He doesn't complain.

Berta appears in the doorway. "Sister Antonia thought you might need me," she says, a huge smile splitting her face like a sunrise. Antonia is right behind her, looking excited, radiating alternating waves of blush pink and purple. Berta tells me I should keep walking around between contractions, so I do, leaning heavily on Amergin or a table or wall whenever the next one comes. I find it altogether strange that my body is doing this all by itself without me willing it to do anything. Actually, I try and will it to slow down or ease off, but that has no effect.

"Lie down and let me check you," Berta says. I've almost gotten used to having her poke around my nether area. She makes approving noises. "It won't be long now," she says.

Suddenly my eyes flood with tears and I begin to sob.

We don't know how to do this. We don't want to. It will tear us apart.

"Don't cry, Meri. I know it's painful, but it will be over soon." Damon's voice. Not Amergin.

There's someone over there by the window, singing quietly. Singing the song of the Old Jade, the Song of the Calumet, the Song that first brought us into the presence of our eldmother Avienne. We see her in the throes of her own birthing, we feel her pains, her struggle. Her immense effort to press this child out of her body into the world. We don't wish to, but we exert that effort, too. One more push and then the sensation of a whole being slithering out of my body. I cry out with release and sorrow. The nen cries out with equal sorrow and surprise, seeing strange lights and movement, feeling new sensations on its skin, hearing sounds slightly familiar but so loud now. Hearing its own voice.

And then the pains come again. Bekanz massages my belly, coaxing the next one into position. Must we do this again? We're coming apart! Can't I keep this one? We need one another.

Meridia, you'll always have one another. But in a different way. Become the separate expressions of the Migrant as you're meant to be. Become three beings, three wills.

I sob into the pain of parting, knowing my eldmother is right. Knowing this is right. No longer one plural being. Becoming three beings, separated at last. I summon the full strength of my will into the final push, surrendering at last, yielding to being Meridia again. Meridia, mother of two nens.

Now there are two voices crying. Separate voices, one tinged with blue, the other an orangey pink. Bekanz and Damon hold them up for me to see. Damon's face glows with golden joy. The damp iridescence of the nens is more beautiful than anything I've ever seen. "Can I hold them?" I say, overwhelmed with a hunger, needing to feel their delicate small bodies in my arms, to inhale their scent, to look into their eyes and know them with all my senses.

Everything becomes a blur. There are careful instructions on how to assist the nens as they begin to suckle from my breasts. Instructions about tending to the cloth coverings that receive the nens' expelled waste. Bekanz has told Damon and me all this before, but it never seemed real then. It barely seems real now, but I try to pay attention. Don't they know that Avienne is here, looking after us? And standing next to her, almost hidden, Maddie is here, too, smiling and clapping her hands in delight.

"Do you have names yet?" Bekanz asks.

"We hadn't really talked about that," Damon says. "Or at least we hadn't settled on anything. We didn't know whether they would be girls or boys."

"It looks like both of them will be girls," Bekanz says, "although that could change in the future."

"The one with the bluer voice is Naomi," I say. "The orangey voice belongs to Odilia."

Damon nods approval, but his eyes skip back and forth between the two nens.

"This one is Naomi," Bekanz says, holding up one of the nens. "Her hair is brownish and looks straighter." *And yes, her voice is bluer.* "And this is Odilia. Her hair is a bit curled and paler." *She's the one with the orangey voice.*

Later Damon will ask me where I found such odd names.

50.

≈

We call them Omi and Odi.

Damon picks up Omi from her basket, hoping to quiet her crying before she awakens Odi. He shouldn't worry. Odilia is a sound sleeper. She doesn't even require suckling as often as Naomi does, but when she sucks, she sucks me dry. Omi needs the comfort of my nipple in her mouth, her body nestled into mine. Or Damon's.

Bekanz says their iridescence won't begin to fade for several tides yet. There will still be traces of it even as they pass from being nens into being young children who can move about at will. With both my mother and my eldmother at such a distance, I rely on Bekanz for guidance. I miss Mother more than I would have thought possible. Avienne feels more present.

I'm surprised at how readily I've come around to being Meridia again. But not the same Meridia. My connection with the two nens is still strong and immediate—I know their needs and moods in an instant—but we're no longer a single plural entity. Or maybe we are, but with a difference. Maybe we all are. All of us are willful entities but linked in a single nexus. Is that it?

During the tides I spent with these nens becoming someone inside my womb, I was also becoming someone. Someone different from what I was before. Someone more eager to find my place in the world. More willing to be the Calumet. I'm still not clear about what that entails, but I'm ready to find out.

For now, my place is with my nens. So many people have offered to help Damon and me look after them. Nens are such a rarity here in New Beniford and having two of them arrive at once has made our cabin a center of attention. Maybe later we'll accept the offers, but for now we want these nens for ourselves. We want ourselves for each other.

Of course Father visits us, and I'm delighted at how he coos over his children. He's as intrigued as I am over how distinct these sister twins are even as newborns. He easily recognizes their respective voices. He shows me how Melfar nens have no need of words to understand things. They're so aware, so complete even at this tender age. He wraps them in gentle colors and sings to them.

"Has the medicine been as effective as we'd hoped? Are all the people getting well?" I'd forgotten to ask Bekanz, so now I ask Father. Caring for the sick had absorbed so much of my time and attention before I fell ill myself. And now that the nens are here, the world beyond my own house has almost ceased to exist for me. I know this will pass, but for now I let it be.

"Yes, it's been a miracle." Father uses words for Damon's benefit. "It took a while for Bekanz to adjust the dosage, but once she got the treatment right, everyone started getting better almost immediately. Some of them wouldn't have lasted much longer without it."

"What about Orban? And Vidvana?" I recall how sick he was, how fearful I'd been for him.

"They're both up and around now, recovering more strength every day."

Father doesn't mention it, but I know they will always have scars from the deep nacreous blisters that covered so much of their bodies. I understand now the scars on Saami's neck and arms, the scars he can't see, though I'm sure that when he touches them, he knows what they are.

"What have you heard from Fayredell?" Damon asks.

"Gerd and Lambert are working on a plan for an event. A public event. A Gathering." *They want us all to come, but it won't happen for a while yet.*

"I'd heard discussion of that," Damon says. "Vidvana says they want us to make a formal presentation of the *Book of All Time*." He glances quickly at me. That's something he hadn't mentioned before.

"That sounds wonderful," I say.

I try to remember the last time I was with Gerd and Lambert. I conjure in my mind the changes I pertanged then within his chamber of mirrors and in the grounds around it. They'd spoken of this Gathering.

The tower is taking shape. It rises from the center of a low, narrow building.

I look toward Damon. "It sounds like a lot of work."

He nods vaguely, not wanting me to know how Vidvana and Zara have been inquiring every day about when he plans to come back and work with them.

"It's important work," Father says.

"Damon, if you're needed to help with whatever it is Zara and Vidvana are preparing for this Gathering, you should go. Father's right. Your work is important."

"I can't go," he says, his heart-verberations soft and rosy as he gazes at Omi, resting in his arms, and at Odi, where she sleeps soundly in one of the baskets crafted by her eldfather Abél. "I can't leave you."

I know he means all of us. "Then Zara and Vidvana should come here. You can do your work at home."

When they arrive, I'm startled at how thin Vidvana is and my heart breaks to see the scars that will forever mark her neck and arms. Her hair looks thinner, straighter. I miss its wildness, but I'm grateful she's alive.

They make little progress during the first few days of work on the *Book of All Time* here. Zara and Vidvana keep wanting to cuddle the nens and are too easily drawn away from the work any time either twin is awake. Zara sings to them and I swear they've already begun to hum along with her as she sings. Especially Odilia. Damon beams with paternal affection at the attention the twins command. But he's begun to wonder if moving his work home was a viable plan.

Today they've invited Elvrid to meet with them. I sit across the room, feeding one nen, patting the other to keep her from waking.

"The *Book of All Time* is still just a stack of notebooks," Vidvana says, "with a collection of photographs to complement it. Now we need to print it. Bind it. Make it into a real book."

"I can do that," Elvrid says. He's thinking about the equipment he'll need for such a project.

Vidvana picks up her notebooks from where they were resting on the floor. As she places them on the table, the stack collapses into a disorderly heap. She adjusts her glasses and begins stacking them again.

"Oh," Elvrid says. "How many pages are you thinking of printing?"

"Well, ideally, we'd like to print all of them."

Elvrid leans away from the table, eyes wide with something resembling horror. "And when is this Gathering you're talking about?"

"In a couple of stints. What do you recommend?"

"Well, most of the books I've printed have been barely more than a hundred pages." Elvrid stares at the pile of notebooks on the table. "We'd need to compile your work into a manageable manuscript. Then there's the typesetting, the printing, the trimming, the binding. The preparation of the binding." Elvrid rubs his forehead, calculating. He thinks it should be done in several volumes and that they'll be lucky to get one volume completed before the Gathering.

"Could we get someone to help you?" Zara asks.

"Yes. I could definitely use some help with a project this big. But mostly I'm going to need my equipment from Temur. If it's still there."

"It's still there," I say. "The Palinjians were only interested in you, not your shop."

Vidvana suggests that one of the Mundani women who has been pestering her for details on the project might be willing to assist Elvrid. Zara recommends a Melfar artist. Elvrid readily accepts both.

"Can we print some of the photographs into the book itself?" Vidvana asks. "Not with the method using Damon's special plates, but photographs based on those images. Printed like the illustrations in ordinary books. I know they wouldn't be as vivid, not alive like the originals. But most Mundani can't see all of what Melfar see in them anyway."

Elvrid says he thinks it can be done, although it's not a skill he's used in his own work. The books he's printed included no photographs, only drawings, and most of them were single copies—ostentatiously singular and highly decorated. He wonders if such elaborations might be appropriate for the *Book of All Time*. "I recall one of the books we had in the shop that contained instructions on how to print photographs for books. I always thought it was something I'd like to try. With Damon's help, maybe I can figure it out. I can collect that book when I get the printing equipment."

"I'm afraid it may be too dangerous for you to go on such a journey, Elvrid," Vidvana says. "Is there someone else we could send?"

"They wouldn't know what to bring. And they might not be able to find the book I need."

"Elvrid should go," I say. "Send a Melfar protector with him. And ask Gerd to send someone from her company, too."

51.

⌒

Elvrid left this morning. Father sent a young Melfar woman called Senja to accompany him. All the Melfar youths are receiving training in the songs at a younger age than used to be customary. Too many adults were lost in the Palinjian attack on Old Beniford.

Damon lent his waif of the Ancient Amber to Elvrid. "If he gets into trouble, you can protect him," Damon told me. I hope Elvrid won't need the stone's special capabilities, its Song of Turning. At least it may aid me in watching over him as he and Senja travel.

Gerd promised to send a trained member of her company to meet up with Elvrid and Senja as soon as they move out from under New Beniford's protection canopy. I watch as they exit, and I'm surprised to see Gerd herself join them. She's armed with a longblade strapped to one hip and a knife thrust into her belt. I know she prefers to fight without weapons of violence, but I also know how determined she is not to fail again to protect someone she's taken into her care.

They exchange greetings and Elvrid's deference indicates that he appreciates who this woman is. Though he only spoke with her a couple of times in Fayredell, he saw the respect she commands among the weftreds allied against the Palinjians.

"If I'm going to guard you, Elvrid, I think I deserve to know exactly who you are," Gerd says.

"I'm Elvrid Conif, bookseller from Temur." He mumbles through clenched teeth.

"I know that's who you've been all your life, Elvrid. But is that all?" Gerd sounds almost teasing. "Wouldn't you like to finally get this off your chest?"

Elvrid sighs deeply, refusing to meet Gerd's eyes. "How do I know my mother was telling me the truth?" he says. "Maybe she made up a story to try and make me feel important." If that had been her intention, she'd failed. Being told that he was the son of Zibal Palinj had not made Elvrid feel important. It had terrified him. That's why, up until this very moment, he had refused to speak it aloud. "But yes," he says, "Mother told me. She said that Zibal Palinj is my father."

There. It was out now. What would Gerd do with it?

"I think she spoke the truth, Elvrid. Her story matches up with what others have said about Zibal. About how he had a relationship with a young woman after his wife's death and how that young woman had suddenly moved away. The story in Benbridge was that she had to take over her father's business after his death."

Elvrid tries to squeeze back the distress that wants to scream into the sunny day, and he ends up emitting some odd squeaking sounds as his face contorts in misery. "I don't want to be him, Gerd. I only want to be my mother's son, my grandfather's heir who took over a wonderful little bookshop and printing business. I liked my life."

Gerd wants to reach out and pat the man's shoulder but she's afraid that might seem condescending. "What you've agreed to do for us you do as Elvrid Conif," she says. "Your talent and skill in printing books have nothing to do with Zibal Palinj."

"That's true," Elvrid says. "I'm a printer who's going to print some books. Maybe help Damon figure out how to print some photographs into the books, too. You're right. None of that has anything to do with who my mother said my father was. And anyhow, he's long dead." Elvrid doesn't add anything about resting in peace.

As they move toward Temur, Senja hums softly, cloaking the trio in a canopy of protection. Ordinary Mundani would see only vague movement as they traverse the ancient Melfar way, nothing more noteworthy than the stirring of leaves and grasses in a breeze. But not all Mundani are ordinary. There are still Palinjian Revelants to contend with, so Gerd remains watchful.

When I tell Father about what I saw, he seems pleased. He says he's relying on me to keep track of Elvrid and Gerd on their journey.

They should reach Temur around midday tomorrow.

52.

~

Father says that the nens' nearly synchronized sleeping pattern is not surprising. They're twins. I'm grateful for the fact that it leaves longer periods of quiet. Damon's work here at the house is becoming more productive. Zara says the images they make here are more vivid and she tries to give me credit for that.

"Do you think it's time to try and make some photographs of Meridia's recent travels with the Migrant?" Zara asks. She turns toward me. "You've traveled deeper into the past than any of the verses in the Canopy of Time. What do you say, Meridia?"

At first I say nothing as I continue to sway with the silent lullaby I'm singing to the twins. I hold them close, one on each arm.

"I think we're all eager to know more about what you've learned," Vidvana says. Her eyes always look unnaturally large through her glasses.

So far, I've only shared accounts of my travels with Father and Brân. Well, they knew some of what happened without my telling them. I've told Damon some of the stories, too, and I've told Zara a little. Maybe it's time I shared my experiences more fully. "How does it work?" I say. I've been watching their process. It looks simple enough, but I'm not at all sure I understand it. Zara sings while Damon manipulates some plates and substances. I pertange the images in Zara's songs and somehow those images end up on the plates. Then later

Damon transfers them onto paper. Vidvana, being Mundani, furiously writes words. Sometimes she also makes marks on paper in a strange hand of circular notations that she's tried to explain to me is a way of writing music. I think it makes more sense than the lines of angular letters depicting words that Mother tried to teach me. Or maybe I find it more beautiful.

"I have no songs like the ones Zara sings," I say. And yet I know I do. They're deep songs. Will I have to go back to where I found them?

"None of us truly understands how the process works," Zara says. "We only know that it does work." She knows I have songs. Incomplete, perhaps, but worthy of sharing in spite of that. She's heard some pieces of them when I sing to the nens. "Consider it, Meridia. We'll only do it if you're willing."

"I'll think about it," I say.

They've finished their work for the day. Damon offers tea and we all sit for a while around the table. Omi has gone to sleep and Odi is on the verge of joining her, rocked in Zara's arms.

"I made some guavacot pudding this morning," Vidvana says. "I meant to bring you some. I'll bring it over a bit later if that's okay."

"That sounds delicious," I say. "Perhaps Damon could walk with you and bring it back. So you wouldn't have to walk all the way here and home again." Vidvana's cabin is at the opposite end of the village from ours. Not a great distance, but an inconvenience to have to do it twice.

Damon readily agrees and soon he and Vidvana leave. Damon loves guavacot pudding.

These nens are so fortunate to be mothered by a Calumet, Zara says.

They began in the worst of circumstances. But they're born into so much love here in New Beniford.

The love of our Calumet and all her people. Zara smiles at me with her head tilted. "That's what you are, Meridia. You're going to have to get used to it."

I return the smile, accompanied by a furrowed brow. *If only I understood what being a Calumet means.*

It means that you're our strongest connection with the Migrant. We're all connected, but there's always one who is more strongly connected with the Migrant than the rest. For us, you are that one.

I sit with that for a while, letting the colors and fragrant notes of its meaning waft into me. Odi begins to whimper and Zara hands her to me. I offer my breast.

Watching you mother Naomi and Odilia, she says, *I see the immensity of your capacity to love and care. And I've seen what a gifted healer you are. These are some of the finest qualities of a Calumet. And already the Migrant has shown you things none of us has known before.* "You're not alone in this, Meridia. You have all our support."

My face glows warm as I hold Odi close, watching her sister twin Omi sleeping in her basket. *I'll help you with the pictures,* I say. *I'll try.*

53.

≈📖≈

Gerd and Elvrid and Senja have reached Temur. Elvrid finds the key he hid behind a loose stone in the foundation of his shop and opens the back door. The stale air inside is thick with the smell of musty paper and mildewed leather, the oily scent of ink. Elvrid starts to open a window and Gerd stops him.

"It's better if no one knows we're here," she says. "Maybe tonight we can open a window, but not now."

"Everything looks like it's exactly as I left it," Elvrid says. He finds a lamp and lights it. He looks around, squinting into the dim corners of the space, making mental notes about the equipment and supplies he intends to take back to New Beniford to reestablish his printing business there. No, not a business. A service. He wishes he could take all the books, too. Well, maybe not all of them. Not the ridiculous self-serving histories of Houses, which contain as many lies as truths.

Gerd walks along a wall of books, head tilted to read the titles on the spines.

Elvrid offers her another lamp. "That wall is all instruction manuals and technical books. I promised Damon we'd bring back the ones on photography."

Gerd removes a book and some of the binding crumbles to dust in her hand. She reads the title, awkwardly sounding out the unfamiliar words. "*Programing Qantum Computhers*. What is that about?"

"I have no idea. That's one of the books we classify as esoteric technica. Nobody really understands what they're about, but people have been recopying and reprinting them for generations. I don't know why. I have a few more like that."

Gerd carefully replaces the book, wipes the dust from her hands, and continues her perusing. There are books on pottery making and metal working and farming and several about something called electronics. She finds a book on photography and hands it to Elvrid. She picks up one called *Piloting and Seamanship* and flips it open. There are pictures and diagrams of all kinds of ships.

Bring that one, Gerd. I don't know why I tell her this.

She looks puzzled for a moment and then places the book on the table on top of the one about photography. She's surprised at the mountain of printing supplies accumulating on the table. "Do you expect us to take all of this back to New Beniford?" she says.

Elvrid takes a step back from the table and glances over his shoulder at some of the things he still needs to add to the collection. "If we intend to print books, we'll need it," he says. "There's a cart in the shed out back. I'm thinking the cart can hold it all."

Gerd is thinking about pulling such a loaded cart all the way back to New Beniford. She reminds herself that she used to make her living carrying things. They'll manage. She moves to another section of books. "What kind of books are these?" she asks. She can't tell from the titles.

"Fantasy," Elvrid says. "They have some amazing drawings in them."

Gerd opens one of the fantasy books and I see illustrations of tall, mirror-covered buildings. Carriages with no equids or pedals. I quiver in recognition. *Bring that one, Gerd.* She hesitates, then adds it to the stack.

Senja sits in a chair observing, humming quietly to shelter the three of them from the awareness of anyone passing by on the street outside.

Outside where it's dark and silent.

Drowsiness causes Senja's protection canopy to thin in places. She sneezes and the canopy frays a bit more. "It's awfully dusty in here," she says. "Do you think it might be alright to open a window now?"

Gerd looks up at the high windows along the ceiling and is surprised to see that night has fallen. "Can those windows be opened?" she says.

Elvrid retrieves a long stick that has a hook at one end and reaches up to unfasten a latch. He pushes the window outward until a brace catches to hold it in place. He opens a second window. The breeze from outside rustles some papers hanging on a wall. It feels cool and fresh. "Is anyone else hungry?" Elvrid says. "We should have something to eat." He pulls a small table from behind a desk and Senja lays out some of their food supplies, continuing her song as she does so.

Gerd can't take her eyes off the shelves and shelves of bound volumes. She's remembering all the books that were burned in the Great Fires. She's thinking of the books that still get tossed into the bonfires that Palinjians light every passage during the Binder. "How did you end up with so many books?"

"My family have been book printers and dealers for generations," he says. "And you know Temur never burned as completely as other towns. We even had a small patch of woods here that lasted for many passages after the last of the Great Fires." His grandfather had taken to lending some of the books for a fee rather than selling them. He did that to keep them from being thrown into bonfires.

"Did you know Madelyn Einkorn and Meridia?"

"Not really. Though it was hard not to know *of* them. There weren't ever more than a few Melfar in Temur that I can recall." Or half Melfar.

I wonder if he might remember my father, Abél. If Abél ever went to Elvrid's mother's shop.

He did go there. I see him arriving to pick up copies of a poem that members of Mother's weftred were learning. Elvrid was a youth then, bending over a printing press, listening absently as his mother chatted amiably with the Melfar man whose name he never knew. A man who disappeared a few passages later.

"Do you have any books of poetry here?" Senja asks.

"Lots of them, but they're in the back," Elvrid says. "We never kept them out here. People had to ask for them. I guess we should take those with us, too, right?"

Vidvana will be happy to have more poems for the *Book of All Time*.

Senja is staring at one of the open windows. She gestures abruptly, signaling everyone into silence.

There's a shuffle of feet on the path outside. A low murmur of voices. And then someone calls out, "We know you're in there! Come out and tell us what business you have here!"

"Go hide in the back and let me handle this," Gerd hisses.

Elvrid grabs up the stack of books on the table and glances fondly at his precious printing equipment. He and Senja disappear.

Once they're safely out of sight, Gerd walks slowly to the front door. She draws herself up to her full height, positions a hand on the longblade that hangs at her hip, and opens the door a crack. She rubs her eyes, feigning sleepiness. "I'm here to do some cleaning up. Doing what I was hired to do. So go along now and let me do my work." She starts to close the door.

"Gerd?" A man has stepped forward from the group. "It *is* you. What the void are you doing here in Temur?"

Gerd recognizes the man as one of the members of her company from Fayredell, a man she's trained with on several occasions in Roqu's sessions. "I should ask what are *you* doing here," she says. What *is* he doing here? Gerd is suddenly aware of Senja at her elbow.

"It's okay, Gerd. They mean us no harm."

The man is speaking again. "We've been keeping an eye on the place, making sure no Palinjians came looking for fuel for one of their ashing fires," he says. "Elvrid Conif is our friend and we don't believe any of the lies the Palinjians are spreading about him."

"They're not lies." The door has opened wider and Elvrid faces the knot of people on the street, which has grown by a few. "Not exactly lies, anyway. It's true that Zibal Palinj fathered me. At least that's what my mother told me with her dying breaths. I can't see she'd have any reason to lie. But it's also true that I wholly and completely reject Zibal Palinj and everything he stands for."

The man speaks again. "And we stand with you, Elvrid. With you and with Gerd."

Donna Dechen Birdwell

There's a murmur of assent from the gathering. "We're with you, Elvrid."

"We follow Gerd."

"Ash the Palinjians!"

This is not what Gerd was expecting. She's overwhelmed by this open show of local support but thinks that the group is getting too loud and might attract unwanted attention from residents who don't share their views. "Come inside," she says. "And let's try to be a bit quieter." They all step into the dusty brightness of Elvrid's bookshop.

I'm overwhelmed, too. Perhaps Lambert Quint is right. Perhaps it is time for Chanters and their weftreds to come out of hiding, to step into the light. The notes of a song bubble into my awareness. I think it might be a piece of the Ancient Obsidian song called Overwhelm with Splendor.

54.

≈≪

Vidvana says she'll watch over Omi and Odi so that I can work with Damon and Zara without being interrupted. I trust her, but I'm not sure I won't be interrupted anyway. The nens and I were one being for so long.

"What should I do?" I say. I'm watching Damon coat some photographic plates with the substance that smells like the snails he kept here at the house before the fever outbreak.

Zara answers. *Call up your memories of being with the Migrant. Listen for the songs. Sing what you hear.*

Where was Naomi when I first met her and Amergin?

She was already deep in the caverns. She was thinking about how she got there. Remembering life at the children's refuge of Saint Odilia before the explosion.

The explosion. A flash of whitest light. Deep blue-black notes strike with staggering force, punctuated by high-pitched crimson screeches of terror. The solid walls of their building crack and crumble like eggshell. Percussive notes of many colors. Another explosion amid a tumbling, discordant collapse. All the high and mid-tones swallowed up, drowned in a deep droning brown as they awaken to darkness and misery. The searching melodies of children reaching out for one another, grasping toward violet hope. Naomi and Amergin's tentative harmonies. Sister Maggie Marie's trumpeting call for calm as they gather around her. I lose myself in the memory of it all as the notes and colors come together, organize, galvanize into clear images and a purposeful song of this band bent on survival.

I sit with them for a while. Listening. Learning their melodies and rhythms. Singing their broken world.

That's beautiful, Meridia. Zara's verberations reach me. *Beautiful and terrible. Can you show us more?*

I follow Amergin as he leads the group through the tunnels, sensing but not quite knowing what lies ahead. He's guided by the songs and colors embedded deep in these stones from a world even more ancient. He synchronizes his own song with these deep voices of time. I listen and learn.

There's a sudden screeching, blue as the sky Naomi knows from before.

No, that's my Naomi, my precious nen. The vision collapses as I take her into my arms.

"I didn't want to interrupt," Vidvana says, "but I'd run out of tricks to keep Omi quiet. Is she hungry?"

"Maybe," I say, as the nen latches onto my nipple. The one on the left. Her favorite. "But she may just want me to hold her." Being cradled in my arms, so close to the familiar beating of my heart, also nourishes her. Now Odi begins to cry.

Damon begins brushing another kind of aromatic liquid onto some papers that he lays over the plates. This part reminds me of working with Father when he was crafting the New Marble Benison. Damon and Zara and Vidvana stare at the papers as if they're watching the hatching of a shama egg. There are murmurs of pleasure. Damon lifts one of the papers and holds it up where I can see.

The paper shimmers and pulses with color. On it I pertange... No, I *see* clear images of Naomi and Amergin and the two older women, Sister Maggie Marie and Sister Berta. "Can you see them?" I ask, my aurynx clutching at the song that wants to rise again, my eyes flooding with wonder.

"We can't be sure we see everything that you do, but the images are clear even to us," Vidvana says. "Can you tell us who these people are?"

I point out each one and tell a bit more of their story. I'm surprised at how easily the words come, how song and printed image and words weave together in my mind, strengthening and clarifying one another.

"Are you telling us that some of these individuals knew how to use the aurynx and gnosic orb?" Zara stares at the image, transfixed.

"Yes. To some extent, anyway. It's why they were sent to the children's refuge. Everyone thought they were mad, that they were imagining things. But they weren't mad. They saw and heard more than ordinary people did. They pertanged. I'm convinced that these must have been some of our first elders." *That's why the Migrant took me there. They wanted us to know where we come from.*

Vidvana and Zara agree that one session a day is enough to expect of me under the circumstances. They don't come every day, but I look forward to printing these pictures from my travels with the Migrant. I love watching the faces of the Sisters and the children emerge onto pieces of paper. I love watching the faces of Damon and Zara and Vidvana as they see these ancient friends. Our eldpeople. I try to explain that some of the pictures, which emerge bathed in light of all colors, are in fact depictions of experiences within the deep, dark caverns where daylight never penetrated.

Sometimes Father joins our sessions. The pictures we make on the days when he's here are clearer than the rest. He's here today.

I'm prepared to sing the joyous notes of Naomi and Amergin's emergence from their long darkness underground, but I keep getting pulled in another direction. I try to apologize.

Don't resist, Meridia. Go where the Migrant wants you. Father tells me this.

But it isn't the Migrant pulling me away this time. It's Brân.

Come see, Meridia. Come see what I've learned.

As if from a great distance, a great height, I see objects fall from the sky, raining down everywhere, landing with huge explosions of white heat. Bombs sent from many different places, each explosion fueled by fear and anger.

Were these like the explosion that sent Amergin and Naomi and the rest below ground?

Yes, Meridia. They very nearly destroyed all the people. A few survived underground, here and in other places as well. Still others were on a remote island that was spared from the blasts.

They came back on a ship, didn't they?

I see them disembarking, sick and frightened, no one there to greet them. I look around for Brân, but he's gone. I listen for a song and find none. A few discordant notes of this ship's strange voyage echo as I settle back into the present.

"What happened?" Zara says. She knows Brân was there. She's not sure about anything else.

Damon's print emerges, showing only a few vague, colorless figures with blurred faces. There's a clearer figure behind them. That one is Brân. I do my best to add to the image they've printed, to explain what I experienced. Words fail me. I find no colors, no music. Few verberations. What I do find feels like anger, hatred, resentment. I know there's more to this story.

55.

Preparations are underway for the Gathering in Fayredell. Here in New Beniford, Damon and Zara work every day on the pictures. Sometimes I work with them. Meanwhile, Vidvana compiles and edits the written stories for the *Book of All Time* so that Elvrid will be able to set the words into type for printing once he returns from Temur. She's conceded that the book will need to be produced in several volumes.

"Could we provide a display of some of our photographs for the day of the Gathering?" Vidvana asks.

Damon and Zara like the idea and begin sorting through images in their minds, trying to decide which ones to include in the exhibit.

"How many copies of the book do we intend to print?" Damon says.

Vidvana closes the journal where she's recorded words describing our latest work. "We'll definitely want to place a copy of the *Book of All Time* in Fayredell so that people there can read it. And of course we'll keep one copy here. We'll want copies for other towns, too, though we won't take them there until we're certain that they'll be safe."

I try to follow their conversation as they discuss how Teagan and her son Rio have taken charge of the abandoned Markham Clauster. They think Brightlea may soon be ripe for new leadership, as well.

Damon is still thinking about the pictures. "If we take pictures to Fayredell, don't you think we should leave some of them there? As a permanent exhibit? At least a few of them. We can always make more here."

Zara and Vidvana like the idea, though Zara points out that the second set of photographs wouldn't be exactly the same images. They never are. Every time a song is sung it contains the hues and verberations of the singer's state of mind on the day. Always a little different. None more accurate or true than any other.

"Elvrid told me that he sometimes printed single pages that people handed out at events. Could we make some of those as well?" Vidvana asks. Damon agrees to speak with Elvrid about it.

I'm keeping busy, too, of course. I still work with Damon and Zara one morning every six, making additional photographs, but I've also begun venturing out to help Bekanz look after sick people. She has me following up with patients who are still recovering from the nacreous fever, helping them know which teas and tinctures will get them back in good health more quickly. Yuli stays with the nens while I do this work.

Occasionally I find time to escape to my green glen to commune with my waifs. With the Migrant. I used to feel that this was a selfish pleasure. Now I know that this, too, is my work. The Migrant has shown me so many things from the past, but now I find that most of the questions I have are concerned with the future—with my future and the future of these people who insist on calling me Calumet. And the future of those elsewhere who want to call me Prophet.

In response to my queries, Zara has gifted me a waif of an Amethyst that holds the Song of the Migrant. She told me what she knows of it. *It's a very old song,* she said, *from the early returns of Razak Pherson's life. Its Benison was erected in Lindmor and the song was shared mainly among the Melfar of Cödweg. That was the only meed in which different groups of Melfar erected different Benisons.*

Damon had told me about that. He said the other Preterit Amethyst was erected in Túl and carried a Song of the Forest.

I have most of the Song of the Forest, Zara says. She learned it from a woman from Túl. *But I only know a few fragments of the Song of the Migrant.*

It was about accepting natural cause and effect. Is that right?

That's how I understand it. Avienne tried to teach me more of it, but I'm afraid I didn't learn it well. This waif that I've given you was hers. I should've paid more attention.

You know so many of the songs, Zara. We can't expect you to remember all of them. I know she expects it of herself.

A little past midday I slip away to the refuge of my glen, leaving the sleeping nens in Yuli's care. The stool isn't here anymore. Now that I'm no longer pregnant, I've returned to my habit of sitting on the ground whenever I can. I like the feeling of being in contact with the earth. Sometimes I still pertange the songs of old tree roots and of other things that live and grow below the surface.

The mat of growing things I sit on is warm from the sun and fragrant with life. I take the Preterit Amethyst between my hands, trying to recall the notes of its Song of the Migrant that Zara passed on to me, the notes she preserved from my eldmother Avienne's knowledge of the song.

Who taught it to Avienne?

I hear the notes now in Avienne's voice. I know it's her voice despite its childlike timbre and color. Tentatively, she follows another stronger, more resonant voice. It's her own mother. My elder eldmother, Meridia.

We knew the whole song, but it was a difficult one. People resisted it.

Why, Eldmothers?

Notes rise like evaporating dew. Songs of birds seeking mates, building nests. Lower notes creep and slither like serpents seeking the birds' eggs, devouring the eggs, laying their own eggs. The high-pitched silver shriek of a falcon as she rises, clutching the serpent in her talons.

We try too hard to be the creative power while denying the destruction that lays the conditions for creation. That's Old Meridia's voice, her verberation.

I feel the turning, the cycle, the rise and fall. I listen to the exquisite music of everything unfolding and folding once more into itself, becoming itself again and again.

Avienne's voice—an adult voice now—rises within the symphony. *What we experience as adversity is only the process. We fall, we rise. Always becoming.*

Together my eldmothers sing the Song of the Migrant and I listen, breathing with my mind. I join them. We sing the colors, the process, the encompassing truth of the Migrant. And then we dance, in great flowing circles, the three of us moving and exchanging places until I no longer know which one of us I am. We are all of us.

"There you are. I thought I might find you here."

Whose voice is that? Were we dancing? I open my ordinary eyes and find myself still seated. My orb is filled with visions of dancing. It overflows with music.

"Are you okay, Meridia? Your nens are asking for you." Yuli's words break through to where I've been. "Damon is there, but they need you."

"Yes, I'm fine," I say. *I didn't mean to be gone for so long. The eldmothers were teaching me things. I got caught in their song.*

I heard a piece of it. What song was it?

"The Song of the Migrant." I pick up the waif of the Preterit Amethyst and tuck it away into the pouch attached to my belt. I turn my thoughts resolutely toward my hungry nens as Yuli and I walk together, going home.

56.

≈≤

"Saami!" Damon is surprised to find the Pherson boy seated alone on the ground next to our cabin. "However did you get here?"

"I followed Zara," he says.

"So you've been here all this time?" I say. "You must be thirsty. Come inside and have something to drink. Maybe a dish of pudding?"

The boy smiles at me. Directly at me. He moves confidently as he enters the cabin. I find him a chair and place his hand on its back.

I offer a goodbye kiss to Damon, who was leaving to go to his workshop when he discovered Saami. Damon needs to finish processing the prints from this morning's work session with Zara and me.

"I hope you don't mind that I was here," Saami says. "I liked listening to you singing. Watching you. I wish I could learn to sing like that. The colors especially."

Zara looks at me with astonishment.

Yes, Zara, he has some abilities of the gnosic orb. He pertanges. I recall my previous conversation with Saami. I'd promised to speak with him again, but I hadn't done it. I'd come down with the nacreous fever and gotten lost. And then the nens were born.

"Was one of the songs about the boy you mentioned to me before? The one who led some people out of an underground cavern?" he says.

"That's right," I say. "I was singing to Zara and Damon about..."

"They were in a very tight space and he led them through it."

"You saw all that?" It's my turn to be astonished now.

"I didn't exactly see it. I don't see anything, you know. I never have. But when I let the notes of your song sort of breathe through me, I felt like that was what was happening. What was the boy's name? I've forgotten."

"Amergin," I say. "Amergin Gorrión." I know he had another name before he came to the children's refuge, but I can't recall if I ever heard it.

"I would like very much to meet this Amergin Gorrión," Saami says. "Where does he live? Can we invite him here? Could I go to visit him?"

Between us, Zara and I try to explain to Saami about the Migrant, about how the Migrant has carried me back in time to experience the lives of people who lived a very long time ago. About how I tell about these experiences by singing the songs I heard when I was with them.

Saami is disappointed. "So I can't meet him."

"In a sense, you already have met him," I say. That doesn't satisfy the boy. I wonder if it would be possible someday to take Saami along on a journey with the Migrant.

We continue our conversation, as Zara and I try to explain about the pictures we're making with Damon. Saami is especially interested in the snails that produce the substance Damon uses to make the photographs. I promise to ask Damon to take him to the workshop one day soon to see the snails.

"Thank you for the pudding," he says, pushing the dish toward the center of the table. "I have one more question, if you don't mind."

"Of course, Saami. You know we welcome your questions."

"Well, after you'd finished with the singing, I heard you talking about some kind of Gathering that they're planning to have in Fayredell. Damon said people were hoping that Elvrid Palinj would maybe be part of it, showing those Palinjians that he's with the Chanters now." The boy takes a deep breath and sits up a bit straighter. "Would it mean anything for a Pherson to be part of it, too?"

Sparks of carnelian-orange fly between Zara and me and the look on Saami's face tells me he saw them. He pertanged something, anyway.

"That could mean quite a lot," I say. "I'll talk with Father about it and we'll consult with Gerd, of course. And she'll discuss it with Lambert. We wouldn't want to put you in any danger, Saami."

He leans forward and slaps the table with an open hand. "Don't vex yourself over me. I don't have to be protected and worried over all the time. It's time for me to stand up and be a man."

I start to say something about the fact that he's only a boy.

"I'll celebrate my twelve passages next stint," he says.

57.

～

Sometimes I feel as if it's all too much. Being the mother of these sister twins—even with all the care they also receive from Damon and Bekanz and Yuli and the rest—is exhausting. They demand my physical body as their own only a little less than they did before they were born. Their budding awareness requires more concentration, more effort as they develop a consciousness that's increasingly separate from mine. I'm also working with Bekanz to tend the sick (although there are fewer of those now) and with Damon and Zara to imprint songs and to help Vidvana put them into words. And amid it all, I'm trying to learn how to be a Calumet.

I've escaped again for some precious moments in my green glen. This time I have no purpose in mind other than solitude. But as always, I have my collection of waifs with me. I hesitate for a few moments, holding the pouch containing the waifs between my hands, close to my heart. I take out the Old Turquoise waif. And the New Marble. I lay these on the cloth in front of me and then find the Old Quartz waif and add it, forming a triangle of the three stones. When I concentrate on the New Marble, a single phrase of the Song of All Songs surges into my awareness: The Preterit Granite's Song of Regret.

Why this one?

Faint shimmers of fibrous sound extend out from each waif to each of the others, joining all three. Without resistance, I fall into their pattern.

I see the great metal ship again, the one Brân showed me. It's landed now and people walk down its creaking bridge onto the shore. Their legs waver beneath them, still attuned to the slip and sway of the ocean. From behind the ruins of a nearby building I feel the eyes of others, watching.

Brân is here.

Who are they, Brân. And why are they so fearful, so angry?

Someday these will be Mundani, Meridia. They've survived horrible disasters. They're angry about the causes of those disasters. And rightfully so. They're fearful about what comes next. No, don't worry about me. I'm well. This part of the story was for me to learn. I'll tell you more soon. As for you, Meridia, you must go and be the Calumet. Our people need you. All of our people need you. All of them are our people. Those who became Mundani and those who became Melfar all came from the same source.

The Song of Regret emanating from the New Marble waif fades as the Ancient Quartz Song of Reconciliation swells. I hum along. In the back of my mind, I also hear the notes of the Song of the Migrant, reminding me that adversity and destruction are part of the nature of things.

Brân is filled with sadness for the suffering of our people, the ones before and the ones now. The strength of his sadness, this surprisingly Mundani emotion, overwhelms me.

His image in my mind grows clearer and more tangible, causing my own Mundani heart to swell with empathy and affection. The shimmering fibers of sound linking my three waifs grow stronger, more strident, more insistent. The fibers reach outward, touching my heart and touching...

"Brân?" I say. A shiver of purest white light pierces my orb and I know he's back. Not back here. There. On Selbourne.

Thank you, Meridia, he says. *I was ready to come home.*

I stare in stunned silence as a crow alights on a rock nearby. It utters one raucous cry and soars skyward.

58.

Abél is overcome with joy at his brother's return and is eager for Brân to rejoin us here in New Beniford. Brân refuses, insisting that he needs to stay a while longer on Selbourne. He experienced eons in that other time-space and he finds it hard to believe that we only experienced his absence for about three tides. He tries to convey to us some of what he learned about the Mundani eldpeople, but even Abél finds his verberations difficult to pertange. He says it's like trying to take hold of a fish swimming in a swiftly moving stream. I'm inclined to agree with him.

Brân has managed to tell us that the region where Mundani and Melfar live has always been afflicted with alternating periods of drought and intense rains. In ancient times, the regular repetitions of the pattern were carefully charted. It was called "The Child." I ask him why it was called that, but he has no explanation.

Gerd and Elvrid and Senja have returned from Temur with their cart loaded down with printing equipment and books. Seeing Gerd always brings memories of Mother. For both of us. In a sense, we're bound to one another through Maddie, and when we reach past the pain of loss, we're grateful for that sense of being family, of belonging to one another.

I tell her about Saami Pherson's desire to take part in the Gathering she and Lambert are planning for Fayredell.

"I think it would be safe enough for him to go," she says. "I was surprised to see how Chanters in Temur are meeting more openly now. Things are changing, Meridia. Encourage the boy. Tell him we'd be happy to have him join us."

The scowl on her face doesn't look at all happy. "You're worried," I say. "You said it would be safe, but I can see that you're worried."

"I'm not worried about Saami. It's you I'm worried about. Far more than Saami Pherson or Elvrid Palinj or Lambert Quint, it's your presence that could be the most important of all."

"Me? But I'm nobody." I feel remorse as soon as I say it. It's a habitual reaction. I was nobody for so long.

"You know that's not true, Meridia. Saami and Elvrid and Lambert are all Mundani. But you're Melfar as well as Mundani. You're the new Calumet of the Melfar. And Prophet of the Mundani if you're willing to accept the role. What could be more important than that?"

"But what about the nens?" I say. "Even though you say it would be safe, I couldn't possibly take Naomi and Odilia into something like this all the way off in Fayredell."

"I knew you'd say that. We're prepared to offer you our sturdiest cart, drawn by our two strongest and fastest equids. You could be there and back in two days. Leave Omi and Odi here in the care of Yuli. No one could take better care of them than Yuli."

"Except their own mother."

"I didn't mean..."

"I know. But I don't see how I can do what you ask, Gerd."

"Will you at least think about it?"

Of course I will. How could I not think about it? The idea is already churning my mind with expectation, trepidation, uncertainty.

Damon is absorbed in studying the book Gerd and Elvrid brought back from Temur, the one about how to print photographs onto the pages of books. He's spending more time in his workshop, which is now Elvrid's workshop, too. Damon says they're making good progress.

I haven't told anyone about what Gerd asked of me. I'm sure Father knows, but he doesn't mention it. I don't say anything to Damon because I'm almost certain he would say "no." That may in fact be my decision, too, but I know this ought to be *my* decision and not Damon's. I know what Father would tell me if I brought it up: He'd tell me to listen to the Migrant.

Today I give in and take my collection of waifs to the glen, leaving the nens with Yuli. She's so good with them. They even seem content to let her feed them cabra's milk out of a bottle.

On my way, walking slowly, I let my mind wander among the songs. Songs I know well and other songs I'm learning from Abél and from Zara. I think about the songs that brought Brân back to us, marveling at how they worked together that day. There was the Canopy of Time and the Song of Regret. Then came the Song of Reconciliation and finally the Song of the Migrant. Fibrous strands of sound linked the three waifs—Turquoise, Marble, and Quartz—resonating with the notes of the songs. I long to ask Brân what he experienced during his return. Did he hear the songs?

I try to remember what Abél told me when he first tried to explain where Melfar songs come from. He said that all of them originate with the Migrant. I wanted to know what they were about, and he said that the songs, whatever we decide to call them, are originally about everything. I remember how it felt when I first met Avienne through the Song of the Calumet from the Old Jade that Damon got from Brân. When I heard that song—pertanged it—I knew at once that it was about everything. But Abél told me that Melfar refine such songs into something... What was it he said? *Something less, which makes them speak as something more.* I want to ask him how it is, exactly, that we refine them.

It doesn't always work. Many of the songs have gone awry, their music obscured, stifled by Mundani words, their intent lost. That's why we're composing the *Book of All Time*, printing words and pictures. We're trying harder to communicate across whatever it is that has separated Melfar and Mundani.

By the time I reach the glen, I'm in a daze, remembering things. Striving to understand something that hovers just beyond my reach. I sit in my usual place and spread my waifs out on a cloth in front of me. I take the New Marble and hold it up to the sunlight. Today it's the Song of All Songs itself that surges into my awareness.

I hear Lambert Quint chanting the words his father Amos put to that song.

Lambert is in his mirrored sanctuary. The verberations of the place are strong. He paces with measured steps, moving slowly from one end of the room to the other and back again, not looking at the mirrors, but keenly aware of the images they reflect, breathing in the reflections, hearing the sound of his own chanting echoing from their depths.

He stops for a moment and gazes into the two mirrors that once belonged to his mother and to his daughter. Another voice joins Lambert's and I see more mirrors. Deeper, darker mirrors. This is Amos Quint's chamber on Selbourne. I listen as the two Mundani men, father and son, chant together. I hear Brân's voice adding music to the words. I breathe with them. I want to sing, but my aurynx refuses.

I want to tell them that they're enough. That Lambert should lead. That they don't need me. And then I pertange a voice—or voices—and I don't know if it's Lambert or Amos or Brân or my father or the eldmothers or the Migrant themselves. The voice is richly layered.

It shatters me.

This is our moment, Meridia. More than ever before, people stand open to the possibility of peace. The possibility of a Prophet of Peace, a Calumet. Go, Meridia. Go and fill their openness with the possibility of peace.

I cover my face with my hands and moan. I have no words. No song.

My will falters. My willfulness collapses.

I surrender, and song rises up all around me.

I sit and let the Song of All Songs embrace me, teaching me the deeper truths of its melodies and harmonies and cadences. Teaching me its intimate partnership with the *Book of All Time*. Teaching me why the song is not enough, why the book needs to be printed, needs to become a solid, tangible thing that can be read everywhere. Not only here in New Beniford, but in Fayredell and Temur and Brightlea and Benbridge and, yes, even in Blanton, even in that last faltering stronghold of the Palinjians.

It's time.

Time to go.

Time to tell Gerd and Lambert that I will join them for their Gathering.

59.

The *Book of All Time* is hefty and beautiful. I feel the weight of it in my hands and admire the printed words on its smooth, clean pages. The photographs turned out well, too, though I prefer the more vivid ones Damon prints with the aid of his snails. Elvrid and the Melfar artist whom Zara sent his way have crafted a cover of finest leather and engraved it with the figure of a tree. Not a tree in flames such as the Palinjians use. This tree is alive with foliage, laden with fruit and the nests of birds. The figure is surrounded by intertwined lines like vines, and within that pattern, there are serpents. In each corner of the cover, a hawk perches, ready to spring into flight. It's the design I suggested.

Zara and Vidvana have selected eleven of Damon's living photographs for the exhibition. One of them shows Amergin and Naomi and the three Sisters. We tried making a photograph from the Song of All Songs, but all we got was a blue-swirled sphere on a black background. Zara insisted that Damon print it anyway. I'm sure it won't be in the exhibition.

When I told Damon about my intention to join Gerd and Lambert and the others for the Gathering in Fayredell, he didn't speak. He just took me into his arms and held me tight, opening his thoughts and his heart to me, his admiration for what I'm becoming.

"So you don't mind?" I say.

"No, Meri, of course not. This is who you are and I am your partner. Of course I'll worry about you." He smiles and caresses my hair. "Isn't that my job?"

Perhaps the decision wouldn't have been so difficult if we'd made it together.

Saami comes to visit me at least once every six. The nens smile and coo at him when he holds them. He knows which one is Naomi and which one is Odilia without being told. Today I'm telling him more stories of my experiences with Amergin and his Naomi.

Saami is thoughtful. "Do you think perhaps I might one day take a partner and have a family? Like Amergin did?" His voice is wistful and I detect a faint lilac tint emanating from his heart.

"I don't see why not," I say.

He lapses into silence again, fumbling for something in his pocket. He pulls out a stone and lays it on the table. "I celebrated my twelfth birth anniversary yesterday," he says. He sits up a little straighter and his voice deepens a bit. "This is my destiny stone."

I'm uncertain what to say. I know very little about the Mundani custom of destiny stones, although Damon told me about his own experience. I attempt to skirt the issue. "I didn't know it was your birth anniversary, Saami! If you'd told me, I would have made you a special pudding to celebrate. How about one for today?" But I know what he really wants is for me to tell him about the stone he found. He hasn't shown it to anyone else yet. He was waiting to show it to me. He was waiting to show it to the Calumet. "Your stone is beautiful," I say, my voice softening. "May I pick it up?"

"Of course," he says, gesturing toward it. "I was hoping you might tell me about it."

"First, tell me what you know," I say, taking the stone and holding it between the palms of my hands. Listening. Breathing.

"Well," he clears his throat to dispel the quaver in his voice. "I think it's bright. I couldn't pick up...pertange any particular colors. I'm not good with colors. But I know there was brightness. And I kept hearing something like... I don't know, maybe like an echo?"

"Your destiny stone is indeed a waif," I tell him. He swells with pleasure at this validation of his discovery. "It's a waif of the New Mica. Well, the old New Mica. I keep forgetting to shift references. We call it the Old Mica now. I've only recently learned its song from Zara. It's the Song of Reflection."

Saami furrows his brow and I notice how his eyebrows are sprouting the longer hairs of Mundani adulthood. "Reflection. Like mirrors? I've always had a hard time understanding exactly what mirrors are like."

"Not exactly like mirrors. Zara told me it was to teach us that whatever we send out comes back to us. Like the image in a mirror. Or an echo. But mostly to show us that how we treat other people is ultimately what we experience in life. It gets reflected back to us."

"So I was kind of right about the echo." Saami is clearly pleased with himself. "I think I understand at least a little about what you say about getting back what we put onto other people." He reaches for the waif and closes his hand around it. "My brother Warreth treated people very badly and you see what happened to him." He places the stone back into his pocket.

"I don't think it's necessarily that simple," I say.

"Warreth had something that he claimed was his destiny stone." Saami rubs the palm of his left hand with his right thumb as he speaks. "He let me hold it once. It was nothing. I couldn't feel anything from it at all."

After Saami leaves, I keep thinking about his mica waif and its Song of Reflection. Thinking about mirrors.

Omi stirs in her sleep and lets out a small cry. It's only an air bubble. I massage her tummy for a moment until she falls back into deeper sleep. Was that really a yellow wisp of gratitude that came from her tiny throat, or did I only imagine it?

I walk toward the door and stop. I'm seized with trepidation about the mirror fragment that Amos Quint had intended Brân to bring back for Lambert but that instead came to me. Why do I find the shard of glass so disturbing?

I take the bit of mirror from the basket where I've kept it and hold it gingerly between my fingers. The sun catches on it and I startle as the reflected brightness penetrates my orb, singeing something into my mind, a milky transparency sparked with blue and orange. But there's a darkness, too. A hollow darkness that reminds me of what I felt when Father described the long returns he spent at Swarthpol. My aurynx shudders with something that sounds to my ears almost like a growl.

What is this strange bit of glass anyway?

I'm not sure I want to know. I've promised to take it to Lambert. But now I'm not certain that I ought to do that. I'm convinced that the shard is a piece of one of the mirrors Amos found in his meditation chamber, the ones that were there long before he ever claimed the space for himself. I reach out, wanting to ask Brân about this, but I can't find him. He's different now and not as accessible as he was before his sojourn among the Mundani eldpeople.

I go to visit Abél instead, leaving the twins in Yuli's care. When I reach his cottage, I find that he knows why I've come. Without speaking, I lay the piece of glass on the table. Father places one of his waifs next to it, and there's an immediate shimmer of fibrous sound between the two objects. Father snatches up his waif and places it back inside his pouch.

I look from Father to the shard and back again. *What just happened?*

I'm not sure, Father says. *But you're right to be cautious about that bit of glass. Brân says the mirrors Amos Quint found on Selbourne may have something to do with activities that the Mundani eldpeople were engaged in around Swarthpol.*

What kind of activity?

Research. Experiments of some sort. Brân doesn't know what the experiments were about.

I'm thinking about the quake. Not the one that plunged Amergin and Naomi into the caverns. I'm thinking about the one that took Brân away after Amos Quint rearranged the mirrors. *Do you think the mirrors had something to do with the earthquake that took Brân away?*

It wasn't an earthquake, Meridia. More like a timequake. A breach? A portal. I'm sure it's how Brân slipped away. And you know he returned to exactly the same spot.

Father is remembering Swarthpol. He refused to think about his experience there for so many meeds, but now he thinks perhaps he needs to remember.

What should we do with the mirror shard, Father? Should we destroy it?

You can leave the shard with me, he says.

Somehow that feels wrong. I'm afraid for Father. I'm afraid of what he's remembering about Swarthpol. *No. I'll take care of it. I'll put it away somewhere until we can learn more about it.* I'm not sure how we'll learn anything more. I'm not convinced we should try.

As I walk back home, I think about what to do with the shard. Perhaps I should bury it somewhere. Yes, that would be best. I'll do that tomorrow. For the moment, instead of returning the shard to the basket where we'd been keeping it, I wrap it in a scrap of paper and place it in the back corner of our highest cupboard.

60.

~

The cloth wrapped around my swollen breasts is damp with milk that my nens will never taste. They're sleeping now, their little bellies filled with cabra's milk. Yuli sends me reassurance, but my heart yearns for my Omi and Odi, my precious nens. *We'll be back soon*, I tell them. And when I say "we," I mean their father Damon and me.

The journey from New Beniford to Fayredell was easy. The cart was sturdy and the equids strong and fast. Damon was anxious about my coming, even though he knew it was the right thing.

"She's our Calumet," Abél had told him. "The time has come for her to be visible."

It's that very visibility that concerns Damon most. He knows the Palinjians are still a threat. He's a constant, nervous presence at my side, so I urge him to go help Vidvana and Zara set up the display of photographs for the Gathering. I'm grateful when he finally goes, leaving me here in the old Landry house.

The others from New Beniford—including Elvrid Palinj and Saami Pherson—left a couple of days ahead of us and are comfortably lodged with various members of Gerd's weftred. Elvrid told us he doesn't mind other people calling him Elvrid Palinj, but that he will always think of himself as Elvrid Conif.

Ann breth Keira has been busy helping her grand-father Lambert with preparations and creating her own display of potted seedlings of many different kinds of trees. She's hoping to recruit more people to assist in replanting forests.

I sleep little. The bed is comfortable enough, softer than my bed in New Beniford. But something gnaws away at the edges of my awareness, causing me to toss restlessly. I keep trying to reclaim the sense of resolve I felt in my green glen, to recall the strength of the song I heard that day. Now that I'm here in Fayredell, surrounded by more Mundani than Melfar, I feel inadequate. It's true that Melfar call me Calumet and that even Lambert Quint now calls me Prophet. But can I be what they need? My heart flutters and my orb buzzes. How can they expect so much of Meridia breth Madelyn, a healer from Temur?

You're also the child of Abél breth Avienne breth Meridia. You come from a line of Calumets.

Yes. That, too, Father. I'm also the mother of two nens who need me. I reassure myself that I'll soon be back with them.

I give in to wakefulness shortly before sunrise and leave Damon sleeping to go for a walk in the house garden. It's quiet in the pale pre-dawn and I wander aimlessly among the verdant trees. I'm aware of someone else here with me.

"Lambert?" I turn toward him.

"Yes, Meridia. I was hoping to have a few words with Gerd about the Gathering, but I'm afraid I've come too early even for her."

"Not too early for me," I say. "I couldn't sleep."

"Yes, I slept little last night myself."

"I had something I was supposed to bring to you Lambert, but I'm afraid in all the bustle and busyness I forgot." Why do I say that? I'd already decided not to bring it. It's true that I gave it no thought as we made our preparations. Why hadn't I buried it as I'd intended?

"Don't concern yourself about it. I'm sure there will be more than enough gifts at tomorrow's event."

"It wasn't like that, Lambert." I feel the need to confess to him. "It was something that your father wanted you to have. First he gave it to Brân, but when Brân disappeared he asked Damon to bring it to me to give to you." Maybe this thing doesn't want to be given to Lambert.

"Another time, then." But now he's curious. He wants me to tell him what it is.

"It's a small thing. A piece of one of Amos' mirrors from Selbourne." I take a deep breath. "A fragment of one of the mirrors that he found there when he arrived."

"Oh," he says. He's aware of my hesitation, my prevarication. "Well, maybe it wasn't destined to be here for this day."

"Maybe," I say.

Lambert lifts his head, gazing over the garden wall to where the sky is beginning to brighten. "Do you think there's any such thing as destiny? Sometimes I think there's not," he says. "Mundani collect rocks—some of them waifs—and call them destiny stones. But the truth is, we have to make our own way, don't we? We make choices. Nothing determines in advance what we'll choose. We make our destiny through our everyday decisions and actions."

I nod in agreement with him. I start to speak, but I see that he's already enmeshed in the further implications of his thoughts.

"There's so much of what we Mundani have always believed that seems somehow misguided," Lambert says.

Should I tell him that I agree with him?

"Vidvana was telling me that Brân has new insights into the origins of the Mundani people. I have no idea how all of that works, but what little I've heard is intriguing. I'm eager to learn more." He wants me to tell him what I've seen. He thinks that hearing it directly from me might make it more believable.

"I've seen very little of the Mundani eldpeople myself, but I do know that Brân found much of his experiences among Mundani eldpeople to be disturbing. They experienced great suffering and started out as an angry people. I'm sure he'll tell us more when he returns to New Beniford."

Lambert sighs, hungry for more insight. "So much of Mundani history is built on anger and revenge," Lambert says. "Oh, how I wish I could go back in time as you have and tell our eldpeople not to fall victim to that. Revenge never leads to anything good."

"Vidvana says that the capacity for anger holds space for the capacity to love."

"Yes, I've heard her say that. She's talking about the vital nexus, the seat of our emotions. She believes that we can choose which emotions we cultivate." He sends me a questioning look.

"I'm sure she's right about that," I say. "In my own vital nexus, I feel it's true."

"You are a remarkable individual, Meridia—both Melfar and Mundani. I'm glad our Sidayens will have the opportunity to hear you speak today." He falls silent for a moment. "We continue to call ourselves Sidayens, but I keep wondering what we ought to do with the commands of the Sidaya. It has many fine words about purity, respect, and honor. But how can there be honor in always seeking to be above others? As for purity...well, isn't everything that exists pure and perfect in its own way, in its natural state? We dishonor that purity when we seek to turn it to our own selfish purposes. To dominate and bend everything to our will. When we accept everything just as it is and embrace one another as equals..." He pauses, grasping for the right words to express the feeling. "We are the myriad expressions of the singularity of existence. We are one."

"Those are the words your father Amos put to the Song of All Songs, aren't they?" I say. I'm thinking how fortunate the Sidayens will be to hear what Lambert Quint has to say.

"Yes. I've been trying to learn their meaning. I have to work hard at this kind of understanding."

"So did your father," I say, following my own thoughts. "The *Book of All Time* has taken a great deal of hard work, too, and was only possible with many of us working together. Vidvana and Zara have discovered connections between Melfar and Mundani that we never knew existed."

"I look forward to reading it. I'm told that a copy will be left in the new tower we've constructed."

"Yes, and some of Damon's photographs will hang in the gallery beside it. What I've learned from the stories they put into the book is that we—both Melfar and Mundani—have faced times of great adversity. So did our elders of long ago. It's how we came to be who we are."

We walk a while longer in silence, until I see Damon standing in the doorway, looking urgently this way and that, searching for me. I excuse myself and go to him.

I'm sure we ate some breakfast, though I don't recall what it was. I kept thinking about what Lambert said to me. What I said to him.

Some of those words are the ones we speak when at last we stand before the group gathered around the greening peppertree on the grounds of the old Quint House. There are more people in attendance than I'd expected. The space is filled and overflows the low wall that still marks the extent of the property. Even more people mill about in the street. Children are there on the shoulders of mothers and fathers, aunts and uncles.

Lambert speaks first and his comments, especially the ones about the Sidaya, are met with nods and exclamations of approval. When he reaches the part about being the myriad expressions of the singularity of existence, there's silence. Whether it's awed silence or the confused silence of incomprehension I can't tell for sure. Maybe a bit of both. Perhaps some degree of confusion is necessary to push us to think beyond our customary patterns.

Lambert introduces Elvrid Palinj and Saami Pherson to the crowd. Each of them says a few words. They speak about letting go of the divisive passions of the past and reaching toward a better future for all our people, a future in which Melfar and Mundani work together in peace as equals.

Vidvana steps forward and reads passages from the *Book of All Time*. She's selected the story about young Razak Pherson and the Calumet called Iria. She reads about the dedication of the New Marble with its Song of All Songs and then moves to a couple of passages about Melfar eldpeople lost in deep caverns and Mundani eldpeople on a lonely ship, surviving illness. Somehow Vidvana has transformed all of this into beautiful poetry, and in the words she speaks I also hear the songs that are imprinted on Damon's pictures.

"This copy of the *Book of All Time* will be housed in the newly constructed gallery you see over there," she says, pointing toward the little tower. "There will also be a collection of some of the photographs that Damon has produced. We invite you all to read the book, study the pictures, and dedicate yourselves to working toward a future of peace between our peoples."

Then it's my turn. I begin by speaking as I did with Lambert in the quiet of the garden. "Our histories show us that we—both Melfar and Mundani—have lived through times of great adversity. So did our elders of long ago. What I have seen tells me that we are all children of adversity. But our eldpeople survived that adversity. Our eldmothers and eldfathers from long ago found ways of living, of surviving, of birthing and raising children, and we are the result. We are their children. Mundani found one way, Melfar found another. Now we've come together. Now we know we were once the same. It would be so sad, after all we've been through, if we destroyed one another now, if we let arrogance and distrust and fear be the end of us."

The people listen attentively, expectantly. I feel their openness. Into that openness, I begin to sing. And as I sing, words come to me, words from the poems Vidvana read and I know as I never knew before how this marriage of words and music belongs to both our peoples and unifies us.

As the song finally dies away into silence, a few voices speak from the crowd.

"Praise to our Calumet!"

"Praise to our Prophet!"

"Let her speak. Let the Prophet speak again."

I'm pushed forward and, breathing with my mind, I open my heart to this Gathering of all our people and more words come. "Let us go forward from this day as one people, singing the songs, both music and words, that belong to all of us. Let's learn from the *Book of All Time* about the struggles and hardships faced by our eldpeople as they became Melfar or Mundani. Learn how they survived. Learn how we have thrived best when we worked together in harmony. Learn these stories and sing them to one another. This is how we grow our peace."

There are more cheers and many flowers are thrown into the air. Bubbles of violet and golden orange light burst from the throats of Melfar and from the hearts of Mundani.

"You did well," Damon says, his arm lying protectively around my shoulders.

"This is not about me," I whisper back. "And it's not about Lambert or Elvrid or Saami. It's about what we can all do together if we only will." I'm grateful for

Damon's embrace, feeling that without it I might dissolve into the Migrant altogether.

A procession forms and we move, with some solemnity and a thrill of murmured conversation, through Lambert Quint's chamber of mirrors and on into the tower that holds the *Book of All Time* and the connected gallery with its collection of photographs.

Finally, we gather for the feast laid out for the celebration. Farmers from every region (except those areas burned by the Palinjians) have brought fresh fruits and vegetables and grains. There are stuffed breads of all kinds and pungent cheeses and pickles and jars of several kinds of tea.

I barely taste the sumptuous delicacies, as the exhilaration of the day begins to give way to a yearning to return to New Beniford, to Naomi and Odilia. Damon never leaves my side. He understands me, understands that though I may be Calumet and though I may even be willing to be called Prophet, I am still his partner and the devoted mother of our nens.

Calumet. Am I truly that? And Prophet? My heart swells with determination to be what is needed in these times. I grasp Damon's hand under the table and attune to the conversation around us, the excited babble of Mundani men and women commenting to one another about the *Book of All Time* and about the pictures in the gallery. Their hearts quiver with pulses of gold and pink tinged with violet. Members of different weftreds embrace one another openly, smiling and laughing with abandon. Melfar walk freely among them, giving and receiving smiles and greetings and joyful embraces.

At last Damon and I bid farewell. We pass outside the wall surrounding the Quint property. It's no longer a wall, really. Only a marker signaling passage into a separate space, a space through which entrance and egress is unimpeded.

Outside the boundary I see two men hurrying away. I pertange a dissipating crimson rage clutching at their two hearts. I know these are Palinjians. We haven't won over all the people. Not yet. But we've made a good start. We've finally reached beyond our Melfar fastnesses, beyond secret weftreds, joining together openly in our shared world.

I wish Father and Brân could have been here, but Father insisted on staying in New Beniford. And Brân is still on Selbourne.

No, he's on his way home, ready to rejoin his brother twin in New Beniford. And to meet Naomi and Odilia.

Damon and I hurry toward the cart and equids that will take us home. Something is disturbing my orb, something that I can't quite name. Does Father know what it is? Does Brân know?

Tell me about the ship, Brân. That's what it is. That's what I pertange.

Their ships have long since rusted to nothing at the bottom of the ocean, Meridia. There's nothing more to tell.

Not those ships. A different sort of ship. A ship made of wood, with great sheets that catch the sun.

I learned of no such ships.

Brân doesn't know, but I do. A great wooden ship is nearing Selbourne. Prickles of crimson dread creep up my spine, invading my orb and vital nexus. The ship feels empty, and yet it makes unerringly for the harbor.

Amos Quint watches it through his spyglass, and his apprehension reaches me here in Fayredell. *Who are these people and where have they come from?*

Donna Dechen Birdwell

APPENDIX 1

EXPERIENCING TIME

Melfar conceptualize time in terms of cycles. They utilize a lunar calendar overlaid on a solar one, measuring time in *tides, returns,* and *meeds*. A *tide* is a full lunar cycle. The only consistently named tides are Darktide, Brightening Symmetide, Suntide, and Darkening Symmetide (corresponding to lunar cycles encompassing winter solstice, vernal equinox, summer solstice, and autumnal equinox, respectively). Other tides receive descriptive labels, which can vary from one return to the next (e.g., Fogtide, Budtide, Fruittide). A *return* is a cycle of all the solar seasons, with a new return always beginning on the full moon closest to the start of Brightening Symmetide.

There are twelve named returns corresponding to the twelve types of stone from which a Benison is crafted to mark the start of each return (see diagram). A full cycle of returns comprises a *meed*, and meeds are named in the same sequence as returns. The completion of a full cycle of meeds is called a *Great Turning*. Returns of the current cycle are called *New*, with previous cycles referred to as *Old, Ancient,* and *Preterit,* in that order. A particular event is "dated" by one saying that it occurred in a "Fogtide of the Amber Return of the Old Jade Meed."

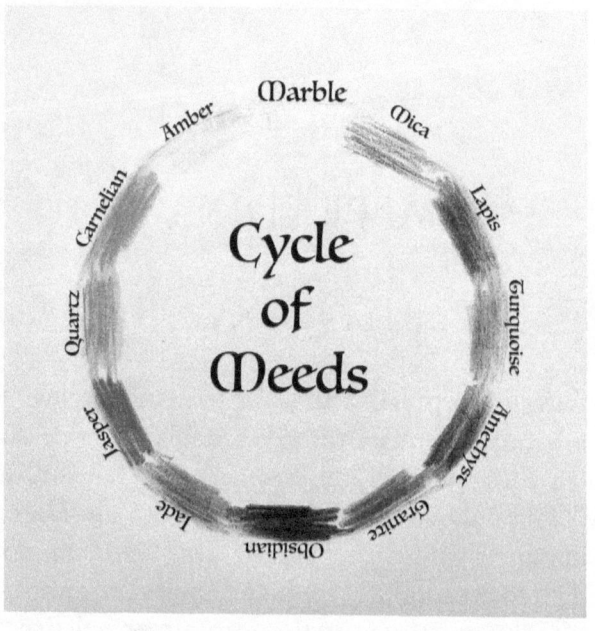

Cycle of Meeds

Marble · Mica · Lapis · Turquoise · Amethyst · Granite · Obsidian · Jade · Jasper · Quartz · Carnelian · Amber

Mundani, on the other hand, utilize a rigidly linear solar calendar. Their equivalent of a Melfar return (our year) is a *passage*. Passages are sequentially numbered, beginning with the birth year of Razak Caloyer, a revered prophet. Each passage is divided into twelve *stints*, each with exactly thirty days, comprised of five *sixes*. These stints are not named, only numbered. To regularize their calendar, they observe a period of five (sometimes six) days at the conclusion of Twelfth Stint. These days are called the *Binder*. The new passage begins on the longest day (summer solstice), which they call Full Sun.

APPENDIX 2: MAP

The map on the following page represents the Mundani world. Melfar don't use maps as such. The eastern "Wasteland" is what was once the Melfar Forest of Cödweg and the southern "Wasteland" is where the Forest of Cesta once stood. The Melfar Forest of Serani lay on the slopes of the western mountains. For the benefit of readers, the map shows the approximate locations of the following places that are important only to Melfar:

1) Beniford
2) Aldbeck
3) Lindmor
4) Woodclasp
5) Gorshfen (on the lake called Glasllyn)
6) Selbourne
7) Túl
8) New Beniford

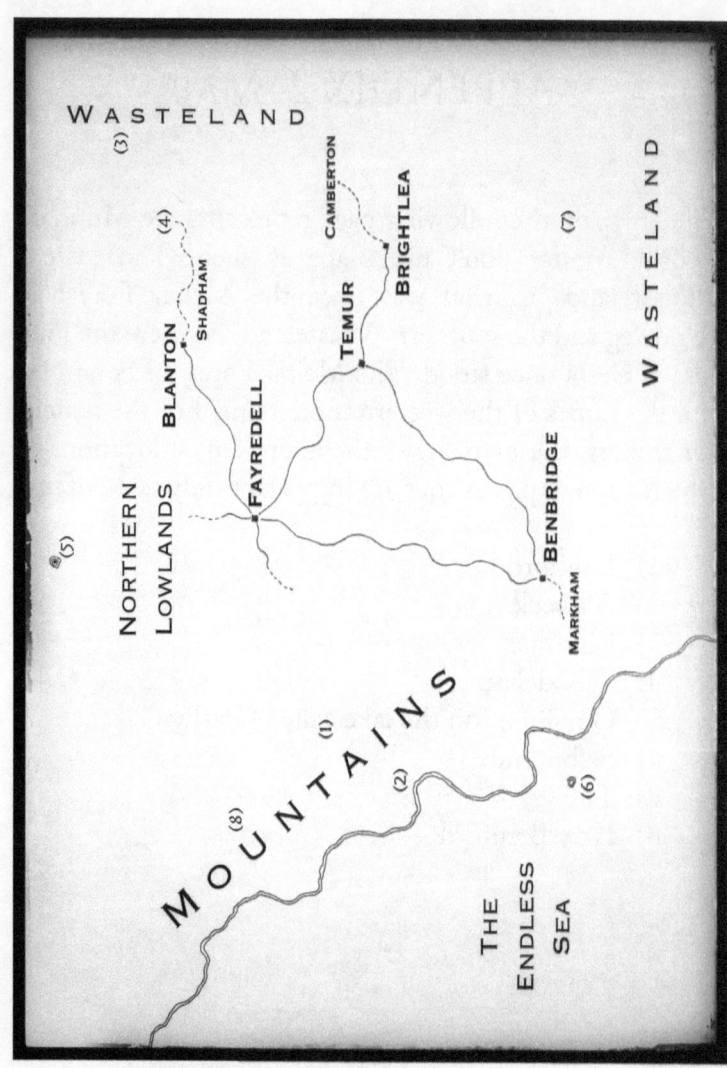

APPENDIX 3

GLOSSARY

aurynx: The organ that sonically verberates biophotonic patterns. It is located in the throat near the larynx.

Benison: A stone monument crafted by Melfar to commemorate the end of one meed and the start of the next. Each Benison contains the imagery of a song.

billbug: A biting insect similar to a mosquito.

Binder: A period of five or six days between passages that calibrates the Mundani calendar. It is considered "time out of time," when rules are often broken.

breth: A kinship term meaning "born of."

cabra: A goat-like mammal sometimes kept for milk.

Calumet: A "peace-bringer" who serves as a respected social and cultural leader among the Melfar.

cavouti: A species of large rodent raised for meat.

clauster: A sacred space surrounding a Mundani temple.

ecphorite: A substance Melfar use in the crafting of Benisons that imprints imagery through sound.

equid: A horse-like mammal kept as a draft animal.

fellspan: The distance to the horizon on relatively flat ground. (Approximately 4.2 miles.)

fireblock: A fabricated fuel made from waste material soaked in groundfat.

fireseed: A spark of energy; an electrical pulse.

gnosic orb: The sensory organ that pertanges biophotonic patterns. It is located in the center of the brow just above the eyes.

kinren: Any employee, servant, client, apprentice, or woman attached to a particular Sidayen.

lamin: An alpaca-like animal kept as a beast of burden and draft animal.

Meed: A cycle of all the seasons (see Appendix I).

Melfar: A "race" of people who traditionally inhabited the forests and who preferentially communicate in images and sounds without words. They are short in stature, stoutly built, with curly blonde or red hair, tawny skin, and eyes generally yellow or green.

Migrant: The ineffable presence that, according to Melfar belief, motivates and empowers everything.

Mundani: A "race" of people living primarily in towns and farms with written codes and formal religion. They are tall and slender, with generally wavy dark hair and dark skin and eyes.

Palinjian: A devotee of Zibal Palinj.

patkány: A very large species of predatory rodent.

passage: Mundani term for a year (see Appendix I).

pertange: To sense in a tangible way the biophotonic and sonic verberations of people and natural things.

return: Melfar term for a year (see Appendix I).

Revelant: An individual who has died and come back to life in the same body.

Sidaya: A code of moral conduct among the Mundani, revealed by their Prophet Razak Pherson. There were six rules: 1) Honor the Creator and the Order His creation ordains. 2) Keep his temples pure. 3) Respect the House of your upbringing and its lineage of fathers. 4) Do not defile your body with impure foods. 5) Do not defile your spirit with impure associations. 6) Do not defile your heart with doubt.

Sidayen: One who adheres to the Sidaya; a high status exclusive to Mundani men.

stint: Among Mundani, a passage is composed of twelve stints of thirty days each and a Binder.

tide: Among Melfar, a tide is a full lunar cycle.

verberate: To sonically generate patterned biophotons.

vital nexus: The energetic network centered around an individual's heart.

waif: A stone associated with a Benison and sharing some of its properties.

weftred: A clandestine network of women and other kinrens among the Mundani.

zaki: A large predatory feline.

CHART OF FAMILIES

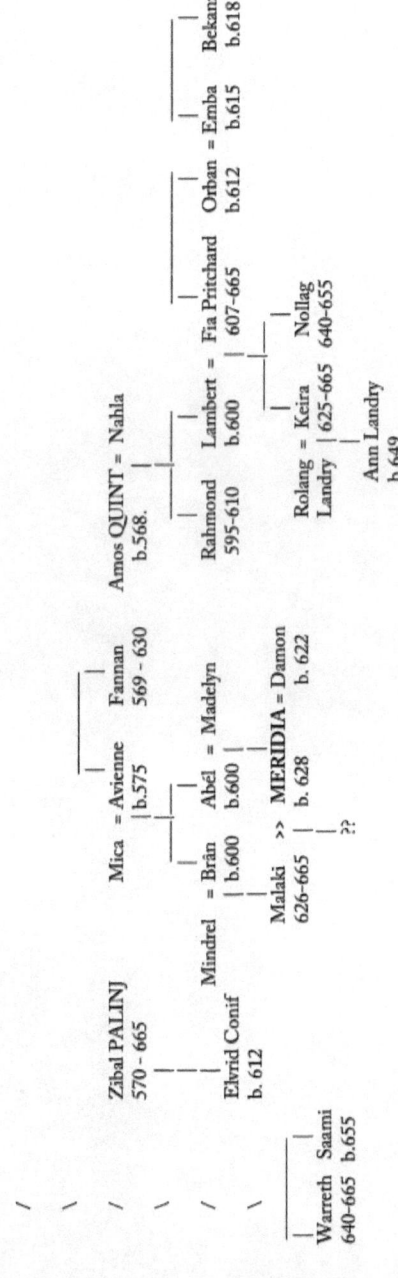

Razak PHERSON
282 - 403

Zibal PALINJ
570 - 665

Elvrid Conif
b. 612

Mindrel = Brän
b.600

Warreth   Saami
640-665   b.655

Malaki
626-665

Mica = Avienne
b.575

Fannan
569 - 630

Abel = Madelyn
b.600

MERIDIA = Damon
b. 628   b. 622

>>

??

Amos QUINT = Nahla
b.568.

Rahmond
595-610

Lambert = Fia Pritchard
b.600   607-665

Rolang = Keira
Landry 625-665

Nollag
640-655

Ann Landry
b.649

Orban = Emba
b.612   b.615

Bekanz
b.618

ACKNOWLEDGMENTS

From the earliest tentative notes scribbled in pencil, I always knew this story would include an epidemic. What I didn't know was that I would be writing about it in the midst of an actual global pandemic. *Song of All Songs* launched (on Zoom) in August of 2020 to welcome words of acclaim. I was eager to finish up *Book of All Time* and put it into the hands of my readers, but the state of the real world presented challenge after challenge—the pandemic, of course, but also an election, an insurrection, and a week-long deep freeze during which I washed from buckets of boiled snow. That sort of weather isn't supposed to happen in Central Texas, but it served as a reminder of why I find it appropriate to write climate calamities into my novels, including this one. I kept slogging on, and roughly a year after Book One of *Earth-Cycles* was launched, here is Book Two.

I'm grateful for the assistance and support of my beta readers—Teresa Roberson, Tony Torzillo, and Cheryl Rooke—and my keen-eyed editor, Katherine Catmull of Yellow Bird Editors. A word of thanks as well to my "fight scene" adviser, Becca Pheasant-Reis. If I still got it wrong, that's on me!

You can find me online at *donnadechenbirdwell.com* which will also lead you to my Facebook, Twitter, and Instagram.

OTHER BOOKS BY
DONNA DECHEN BIRDWELL

Not Knowing, 2019

THE RECALL CHRONICLES

Way of the Serpent, 2015

Shadow of the Hare, 2016

Flight of the Owl, 2016

EARTHCYCLES TRILOGY

Song of All Songs (Book One) 2020

COMING SOON
Beyond the Endless (Book Three)